Early praise for Patrick Craig's *A Quilt for Jenna*...

Patrick Craig writes with an enthusiasm and a passion that is a joy to read. He deals with romance, faith, love, loss, tragedy, and restoration with equal amounts of elegance, grace, clarity, and power. Everyone should pick up his debut novel in Amish fiction, turn off the phone and computer and TV, and settle in for a good night's read. Craig's book is a blessing.

Murray Pura, author of *The Wings of Morning* and *The Face of Heaven*

A good storyteller takes a fine story and places it in a setting peppered with enough accurate details to satisfy a native son. Then he peoples it with characters so real we keep thinking we see them walking down the street. A great storyteller takes all that and binds it together with, say, a carefully constructed Rose of Sharon quilt and the wallop of a storm of the century that actually happened. *A Quilt For Jenna* proves Patrick Craig to be a great storyteller.

Kay Marshall Strom, author of the *Grace in Africa* and *Blessings in India* trilogies

A Quilt for Jenna

Patrick E. Craig

HARVEST HOUSE PUBLISHERS
EUGENE, OREGON

Cover by Garborg Design Works, Savage, Minnesota

Cover photo © Chris Garborg; author photo by William Craig—Craig Propraphica

Published in association with the literary agency of the Steve Laube Agency, LLC, 5025 N. Central Ave., #635, Phoenix, Arizona 85912.

A QUILT FOR JENNA

Published by Harvest House Publishers
Eugene, Oregon 97402
www.harvesthousepublishers.com

Library of Congress Cataloging-in-Publication Data
Craig, Patrick E., 1947-
A quilt for Jenna / Patrick E. Craig.
p. cm.—(Apple Creek dreams series ; bk. 1.)
ISBN 978-0-7369-5105-0 (pbk.)
ISBN 978-0-7369-5106-7 (eBook)
1. Quiltmakers—Fiction. 2. Traffic accidents—Fiction. 3. Amish—Ohio—Fiction.
4. Foundlings—Fiction. I. Title.
PS3603.R3554Q55 2013
813'.6—dc23

2012026072

Printed in the United States of America

13 14 15 16 17 18 19 20 21 / LB-NI / 10 9 8 7 6 5 4 3 2 1

To my daughter Cheryl
and my granddaughter Terra Lynn

Acknowledgments

To my wonderful wife, Judy, for her tireless proofing and editing work on the first six drafts of this book and her ceaseless prayer on its behalf.

To Dan Kline for his initial editing of this book, his great suggestions and input, and his invaluable friendship.

To Sue Tornai for keeping me in the active voice.

Contents

A Note from Patrick Craig

Apple Creek is a real place. It is a village set in the heart of Wayne County, Ohio, eleven miles from Dalton and ten miles from Wooster. It has real streets and real people.

Apple Creek and the surrounding area are home to a large Amish community and have been since the mid-1800s. Not far to the east lies Lancaster, Pennsylvania, where the Amish first settled in America in 1720.

I chose Apple Creek as the setting for *A Quilt for Jenna* while doing research on the Amish in Ohio and in particular on Amish quilt makers. Apple Creek, Dalton, and Wooster are known for the marvelous Amish quilts produced there. Dalton has one of the biggest quilting fairs in Ohio.

A town named Apple Creek was just too good to pass up as a location, so I started my story there. I used the actual streets and highways, the localities, and even local family names in *A Quilt for Jenna* even though all the characters are fictitious and not based on real people.

As I mentally planted myself in the heart of Apple Creek, the characters in the book began to spring out of the earth, fully grown, with lives and stories, joys and sorrows. The story was easy to write because it seemed as though I were reading someone's journal as I wrote it.

The more I explored Apple Creek, the more I realized how connected I was to the village. My great-great-grandfather, Anthony Rockhill, was born forty-nine miles from Apple Creek in Alliance, Ohio, in 1828. Apple Creek is eighty-five miles from the site of Fort Henry, West Virginia, on the Ohio River. Fort Henry was the site of Betty Zane's run for life during the British and Indian siege during the Revolutionary War in 1782. The book *Betty Zane* by Zane Grey was a childhood favorite and still has a place on my bookshelf.

As a child I poured over stories about Lewis Wetzel and Jonathan Zane and followed them through the trackless Ohio wilderness only a few miles from what would become the village of Apple Creek. Though I've never been there, I feel I know the area like the back of my hand. And so it was no coincidence that I came to choose Apple Creek. Though the characters in this book are fictional, they have become very real to me, as I hope they will become to you.

And by the way, the horrific storm in *A Quilt for Jenna* is also real. Historians have called it the Great Appalachian Storm or even the Blizzard of the Century. At the time, of course, the people who lived in the path of this monster didn't have a name for it. They just hunkered down and tried to endure it.

I hope the story of Jerusha Springer and her struggle to survive will touch a place in your heart as you read. Perhaps something of your own life will be changed for the better by the end of the book. So as I think about it, maybe it was coincidence that I chose Apple Creek. After all, coincidence is just God choosing to remain anonymous.

The First Day

Wednesday, November 22, 1950

Chapter One

The Quilt

◇◇◇

Jerusha Springer reached behind the quilting frame with her left hand and pushed the needle back to the surface of the quilt to complete her final stitch. Wearily she pulled the needle through, quickly knotted the quilting thread, and broke it off.

Finished at last. She leaned back and let out a sigh of satisfaction. It had taken months to complete, but here it was—the finest quilt she had ever made.

Thousands of stitches had gone into the work, seventy every ten inches, and now the work was finished. It had been worth it. The quilt was a masterpiece. *Her* masterpiece...and Jenna's.

She grabbed a tissue and quickly wiped away an unexpected tear.

If only Jenna were here with me, I could bear this somehow.

But Jenna wasn't there. Jenna was gone forever.

Jerusha glanced out the window as the November sun shone weakly through a gray overcast of clouds. The pale light made the fabric in the quilt shimmer and glow. A fitful wind shook the bare branches of the maple trees, and the few remaining leaves whirled away into the light snow that drifted down from the gunmetal sky.

Winter had come unannounced to Apple Creek, and Jerusha hadn't noticed. Her life had been bound up in this quilt for so many months—since Jenna's death, really—that everything else in her life seemed like a shadow. She stared at the finished quilt on the frame, but there was no joy in her heart, only a dull ache and the knowledge that soon she would be free.

She had searched without success for several months to find just the right fabric to make this quilt, and then she stumbled upon it quite by accident. A neighbor told her of an estate sale at an antique store in Wooster, and she asked Henry, the neighbor boy, to drive her over to see what she could find. The *Englisch* had access to many things from the outside world, and she had often looked in their stores and catalogs to find just the right materials for her quilting.

On that day in Wooster she had been poking through the piles of clothing and knickknacks scattered around the store when she came upon an old cedar chest. The lid was carved with ornate filigree, and several shipping tags were still attached. The trunk was locked, so she called the proprietor over, and when he opened it, she drew in her breath with a little gasp. There, folded neatly, were two large pieces of fabric. One was blue—the kind of blue that kings might wear—and as she lifted it to the light, she could see that it seemed to change from blue to purple, depending on how she held it. The other piece was deep red...like the blood of Christ or perhaps a rose.

The fabric was light but strong, smooth to the touch and tightly woven.

"I believe that's genuine silk, ma'am," the owner said. "I'm afraid it's going to be expensive."

Jerusha didn't argue the price. It was exactly what she was looking for, and she didn't dare let it slip through her fingers. Normally, the quilts that she and the other women in her community made were from plainer fabric, cotton or sometimes synthetics, but lately she didn't really care about what the *ordnung* said.

So, pushing down her fear of the critical comments she knew she would hear from the other women about pride and worldliness, she purchased it and left the store. As she rode home, the design for the quilt began to take form in her mind, and for the first time since Jenna's death, she felt her spirits lift.

When she arrived home, she searched through her fabric box for the cream-colored cotton backing piece she had reserved for this quilt. She then sketched out a rough design and in the following days cut the hundreds of pieces to make the pattern for the top layer. She sorted and ironed them and then pinned and stitched all the parts into a rectangle measuring approximately eight and a half feet by nine feet. After that she laid the finished top layer out on the floor and traced the entire quilting design on the fabric with tailor's chalk. The design had unfolded before her eyes as if someone else were directing her hand. This quilt was the easiest she had ever pieced together.

The royal blue pieces made a dark, iridescent backdrop to a beautiful deep red rose-shaped piece in the center. The rose had hundreds of parts, all cut into the flowing shapes of petals instead of the traditional square or diamond-shaped patterns of Amish quilts. Though the pattern was the most complicated she had ever done, she found herself grateful that it served as a way to keep thoughts of Jenna's absence from overwhelming her.

Next she laid out the cream-colored backing, placed a double layer of batting over it, and added the ironed patchwork piece she had developed over the past month.

On her hands and knees she carefully basted the layers together, starting from the center and working out to the edges. Once she was finished, she called Henry for help. He held the material while she carefully attached one end to the quilting frame, and then they slowly turned the pole until she could attach the other end. After drawing the quilt tight until it was stable enough to stitch on, she started to quilt. Delicate tracks of quilting stitches began to make their trails through the surface of the quilt as Jerusha labored day after day at her work.

The quilt was consuming her, and her despair and grief and the anger she felt toward God for taking Jenna were all poured into the fabric spread before her.

Often as she worked she stopped and lifted her face to the sky.

"I hate You," she would say quietly, "and I'm placing all my hatred into this quilt so I will never forget that when I needed You most, You failed me." Then she would go back to her work with a fierce determination and a deep and abiding anger in her heart.

And now at last the quilt was finished—her ticket out of her awful life.

"I will take this quilt to the Dalton Fair, and I will win the prize," she said aloud. "Then I will leave Apple Creek, and I will leave this religion, and I will leave this God who has turned His back on me. I will make a new life among the *Englisch*, and I will never return to Apple Creek."

She stared at the quilt. *I will call this quilt the Rose of Sharon. Not for You, but for her, my precious girl, my Jenna.* The quilt shone in the soft light from the window, and Jerusha felt a great surge of triumph.

I don't need You—not now, not ever again.

And Jerusha turned off the lamp and went alone to her cold bed.

Chapter Two

Bobby

Bobby Halverson stood in the rolled-up doorway of the diesel repair shop, smoking a Camel and watching the gray storm clouds blowing in from the south. The wind carried a biting chill, and flurries of snow had become a steady fall. Behind him in the shop, Dutch Peterson was complaining out loud as he worked on Bobby's old tractor.

"These glow plugs are shot, Bobby! Only three give me enough current to start it up. And the compression release is jamming up. If you get stuck out in the cold and she sits for a while, you're going to have a heck of a time startin' 'er up again."

"Well, can you get me some new plugs, Dutch?" Bobby tossed away his cigarette and came back into the shop.

Dutch had parts spread all over the place and was knocking dirt out of the air cleaner as he continued his grumbling. "This old hunk-a-junk belongs in the junkyard."

"Come on, Dutch, you've got to get it going for me. There's a big storm coming in, and I'm the only plow in Apple Creek. What about all those Amish folks with their buggies? If I don't keep the roads clear, they'll get stuck for sure. A lot of people will be on the road tomorrow for Thanksgiving, and it'll be even worse when they come back home Friday. I've got to keep the roads open."

"Okay," Dutch said. "Don't get all het up. I think I can get you some new plugs by Monday if I can get up to Wooster, but until then you be real careful. Once you get 'er running, don't let 'er stop, or you'll be up against it, no joke."

Bobby stepped over to the barrel stove that heated the shop and threw another shovelful of coal into the bottom bin. The barrel was already glowing red hot, but it did little to dispel the cold inside the shop. Bobby slapped his arms against his chest and stamped his feet on the concrete floor.

"Man, it's freezing cold," he said. "I bet the temperature's dropped ten degrees in the last hour. I'm sure glad I had you build that cab on the plow. This wind's going to get really fierce before the storm is over."

Dutch kept about his work, and slowly the parts he had cleaned went back into the old engine. He stopped and held up an injector to the light.

"Bobby," he said, "you're a good-hearted soul, and you help a lot of people, but you don't know nothin' about keepin' this old rig going. You're dang lucky to have me to help you, because otherwise, this old hoss would have been sitting in a pasture somewhere years ago."

"I know, Dutch," Bobby said, "and I sure do appreciate it. Now, if you don't mind, maybe you could stop with the jawin' and get this old hoss back on the road."

Bobby Halverson was Apple Creek's one-man snow-removal department because he had the only plow within about ten miles. In a big storm, the County workers usually concentrated on Wooster and the bigger towns, leaving Apple Creek to fend for itself. He had rigged up the plow on his tractor three years ago with Dutch's help and had been able to keep the roads mostly clear that year. The locals were so grateful they pooled some money to create a snowplow fund to help Bobby with expenses. It wasn't a lot, but it helped keep the tractor running and get a few extras, which was nice—especially this year, with Thanksgiving tomorrow.

Bobby walked back to the open door of the shop and surveyed the sky. The wind was blowing in from western Pennsylvania, and the way it was picking up, along with the big drop in temperature, told Bobby that a humdinger of a nor'easter was coming through. The weatherman on the radio had called it an extratropical cyclone, whatever that meant, and warned about high winds and even tornadoes along the path of the storm. Many of the outlying farms would be snowbound, and there would definitely be some downed power lines and blackouts. So it was critical that Dutch get the old plow in shape because it would be a long haul until Monday.

Bobby stared out at the street. The wind was gusting and the snow was falling softly on the road. The asphalt still held enough heat to melt off some of the snow, but it wouldn't be long until the roads were covered and icy. A few cars made their way toward the center of the village, probably headed for the creamery or the grocery store to do some last-minute Thanksgiving shopping.

"Okay," Dutch said, "stop your mooning and get over here and crank the starter. Let's see if we can get 'er going."

Bobby jumped up into the covered cab and watched Dutch spray some ether straight into the manifold port. "Crank it!" Dutch yelled, and Bobby turned her over. The old tractor jumped a little and then fired right up. Ka-chug, ka-chug, ka-chug...the old two-stroke engine labored to life.

Dutch closed the hood and stepped over to the cab.

"Leave her running for a while to clean out any gunk that's still in there. And remember, the glow plugs have to warm up for at least ten minutes in this weather or she'll never start. And don't kill the engine out there, or you'll have a mighty cold walk home."

Chapter Three

The Crash

◇◇◇

The old Ford station wagon sped west through the growing darkness on County Road 188 toward Apple Creek. The man behind the wheel had a two-day growth of beard and bloodshot eyes. Beside him, shoved down between the two front seats, sat an open whiskey bottle. Every few minutes the man pulled it out, put the bottle to his lips, and drank. The snow was coming down harder now, and the man was singing at the top of his voice.

"Jingle bells, jingle bells, jingle all the waaayyyy."

When he heard a sob from the backseat, he turned to look at his passenger—a little girl, her eyes wide, her thin summer coat pulled tight around her body. She was about four years old with wavy strawberry-blonde hair, and under the coat she was wearing a dress, a wool sweater, some tights, and a pair of sneakers. Her skin was pale, and her lips were cracked from the cold.

"Whatta ya cryin' about?" he snarled. "I told your mama not to take that stuff. I told her over and over that she was in over her head. But would she listen to me? No. She just kept whining. 'I need to get high, Joe, I need to get high.' Well, she got *too* high, and now she's gone and we're stuck with each other—and you're not even my kid."

Joe took another long pull on the bottle. The little girl in the back was clinging to the door handle with all her strength as Joe fishtailed down the road.

"Mama," she said softly.

"Shut up about your mama," Joe snapped. He leaned back over the seat and took a drunken swing at the girl with his open palm. The car went into a skid and headed toward the bank alongside the road.

"Whooee, this road is getting slick," Joe said as he steered the car out of the skid.

The girl began to cry—barely a whimper—as she whispered "Mama" once more.

Joe ignored the cry this time and reached for the bottle again, and taking another long pull, he drained it. As he did the car again swerved, and the little girl cried out, "Mama...Mama!"

"That's enough about Mama!" Joe shouted as he threw the empty bottle down in the corner of the car. "I've had it with your sniveling." He reached back and grabbed at the girl but missed. Her cries now became shrieks of fear as Joe turned from the girl to the steering wheel and then back at the girl, screaming, "Just shut up, shut up, shut up!"

Looking away from the road, he didn't see the sudden corner, and before he could turn back to the wheel, the car went straight off the road, down an embankment into a wooded area, and over a mound that sent the car airborne. The old Ford slowly turned in midair as it sailed over a rise and then crashed down on its side and slid down a bank. The car finally hit up against a big pine, spun completely around, and crashed into a rocky outcrop, which swung the car downhill again. They slid for several more feet and then slowly came to a halt.

Everything was quiet for a few minutes, and then Joe groaned. He had been thrown facedown on the passenger side and ended up in a ball against the door. The little girl had disappeared down behind the front seat and lay there, quiet and still. Joe turned himself around and tried to pull himself up the seat to the driver's door. His face was bloody, and pain shot through his arm like fire. The car shifted as he moved and slowly rolled over onto its roof. Joe cried out in agony as he fell back against the passenger door. He tried the door, and it creaked open, so he slowly crawled out, cursing with every movement. The car jutted partway out on what looked like a large snow-covered meadow. Joe struggled to his feet, kicked the door shut, and looked around. Behind him, the marks of the car's journey down the hill showed him the way back to the road.

"Well, isn't this handy?" he muttered. "I can get rid of my little passenger, and if anyone asks, I'll tell 'em she got killed in the wreck."

Joe stepped to the back door. "Come out, come out wherever you are," he sang as he reached for the door handle.

He bent down to look in the window. The little girl looked out at him with terrified eyes.

"Peek-a-boo, I see you."

Joe grinned and pulled on the handle. The door was jammed shut, and he couldn't budge it, so he stood up and began to kick the window.

"Come on out, honey," he grunted in pain. "I'm gonna help you find your mama."

He didn't have enough strength left in his leg to continue kicking, so he looked around for something to break the window. A few feet away he saw a long piece of metal that had broken off the car as it hit the ground. He walked over and bent down to pick it up. As he did he heard an ominous cracking under his feet. He stopped and listened.

He heard the cracking again, only louder this time, and then in an instant he knew where he was. This wasn't a large meadow—it was a frozen pond. Terror gripped him. The ice groaned again, and a long fracture shot out from between his feet. Desperately he took a running leap, but the ice broke beneath his feet, and he plunged into freezing water. He struggled to climb out, but his right arm, still in pain, couldn't keep a grip on the edge of the ice. Each time he took hold, the edge broke away.

Finally, in desperation, he called out, "Help me! Please, God, help me!"

Panic-stricken, he began thrashing wildly at the edge of the ice, trying to pull himself up. But the more he thrashed, the weaker he felt.

"Oh God, oh God, oh God!" he screamed, and then his water-soaked clothing dragged him under. He struggled back up, but he swallowed water as he gasped for breath and then sank again. There was a wild momentary thrashing under the water, and then a stream of bubbles broke the surface. Then everything was quiet and the water became still.

In the car, the little girl's eyes were fixed on the surface of the water where Joe had disappeared. She had slipped down into the space between the front and back seats when Joe was grabbing for her before the crash, and that had saved her life. Now she lay on the ceiling of the upside-down car clinging to a dislodged seat cushion. She had a small gash over her eye, and with Joe's disappearance into the water, she cried, "Mama...Mama, come find me...Mama!"

Then she slipped into unconsciousness, and it grew quiet in the car. Outside, the wind began to blow harder through the trees, and the snow began to fall.

◇◇◇

Jerusha sat up in her bed.

It had been a horrible dream. Jenna had been lost in a dark place, crying for her. Jerusha wanted to scream, "I'm coming, baby, I'm coming," but no sound would come out. And then Jerusha woke up. She put her face in her hands and sobbed until the light began to break in the east.

The Second Day

Thursday, November 23, 1950

Chapter Four

The Journey Begins

The gray light of dawn crept slowly into Jerusha's room. Outside, the wind whistled around the eaves and through the trees. Jerusha lay in bed staring at the ceiling, the deep ache in her heart pounding like a throbbing wound. She had often dreamed of Jenna but never as vividly as last night.

She slowly swung her feet over the side of the bed and sat for a long time with her head in her hands. Then she rose and headed for the simple bathroom. Before she turned on the shower, she ran cold water into the sink until it was full and then put her face under the water. The shock brought her quickly awake, clearing the fog from her mind. As she toweled off her face, she couldn't shake the memory of the dream. Jenna was near but lost in a dark place, calling to her.

She looked up into the mirror and stared at the face she saw there. She had been a lovely girl once, but grief and loss had carved their cruel imprint on her features. The once-smooth skin had frown lines that made her look much older than she really was. Her eyes, once bright and expectant and full of life and faith, now had a dull, lost look.

The sound of the grandfather clock tolling six times broke into her thoughts and brought her back to reality. If she didn't hurry, she'd be late.

Hurriedly she stepped into the shower. As she stood under the barely lukewarm water, her thoughts pressed in on her again.

When I leave here, I'll never have to worry about hot water or heat again. I won't have to share the propane with my neighbors. I'll get a car and go wherever I want to go. I'll have Englisch *friends, and I'll call them on the phone. Maybe I'll even have a television set!*

Jerusha was startled by the sudden sense of shame that swept over her.

"And I won't feel guilty about anything I do!" she said out loud, glaring toward the heavens, where she imagined this Amish God was sitting on His terrible throne laughing at her. As she stepped out of the shower to towel off, she continued her rant. "I won't feel guilty ever again, and I'll do what I want to do, and You'll never stop me..."

Jerusha trembled at her own words but then added, "She's gone, and You took her from me. I hate You! I hate You! I hate You."

A knock on the front door caused her to take hold of her emotions.

"Missus Springer?"

It was Henry, the *Englisch* neighbor boy who was going to drive her to Dalton. She opened the bathroom door and called out, "I'm running a little late, Henry. Can you come back in twenty minutes?"

"Sure thing, ma'am," the boy said through the door, "but if we're going to get up to Dalton before the storm hits, we have to get going."

"I'm sorry, Henry," she called. "I'll be ready in a jiffy."

Jerusha quickly slipped into her clothes, rolled her braided hair into a knot, and pulled on her prayer *kappe.* She gathered her things and then went into the sewing room, where the quilt lay neatly folded on the table. She unfolded it and began to examine every detail one more time. She checked the stitching but could not see any mistakes or overruns. The pattern was totally unique, and the material was beautiful. As it lay on the table before her, the colors shimmered and shifted in the light. The quilt felt alive to her, and in a way it was. She had poured her memories of Jenna's life and her anguish and grief into this quilt, and the result was truly a masterpiece, a symphony in color and design. She carefully refolded the quilt.

I put all of my skill and all my feelings into this quilt. I'm going to win that prize, and with the money, I'll get a new start. I'll be free. Free to do what I want to do and go where I will. This is a quilt for Jenna and for me. It's my ticket away from here and from You.

"You don't own me anymore!" she hissed into the silent room.

She then placed the quilt in a cardboard box and folded the flaps together. On the side of the box she wrote, "The Rose of Sharon—quilt by Jerusha Springer."

A knock on the door startled her, and Henry called out from the porch. "We got to get going, Missus Springer. The storm is picking up, and it will take us a long time to get there as it is."

"I'll be finished in a minute, Henry," Jerusha said as she opened the door. "Please, could you carry my things to the car?"

"Glad to, ma'am," Henry said with a look of relief on his face. "I hope you dressed warm."

"Indeed I did," Jerusha said as she pulled on her long winter coat. She handed Henry the box that held the quilt and slipped her galoshes over her lace-up shoes. She started out the door but then paused and looked back into the house.

This place used to ring with laughter, and joy and blessing overflowed. I had my life and my good husband and my little girl. It was as if the angels stood round about this house and guarded it from any harm. And then You took her from me and You stripped away every bit of joy and left only this darkness and pain. Soon I will leave this place and I'll not look back.

Jerusha collected her thoughts and then stepped out and closed the door. The clicking of the latch had a final sound that pleased her. She turned to the young man who was standing expectantly on the porch.

"I'm ready, Henry. Thank you so much for taking me." She smiled quickly and then stepped out into the cold. The icy snow hit her face like needles.

Henry walked down the steps and opened the door to the backseat of his sedan.

"I've got chains if we need them," he said. "But these snow tires ought to keep her on the road. She's real heavy and she goes through the drifts like a truck. I figure we'll take the county highway to Carr Road and then cut over to Kidron Road. Bobby usually keeps that plowed pretty good during storms, and it's the quickest way into Dalton. Are you sure they're going to have the quilt fair, Missus Springer, given the weather and all?"

"They have never cancelled this fair, and even if they postpone it, I need to see the fair manager. I've arranged for a place to stay, and I'll be fine. I have your phone number, and I'll go to the store and call you to make arrangements to get back home, or I'll take the bus."

"Okay, Missus Springer, whatever you say. If I didn't have to get up there myself today for Thanksgiving at my grandma's, I might be having second thoughts about going."

Henry had a grim look on his face, but Jerusha dismissed his frown.

Today is Thanksgiving. I completely forgot. But then, what do I have to be thankful for?

Jerusha climbed into the car, and Henry got in behind the wheel and started the Buick. He headed the car out of the driveway, the tires crunching on the new-fallen snow as he turned onto the long gravel road to the county highway. Suddenly a powerful sense of expectancy swept over Jerusha, a feeling so intense that she nearly cried out for joy. But she held her words and sat in the backseat trembling as they began the journey, out and away, away from this place and from these people and from this God—the God of broken dreams and lost hope and beaten-down faith.

CHAPTER FIVE

The Storm

BOBBY HALVERSON WAS OUT EARLY on Thanksgiving morning. Snowfall had been steady all through the night, and the temperature had dropped into the twenties. Bobby had been running his plow up and down Highway 30, the main route between Wooster and Dalton, since five.

The old tractor had been running pretty smoothly, and the heated cab kept Bobby fairly warm. On his second pass toward Dalton, he turned south onto Carr Road and headed back toward Apple Creek. He crossed County Highway 188 and continued toward Dover Road. Along the way he checked the driveways and lanes that opened out onto the road. Many of his Amish friends lived on farms along here, and they didn't have powerful enough equipment to clear their roads in a major snowstorm. So far the area had received only about five inches, but Bobby knew more was coming.

As he plowed south along the road, he saw Henry Lowenstein's old Buick coming toward him. As they pulled alongside each other, Bobby throttled down the tractor and stopped. Henry pulled up alongside and rolled down the window of the old sedan. Bobby leaned out of the window of his cab and called over the sound of the rising wind.

"Hey, Henry, where you headed in this weather?"

"Hey yourself, Bobby," Henry called back. "I'm headed to Dalton to my grandma's house for dinner. Takin' Missus Springer up to the quilt fair."

Bobby hadn't noticed Jerusha in the backseat. He had once been close to Reuben and Jerusha. He and Reuben had been like brothers.

"Howdy, Jerusha," Bobby called down with a smile.

"Hello, Bobby," Jerusha answered, looking straight ahead.

Bobby understood and let it pass. He turned to Henry.

"You better get a move on. The wind has picked up quite a bit, and the snow is really gonna start coming down. It's getting colder too. I sure don't like the looks of this storm. It's gonna be a whopper."

"Don't worry about me, Bobby," Henry called back. "This old warhorse is like a tank. Got a great heater, and she's heavy enough to go right through the drifts."

"Okay, then," Bobby said. "But keep your eyes on the road. There's a lot of black ice between here and Dalton, and the snow has been filling in behind me as I plow. I'm expecting the main part of the storm to be on us a lot quicker than we expect."

"Will do, Bobby!" Henry yelled over the wind. He put the car in gear and chugged up the road.

Bobby had an uneasy feeling as he watched Henry head north. He pushed on the tractor's throttle and began heading south to the county highway. About a quarter of a mile down the road, he turned left and pulled into the Borntrager farm, plowing the snow into the ditch as he headed down the lane. Amos was out in front of the barn getting his cows inside. He waved as Bobby rumbled up.

"Everything okay, Amos?" Bobby asked from the cab.

"Doin' fine, Bobby, just fine," Amos answered. "Thanks for plowin' her out for me. I got lots of propane and plenty of food, so I think we'll be all right until she blows over."

"Well, I'll look back in on you next pass through," Bobby called as he turned around in the farmyard and headed back toward Apple Creek. He turned south onto Carr Road and passed the Albrecht place and then the Kopfensteins'. Bobby could see the families out battening down their barns and sheds and getting their livestock under cover. He then pulled onto the county highway and headed west into Apple Creek. The wind began to howl, and Bobby noticed that his cab was considerably colder.

She's coming, and she's a mean one. This is gonna be nasty. The tractor throbbed beneath him as he headed west. Bobby Halverson had a very bad feeling about this storm.

He had a good reason to fear this storm. Two hundred fifty miles to the east, the wind was gusting at over eighty miles per hour. Large areas of the Northeast were experiencing massive tree damage and power outages. Coastal waves and tidal surges from the high winds breached dikes around LaGuardia and flooded the airport runways, shutting down the air traffic there. In Pennsylvania, the Schuylkill River reached flood stage as more than thirty inches of snow accumulated in Pittsburgh. Two fronts of the storm, one moving down from Canada and one up from the south, joined over Lake Erie and moved west and south, bringing freezing temperatures and record snowfall. The barometric pressure inside the storm had plummeted over Washington DC, and the storm began to rotate counterclockwise, transforming into a huge, six-thousand-foot-high cyclone with winds that would eventually top a hundred miles an hour.

◇◇◇

Henry reached Kidron Road and turned north. He was looking for the turnoff to Nussbaum Road. That was the shortcut that took almost a mile off the trip into Dalton. The wind had picked up, and Henry could feel the car shake as the gusts struck. The snow was thick, and visibility was only about three hundred feet. Still, Henry wanted to get to Dalton before the worst of it hit, so he picked up speed. He leaned forward, peering through the window as the snow closed in. Visibility was decreasing.

He slowed down a bit. What was that ahead? Something in the road, but what? It was some black...Before he could finish the thought, the cow turned toward the car and into its path. Henry pulled the car to the right to swing around the animal and then jerked the wheel to the left.

The confused cow stood her ground as the car hit her in the hindquarters. She spun around and then staggered off up the road.

Henry tried to turn into the skid as he felt himself sliding off the road, but the big Buick lost traction, and the rear end began to swing around, guiding the car over the side of the road backward and into a ditch.

When the car settled, Henry took stock of himself and asked, "You okay, Missus Springer?"

"I think I twisted my neck," Jerusha said. "But other than that I seem to be all in one piece."

Henry climbed out of the car and went around to the back to look at the now-blown tires.

Then he made his way up the ditch and onto the road to see if he could find the cow. She lay in the ditch about fifty feet away, jerking in spasmodic death throes. He cursed under his breath and then walked back to the car and climbed into the front seat.

"We're stuck good, ma'am," he said. "I only got one spare tire, and both the back tires are blown. Don't think I could get us out of this ditch even with both tires. We're going to need a tow truck."

"What'll we do?" Jerusha asked.

"I know where we are," Henry said. "That was one of old man Johnston's cows—I can tell by the cut ear. That means we're about four miles out of town. I think you should stay here and keep as warm as you can while I go for help. I got an extra blanket in the trunk, and you're dressed pretty warm, so you should be okay."

"Are you sure you shouldn't just stay here, Henry?" asked Jerusha, her voice sounding a little frightened. "Surely someone will come by and see us."

"No, ma'am," he answered. "With the storm pickin' up, there might not be anyone along here for a good while. Most people would take Highway 30 in this storm. Besides, the ditch is just deep enough to keep us out of view. I can make it into town well before dark and get somebody to come for you. You just wait here. I'll be back in no time."

Henry closed the door, went around to open the trunk, and pulled out the shipping company blanket he kept there. It was thin and dirty, but it was all he had. He closed the trunk and handed the blanket in through the back door to Jerusha. He tried to keep up a good front as he said, "Don't worry none, Missus Springer. I'll be back before you know it. I'm going right up to Nussbaum Road, over to the Township Highway, and then right into town. I'll probably get picked up before I even get there. Just bundle up and don't leave the car. I need to know you'll be here when I get back."

"Don't worry, Henry," Jerusha said. "I don't think I'll be going for a walk or anything."

Jerusha managed a wan smile as Henry patted her on the arm. He handed her the car keys.

"If it gets really cold you can turn the car on for a few minutes. She's got a good heater and she'll warm up pretty quick. But don't leave 'er on too long—five minutes at most. You don't want to get carbon monoxide poisoning."

He closed the car door and started off up the road to Dalton. The white snow closed in around the car, and in a few seconds Henry had disappeared. Jerusha sat still, staring into the gathering storm.

This is Your fault, Jerusha thought. *You are still punishing me. What did I do to make You hate me so much?*

◇◇◇

Not far away lay another wrecked car, still on its roof, partway out onto the frozen pond. Inside the car lay the little girl. The seat cushion, some extra clothing, and a lone blanket that had piled up around her during the crash were all she had to keep her from the bitter cold. Her eyes fluttered open, and she looked out through the window of the upside-down car. She remembered the look on the bad man's face as he sank beneath the water. He had stared right at her as he clutched the edge of the ice with one arm. Then the water had dragged him down, his open mouth filling with water as he choked out one last scream. Now she was alone in the storm, and there was only one person she wanted to comfort her, to hold her close…but that person was gone.

The girl stirred weakly and began to cry. "Mama, I'm cold," she said. "I'm so cold…"

Chapter Six

Apple Creek

◇◇◇

Jerusha sat in the back of Henry's car, wrapped in the thin blanket the boy had given her. She felt as if she had been sitting for hours, waiting for Henry to return. As time wore on, her thoughts crowded in on her. Reuben's face was before her now, staring at her with that empty look that had filled his eyes on the day he went away after Jenna's death. Jerusha closed her eyes and shook her head as she tried to keep her thoughts on her present situation.

She didn't want to think about Reuben or Jenna or Apple Creek, but she couldn't stop the thoughts. While she had been making the quilt she had been intent on her work, and her single-minded determination kept at bay the demons that wanted to devour her soul. She remembered the moment she had finished the quilt.

Always before, she had followed the Amish tradition of deliberately sewing a mistake into her quilts to avoid offending God with human perfection. But she hadn't done that this time. This quilt *was* perfect, and she had made it. If that was a sin, then so be it.

When she had come to the place where she normally would have sewn a mistake into the patchwork, she had paused. The quilt was stretched tightly on the frame, the beautiful silken fabric glowing in the last rays of light coming through her window. The effect was almost sublime in its perfection, and she had leaned back in her chair to admire her work.

She remembered how she had broken the last thread of the perfect quilt in defiance, and suddenly a weariness overcame her. Her head nodded as she sat wrapped against the cold in the back of Henry's car. Her thoughts, once churning like the water in the millrace behind her father's gristmill, began to still themselves. The days of planning and sewing and hating had taken their toll, and in the cold light of the gathering storm she remembered the days of her happiness...before.

◇◇◇

The days of Jerusha's childhood had been good days, filled with the comfort of a stable family and the practice of her faith. Her family was Old Order Amish, and she loved the ways of her people. The Hershbergers lived on one of the largest farms in Apple Creek. The family had been in America for more than two hundred years—since the Plain People accepted William Penn's offer of religious freedom. Even before that, when the first Amish came to Pennsylvania from Switzerland in 1720, the Hershbergers were among them.

When the Amish moved west in the early 1800s, the Hershberger family had followed, arriving in the village of Apple Creek in 1857. The land was fertile and open, and it greatly suited the Amish folk and their agricultural skills. The Hershberger family had homesteaded a tract of land outside the village, and over the years they had purchased neighboring farms. Now they held more than two hundred acres of the most fertile land in the township, and Hershberger milk and cheese were renowned throughout Wayne County.

During her childhood, the rest of the nation was suffering through the Great Depression, and the Amish were not sheltered from the turmoil of those years. But the Amish were accustomed to doing more with less. The Hershberger family and their neighbors simply pulled inward and depended on each other, so Jerusha grew up in an atmosphere of love, self-sufficiency, and community. The Amish of Apple Creek remained an island of safety and prosperity in those troubled times.

Jerusha's days were filled with the simple tasks of a farm girl—planting in the spring, tending the animals, and cooking for her father and brothers as they harvested the corn and wheat. She watched her grandmother and mother can and preserve the garden produce and put up the fruit for the winter. They filled the root cellar with potatoes, onions, and barrels of apples. Her father brought ice from the winter pond and packed it into the cold house, which was dug into the side of a hill behind the house. Then they prepared hams, chickens, and sides of beef and stored them away for the festive dinners and holiday celebrations that were the hallmarks of her youth.

Jerusha's father was an *Armendiener*, a deacon, and she loved to sit quietly while he read from the Bible during the Sunday meetings. The scriptures came alive to her as he read, and his rich baritone voice soothed her and filled her with a certainty that the God her family served could only be a good and loving God.

When she was old enough, her father gave her the job of bringing home the milk cows every evening, a job she thoroughly enjoyed. Like most farm children, she liked being alone. In those days, before World War II, the fields around Apple Creek were open to the horizon, and there were many stands of trees with small creeks and ponds. Jerusha found great comfort in the simplicity of her life as she wandered through the fields and woods. Every so often she would hear the train chugging along the tracks to parts unknown, its mournful whistle seeming to warn of the dangers and sorrows of a complicated modern world.

At these times Jerusha would kneel down on the earth and touch the grass or stop by a cold clear brook and dip her hands in the water, feeling the coolness on her skin and letting her thoughts focus on the God who could create such beauty with a spoken word. She didn't comprehend the deeper theological issues that surrounded her faith, nor did they really interest her. She only knew that at some time in the past, wise men had led her people away from the traps and pitfalls of a world that catered to men's basest natures and distracted them from this God of wonders who revealed Himself to her in every wooded path and every spring flower.

Many days, after her chores were done, Jerusha found her way to the old red barn and climbed up the wooden rungs into the sweet-smelling hayloft. She would lie on her back in a soft mound of hay and fix her thoughts on the psalms and prayers that were the staple of her people's life and daily work. Often she brought her family's copy of the *Ausbund*, the ancient Amish hymnal, and read the lyrics to herself. There was no musical notation in the book, but the melodies had been passed down from generation to generation and were as familiar to her as the stars of the night sky. Her favorite was the *Loblied*, the praise song, which was sung every time the people gathered for church, and her sweet voice would lift in praise to her God. As she sang, she often felt that she was wrapped in God's comforting arms. Often her father, passing by on his way to some part of the farm, would stop and listen as Jerusha's clear soprano floated down out of the hayloft like a sweet angel voice singing the praises of God.

"*Kumme, dochter*, there is work to be done," he would call up to her, yet the tone of his voice would let her know that he took comfort in a daughter so grounded in the faith.

Jerusha would climb down and walk with her father in silence. He did not often speak of tender things, but a gentle hand on her shoulder would fill her heart with acceptance and love.

The days of her young life invited a future that, while unknown, need not be feared, but rather welcomed. This life, uncomplicated and innocent, was all she knew, and it held her secure just as a mother's tender arms hold a newborn. Time was not to be counted in hours and minutes, but rather in revelations and discoveries, in long dreamy summer days that never seemed to end and cold winter nights sitting by a warm fire, watching her mother and grandmother at the quilting frame.

And so it was that when she was ten years old her grandmother brought her into the *dawdy* house where she had lived since *Grossdaadi*'s death.

"*Kumme,* Jerusha," she said, "it is time for you to learn to quilt. See here now, *onest.*" And she began to teach Jerusha.

"The first thing that needs to be done before any quilt is made is to decide which kind of design we will use," she had said. "We must know in our heart what the quilt will look like when it is finished, because it can take anywhere from four hundred to six hundred hours to put together just one quilt. You can sew the most perfect stitch, but without a good design it means nothing. If the design is not pleasing to the eye from the start, that's wasted time, and to waste time is to try God's patience."

Sitting at her grandmother's side, she watched her sketch out what she called a "star" quilt. The design was beautiful but simple. First a starburst in the center, then eight branching pillars, surrounded by another circle. On the outside of the circle she drew more pillars that were set between the inner pillars with the outer circle separating them.

"On the tops of the pillars we will make flames of fire," her grandmother said softly. "They will be just like the lampstand in *der Heilige Platz*, where God spoke to the high priest."

Once the design was created, Jerusha watched as her grandmother cut the chosen pieces of fabric into perfectly matching parts.

"If the quilt is going to be even and symmetrical, the pieces must be true," she said.

She let Jerusha try her hand, and even on her first try Jerusha cut the pieces straight and perfect.

"*Ja, das is gut,*" Grandmother said. "You will be a fine quilt maker, my girl."

Once the pieces were cut correctly, Grandmother pieced them together with pinpoint accuracy.

"If the quilt is not aligned properly, even in just one small part, the whole thing will look off balance and might pucker," she had said. "If the design is to be even and pleasing to the eye, each individual piece of fabric must be stitched together just right in order for it to fit together properly. You must trust your own eye and sewing skills for measurement and accuracy. It is a gift not every quilter has."

Over the following days as *Grossmudder* began to patiently open the quilting way to Jerusha, the girl felt something growing in her—the absolute certainty that God had given her an eye and a gift for this work. As her grandmother pieced together the layers of fabric, she allowed Jerusha to help her stitch them together. First, she placed the patterned top piece on a layer of batting, and then sewed the whole design to a black backing piece. Then, with the quilt stretched tightly on the quilting frame, Jerusha began to learn the even, beautiful stitch of the quilter.

"Dummel dich net," her grandmother would say. "Take your time, don't hurry."

Once, when her mind wandered while she was stitching a piece, she made a mistake and went past the place where she should have stopped.

"Halt ei, sell geht su weit!" her grandmother exclaimed. "You have gone too far. You must concentrate on what you are doing, my girl."

Jerusha had watched with downcast eyes and a flame burning in her cheeks as her grandmother carefully removed the errant stitches.

"Never hurry, always pay attention, and do the work as unto the Lord," she told Jerusha in her gentle voice. "You have been given a way to give back to the Lord, as He has given to you. This is a special gift not everyone is given. But to whom much is given, much is required. You must always give back to God from the gift He has given you. And there are dangers along the way. If you become a good quilter, it is quite possible for you to become prideful, thinking that somehow you are more special than others. That is why we put a small mistake in the quilt before we finish. This is so we do not make God angry with us for being too proud."

Jerusha did not understand until many years later why she felt the small twinge of fear, the first she had ever felt, when her grandmother spoke those words.

Chapter Seven

Deep Roots

The next few years flew by for Jerusha. She had found her calling as a quilter, and within a year she was sewing whole sections of her grandmother's quilts on her own. Her stitch was fine, almost invisible, and while most quilters would put seventy thousand stitches in a quilt, Jerusha sewed more than ninety thousand stitches into her first complete quilt.

"*Ja*, your stitch is so small and even," her grandmother said as she looked over Jerusha's first quilt. "It is as though you've been quilting all your life."

Grandmother Hannah also helped Jerusha with her schooling, which allowed Jerusha to spend more time at home working on the quilts. Her grandmother was careful to see that she did her chores and helped around the house as all the Hershberger children did, but when the moment came each day to sit down at the quilting frame, Jerusha lost herself in the work.

One day when they were working on a new design together, Jerusha asked, "Grandmother, has our family always lived in Apple Creek?"

"We have been in Apple Creek almost a hundred years."

"How did our family come to Apple Creek?"

Hannah paused and looked at Jerusha over her reading glasses, which she wore down on her nose. Then she put down her work, and taking Jerusha by the hand, she led her to a small chest in the next room. Hannah opened the chest and took out two books. She held up the first. It was titled *The Martyr's Mirror*.

"To understand how we came to Apple Creek, you must first ask, 'Where did the Amish come from?' This book was first printed in the year 1660 in Holland," Hannah said. "It tells the story of the Anabaptists and their fight for religious freedom.

"And this book," Hannah continued, holding up a small volume with a plain leather cover, "tells the story of Jonathan and Joshua Hershberger. It tells of the choices the twin brothers made after Indians massacred their family near Fort Henry on the Ohio, and the effect those decisions had on generations of Hershbergers. One brother forsook the Amish church, and all his descendants went out into the world, so there are many with the name Hershberger who are not Amish. The other brother, Joshua, stayed in the church and remained faithful, even under the most difficult conditions. Joshua was your great-great-great-grandfather. His grandson, my father, came to Apple Creek in 1860 as a boy. It is because Joshua stayed true that you are here today."

Jerusha lifted her chin and said proudly, "Grandmother, I will always stay true to our family and our ways. I swear it."

"Be careful what you swear, child," said Hannah softly as she stood up and put the books back into the chest. "One day God may hold you to it."

◇◇◇

Jerusha shifted in the backseat of Henry's car and moaned slightly. Her eyes fluttered open and then closed again. For a moment she couldn't remember where she was. *There was an accident. A cow.* She pushed herself up in the seat and stared around.

The memory of her grandmother's words resounded in her mind. "*Be careful what you swear, child. One day God may hold you to it.*"

Jerusha realized with a start that she was breaking the vow she had sworn to Hannah so many years ago.

But I'm not the guilty one! You're punishing me, and I didn't do anything! I was a good Amish girl. I kept the ordnung, *and I've been faithful in all my ways. You are the one who is wrong. But since You're God, You don't get punished, is that it?*

Jerusha felt the flush of anger rise in her face. The empty days since Jenna's death and Reuben's disappearance crowded in on her, and her thoughts became incoherent and jumbled.

Get hold of yourself, Jerusha. Conserve your energy. You have to wait patiently until Henry returns.

Jerusha clutched the blanket closer around her and found herself thinking about her grandmother again.

It all started when You took her from me. She was my teacher and my friend and I loved her so, and yet You let her die a horrible death.

Suddenly Jerusha was startled to realize that her anger had begun that day, the day her grandmother died.

That was the day I started to see You as you really are—vengeful, controlling, and to be feared. You are not the God I thought I loved, but a God who has taken everything I held most dear. I won't forget and I'll never forgive...

Chapter Eight

Reuben

◇◇◇

Seventeen-year-old Jerusha stood in front of her mirror. The black dress was simple and severe, and yet it couldn't hide the lovely young woman she had become. Even in her sadness, her face shone.

Outside her bedroom, a plain wooden coffin stood in a room that had been stripped of all furniture. In the coffin lay her beloved *grossmudder*, Hannah. Hours after her death, Jerusha and her mother had carefully washed Hannah's body and then dressed her in the plain white dress Hannah had worn on her wedding day.

Even in death, Grandmother's face was serene and gentle, and somehow she looked younger than the years that had finally taken her. When the family learned Hannah was dying of cancer, they began preparations for this day. Two days before her death, Jerusha's father made the coffin with his own hands. Jerusha watched with a heavy heart as he skillfully prepared the simple pine boards.

"We all face this day, *dochter*," he said to Jerusha as he worked. "Your *grossmudder* has lived a rich life and is beloved in her community. She lived the way our people have been taught to live for three hundred years—love your enemy, do good to those who harm you, and pray for those who despitefully use you. She planted seeds of love in the hearts of many members of our church and will leave treasures behind that will work in people's lives for many years to come. She lived by a simple rule: *Alli mudder muss sariye fer ihre famiyle.* She especially loved you and has imparted a special gift to you. Now that she's gone, you must never forget what she taught you. The gift you have is from God and must be given back to Him with each quilt you make. You have become well known in this area for your skill, but you must always remember that Jesus is the vine and you are only the branch. Without Him you can do nothing. There may come a day when you must give all back to Him. Do not let pride take root, *dochter.*"

Jerusha's heart ached with sorrow as she stood before the mirror. Her grandmother had not only taught her to be a quilter, she had schooled her in the practices and roots of their faith.

"Jerusha, it's time," her mother called from the next room.

Jerusha opened the bedroom door and entered the viewing room quietly. It was the third day since Grandmother's death, and four older men who had been friends of her grandfather stood next to the coffin, preparing to carry Hannah outside to the plain black horse-drawn hearse. Jerusha went to the side of the plain pine box and stared down at Hannah, trying to fix the image of her grandmother's beautiful face in her mind forever.

I must not cry or show emotion, she thought. Her hands clenched the edge of the box, and as the grief rose in her she began to feel something she had never felt before—anger toward her God.

This is blasphemy, said a strident voice within her, and she found herself trembling in fear as she stood there. She wanted to cry out or fall sobbing on Hannah's breast, but instead she gripped the coffin until her knuckles turned white. Then she felt her father's hand on her shoulder and heard his quiet voice in her ear.

"Come, *dochter*, we must let her go," he said.

Slowly she let go of the coffin and stepped back. The four men picked up the box and walked slowly and silently out the door. Jerusha and her parents and brothers followed. Outside, a long row of wagons and buggies was stretched along the road. The coffin was placed into the hearse, and the pallbearers climbed on board. The wagon started off at a slow pace, and the mourners stirred up their horses and fell into line. The solemn caravan began to make its way south toward Millersburg and the Amish cemetery. The twenty-mile journey took three hours, and Jerusha dreaded every minute. The rising of the sun burned off the early morning coolness. Jerusha felt the sun's heat on her back. Ahead of them was a wagon with a family she didn't recognize. She leaned over to her mother and asked, "Who are those people, Mama?"

"That's the Springer family. Mr. Springer is a widower with two sons. He's come from Wooster to court Abigail Verkler, who lost her husband last year."

Jerusha looked with curiosity at the buggy ahead. She could tell that the woman in the buggy was Abigail, for her mourning clothes didn't conceal her small stature and stout body. The man seated beside her wore the black broad-brimmed hat peculiar to her people. Seated in the back of the buggy were two boys, one a young man already. They stared straight ahead, their longish hair curling out from under their hats.

The miles crept by, and Jerusha found herself thinking about the moment of anger she had felt while she was standing by the coffin. She felt ashamed that such a strong emotion should arise in her heart. She had always been a child of God, and to feel anger toward Him was a new and puzzling sensation.

Will I have hope of salvation if I show anger toward God? I've tried to be a good and faithful girl. I know He died for me, and I hope I'm saved, but can I offend Him enough that He would keep me out of heaven?

She pondered on that for a while until the rhythmic clopping of the horse's hooves lulled her to sleep on her mother's shoulder.

They arrived at the cemetery at midday. The graveyard was on a private farm because her people didn't like being buried with the

Englisch. The people climbed out of their wagons and buggies and slowly made their way to the simple farm building where the service was to be held.

The pallbearers carried the coffin to the front of the room, placed it on two sawhorses, and opened it so the family could view Hannah one last time. None of the mourners showed any emotion as they sat on the simple benches. A *Volliger Diener*, a bishop, delivered the two-hour sermon in Pennsylvania Dutch. His words were not a eulogy of Hannah and her goodness but rather an exhortation to give thanks and praise to God. No one shared stories about Hannah, but Jerusha wished she could go up to the front and tell everyone how much her grandmother meant to her. At the end of the service, the bishop mentioned Hannah's name, the name of her husband, and her birth and death date, and that was the end.

Jerusha looked around at the people, and to her surprise, she felt the anger rising in her again.

She was so good to me, Lord, she prayed. *Why did You take her from me in such a horrible way? Did I do something wrong? Are You punishing me?*

She wished with all her heart that the people would cry out and throw themselves weeping on her grandmother's coffin, but the room was still as the pallbearers picked up the pine box and carried it out to the gravesite. Small beams of light came through cracks in the wall and lit up the dust motes floating in the air.

There was no music. The shuffling of feet on the dirt floor made the only sound in the simple farm building as the people followed the coffin out. Breathing hard, Jerusha leaned forward and slowly stood to her feet with her elbows bent and her fists clenched. Just as she was about to scream the name of her grandmother, a firm hand took hold of her shoulder, and she heard a quiet voice say in her ear, "Don't."

Jerusha turned slowly and saw the chest of someone very tall. She lifted her head and looked into the bluest eyes she had ever seen. Dark, long hair framed a face that was remarkable in its symmetry and strength. The black hat, tilted back on his head, gave the young man a slightly rakish look. Behind the stern set of his face, Jerusha saw that his eyes were kind toward her.

"I know you want to scream, but don't," he whispered. "My mother died last year, and I wanted to scream at her funeral too. Believe me, now is not the time."

In the grip of his strong hand, Jerusha felt the tension and anger drain out of her, leaving an empty, aching sorrow, and then she found herself walking slowly along with him out to the grave.

The bishop who led the funeral went ahead of the mourners to the graveyard. When all had gathered beside the grave site, he gave a final prayer, and the pallbearers closed Hannah Hershberger's coffin for the last time. They placed ropes under the coffin and used them to lower the coffin into the ground. Members of Jerusha's family stepped forward and threw a handful of earth onto the coffin. Jerusha stood a long time with the dirt in her hand before she dropped it into the grave. When the clod hit the top of her grandmother's coffin, it sounded like a door slamming. A knife twisted in her heart as in that moment she came to grips with the reality of death and its finality. Jersusha stepped back, and as the mourners watched, the pallbearers filled in the grave. And then it was over. There were no flowers or foliage near the grave. The plain tombstone lay on its side, waiting to be set in place.

Hannah Hershberger, 1862–1941, 79 years, 2 months, 5 days.

That was the summation of her grandmother's life. Somehow it seemed not enough.

As Jerusha slowly walked back to her father's buggy, the young man who had stopped her from crying out stepped in beside her and spoke to her. The sound of his voice was rich and masculine, and she suddenly felt herself blush. She plucked up her courage and looked into those startling blue eyes. They were still smiling at her, and then she heard his words coming to her as though from a long distance away, and slowly she realized what he was saying.

"I'm Reuben Springer, and you're the girl who makes those quilts," he said. Then he turned and walked back to the road.

◇◇◇

The upside-down car teetered back and forth in the wind like an old rocking chair. Inside, buried in a pile of clothing, blankets, and a seat cushion, lay the little girl. She had reddish-blonde hair and a determined chin. Her skin was blue from the cold, and over the hours she passed in and out of consciousness. The front of the car lifted up, settled down again, and then lifted up again. The wind blew harder and then eased off. The car moved a little, sliding a few inches more out onto the ice. The snow had blanketed the surface of the pond, hiding the hole that had been there only hours before.

As the car rocked gently, a picture came into the little girl's mind. She was warm and safe in her mama's arms, and her mother was singing a song as she gently rocked back and forth, back and forth.

Suddenly the wind picked up again, and a strong gust hit the car. The front end reared up like a horse and then smashed back down onto the ice. The ice groaned and cracked, and then a small fracture began to run out from under the front of the car like a lightning bolt.

Chapter Nine

Changes

IN THE SPRING OF 1941, distant rumblings of the conflict in Europe had come to Apple Creek from time to time, but for the most part the Plain People did not involve themselves in discussions about England's battle against the Nazis. Their firm belief in nonresistance precluded any discussion of a possible global war. The people remembered that in World War I the government had drafted Amish men, but most refused to fight, and the whole community had suffered persecution and scorn as a result.

And now, before another war erupted, the elders of the faith were working with the government to provide honorable alternatives to actual combat. However, the possibility of being forced into combat was a source of some concern among the young people. Even so, on this lovely spring morning, thoughts of the war and the world outside Apple Creek were far from Jerusha's mind.

Jerusha hadn't seen Reuben Springer since her grandmother's funeral, but she thought about him often. She remembered his gentle touch and soothing voice. She especially remembered his deep blue eyes and the effect they had on her. She was bothered that someone of the opposite sex could command her thoughts the way he did, for she had kept herself apart from the company of young men, even at the Sunday night singings, where discrete courtship was encouraged for young people past the age of sixteen.

Jerusha had no interest in marriage. Her life was centered in her family, the dawn-to-dusk work of a farmer's daughter, and quilting. As a result, this newcomer's constant intrusion into her thoughts was aggravating. Yet she also found her heart being stirred in a way she had never known before. She remembered the smile hidden behind his stern eyes, the breadth of his shoulders, and the easy, confident way he carried himself. Jerusha was not a young woman without passion and had experienced moments of deep love and wonder in her young life—for her family, for her God, for the beauty of a sunset, for her grandmother. But these feelings she had when she thought of Reuben were unlike anything she had ever known. In one moment they were deep and still, like her father's millpond at sunset, and the next minute they would carry her over rushing rapids, tumbling her thoughts and shaking the very foundations of her emotions.

And so it was that she was lost in reverie as she walked the familiar path into the village to visit the store, not paying attention to what was going on around her.

"Well, here's one of them Amish gals," said a thick voice, startling her. Ahead of her on the path stood two men, one holding a half-empty bottle in his hand.

"And a mighty pretty one at that," said the second man.

The first man stepped forward into Jerusha's path. He towered over her, his eyes bloodshot and his face grizzled with several days' growth of beard.

"They told us over in Indiana that there was some holy gals out here, unspoiled, so to speak," the first man said. "But we didn't reckon they was as pretty as you." He leered at Jerusha with a sly grin.

"Please excuse me so I can go about my business," Jerusha said, uncertainty in her voice.

"Well, we was thinking we might go about some business with you, say...in those trees over there. Just a few minutes of your time, and then we'll be on our way. What say you?" As he spoke he reached out and caught Jerusha by the arm.

The second man, who was small and thin, had edged around behind her and suddenly clapped his hand over her mouth. "Like he said, just a few minutes of your time, darlin'," he whispered thickly in her ear, "and then we'll be off. We'll never tell, and you can keep your secret. It's mighty lonesome out on the road, and we're in great need of some female companionship." His breath was foul, and he began to paw at her, his filthy hand fumbling at the snaps of her dress.

Jerusha tried to scream, but the man tightened his grip on her mouth. She struggled in his grasp, but he was too strong for her. She bit down on his hand as hard as she could and tasted his blood in her mouth.

"Owee! She's a spitfire!"

"Hold her. I'll quiet her down," the first man said. He drew back his fist, but suddenly there was a *thud*, and he seemed to disappear. The second man suddenly loosened his grip on Jerusha and turned away from her. Jerusha collapsed to the ground, gasping for breath. There was a series of cracking sounds, another *thud*, and then quiet. A gentle hand touched her shoulder.

"Come along, little Miss Quilter," said a familiar voice. She looked up into Reuben Springer's face. Behind his blue eyes she saw the same smile she had seen before.

"But those men," she gasped. "They...they wanted to..."

"They appear to be taking a little nap, so that's probably the last thing on their minds right now."

Jerusha looked behind her and saw the two men stretched out along the path. The first one began to stir. Reuben stepped over and slapped the big man's face. His voice took on a dangerous edge as he roused the semiconscious man. "Get up, you pig, or this will be the last place you'll ever sleep."

The big man rubbed his jaw as he slowly struggled to his knees. He looked around for a weapon. Reuben quickly stepped in with two powerful blows to his head, and the big man crumpled in a heap. He lifted his hands in a gesture of surrender.

"Now, if I were you and I didn't want to spend the rest of my short life getting the stuffing whipped out of me, I'd collect your pal and hit the road," Reuben said as he stood over the fallen man.

"Okay, okay, we're going. But I never heard of no fightin' Amish before."

"If I ever see you in this town again," Reuben replied, "I'll rewrite that notion on your thick skull. Now git!"

The first man stood up shakily and walked over to his friend, who was just coming to. He gave him a kick in the leg and said, "Come on. Seems we're not welcome here."

The second man dragged himself to his feet, and the two staggered away. Reuben returned to Jerusha's side, took her arm, and helped her up.

"There now," he said softly, "all's well."

Jerusha looked up and stared straight into Reuben's eyes. Immediately she blushed and looked down, totally flustered by the turn of events. Her expression did not escape Reuben's notice.

"So, Miss Hershberger, do I really have that much of an effect on you?" he asked. "I must say, it's encouraging and rather flattering."

"Well, thank you for your help," she shot back, alternately flushing red and going pale. "But don't give yourself airs. I was just attacked, and then I watched you beat the tar out of those men. How am I supposed to react?"

"Oh, so I'm not so grand as I thought," he said, chuckling. "Well, that's fine. As for beating the tar out of those men, I'd do it twice over if it meant your safety."

"You're a strange sort of a pacifist," Jerusha said. "I'm not sure the elders would agree with you."

"Well, as you get to know me better, you might find that I have some...well, unorthodox views as far as the elders are concerned."

"What makes you think I want to know you better?" Jerusha asked. "I don't even know you at all."

"But I would like to know you better," Reuben said, "and if it takes thrashing a couple of thugs to get an introduction and win your admiration, then I'll do what it takes."

Jerusha softened. "I'm sorry. After all, you did save me from an awful fate, I'm sure." She blushed again and then said, "I probably should be going." She took a few tentative steps toward the village.

"Where to?" Reuben asked, falling in beside her.

Jerusha tried to bring order back to her emotions. "Well, if it's any of your business, I'm going to the store. I have to get some things and then go right home."

She managed a glance his way and took him in. At her grandmother's funeral she had assumed he was in his teens, but now she saw that he was older, maybe twenty or twenty-one. Something about him seemed different from the boys who had tried to impress her in school or at the evening singings. He carried himself with an assurance that most of the boys lacked. She felt it both attractive and at the same time disconcerting.

"Where did you learn to fight like that?" she asked quietly.

"I have an *Englisch* friend in Wooster who's in a boxing club, and he showed me a few things."

"But we aren't supposed to be friends with the *Englisch*," Jerusha said.

"When I turned sixteen, my *daed* looked the other way at some of the things I wanted to find out about."

"Oh, running around," said Jerusha. "*Rumspringa*."

"Well, I guess that's the name for it," Reuben answered, "but to me it's just getting to know this wide world we live in a little better."

"Is that why you're not married?" Jerusha asked.

"That, and the fact that I've never seen a girl I was interested in," he said. "That is, until I saw you."

Jerusha felt a strange falling sensation take hold of her. She found nothing to say as the two walked on in silence for a moment, and then Reuben took her arm and stopped her.

"I don't want you to think me too bold, but I want to ask your permission to talk to your father. I would like to court you," he said quietly.

Her thoughts swarmed through her head like bees, and then she heard herself say quietly, "All right, if that's what you want."

And then she quickly turned and walked away from him toward the village.

Chapter Ten

Troubles

WHEN JERUSHA ARRIVED HOME, she ran straight to her room, threw herself on her bed, and tried to quiet her emotions.

Why did I tell him he could talk to Daed*?*

The events of the day flooded in on her—the attack in the woods, Reuben appearing out of nowhere to save her, the beating he gave those men, her acquiescence to his request to speak to her father. It had all happened so fast, she barely had time to think. But now, alone in her room, she couldn't help her mind from replaying it again and again.

How did Reuben happen to be there at just the right time? Was he following me? He beat those men terribly. It should have made me sick, but it didn't. Oh, Reuben, what am I supposed to do with you?

Suddenly Jerusha's life had become very complicated. Her simple childhood and the years she had spent by her grandmother's side had all seemed so easy. Family, farmwork, and quilting had been her life. Now a whole new element had been thrust upon her in the person of Reuben Springer. She turned onto her back and stared up at the ceiling.

Late the next afternoon, Jerusha's father came in from his work. He cleaned up and then went to Jerusha's door and knocked.

"Jerusha, are you in there? I need to speak with you."

Jerusha opened the door slowly. "What is it, *Daed*?"

"The Springer boy came to see me this morning."

So soon!

"What did he want?" she asked, feigning ignorance.

"He wants my permission to court you," her father said. "I told him he could not."

Inwardly, Jerusha gave a sigh of relief. Controlling herself, she asked, "What reason did you give him?"

"The Springer boy is a pleasant young man. He is older, and my understanding is that he is a hard worker. But I have heard stories about his adventures while he has been in *rumspringa*—drinking, fighting, dancing, and other activities that cannot be mentioned. It is said that he owns a car and keeps it in a garage somewhere in Wooster and that he has traveled as far as Akron and Indianapolis dressed as an *Englischer*."

"But many of the boys try out the things of the world during *rumspringa*," Jerusha said. "Does that make him a bad person?"

Her father frowned. "*Nee*, but the most important reason I won't allow it is that although he is twenty-one, he has not been baptized or joined the church. This disqualifies him for marriage. I do not think he is right for you."

Jerusha found herself rising to Reuben's defense. "But, *Daed*, Reuben was so kind to me at the funeral and he—"

"Kindness isn't the measure of a man, especially in our way of life. A man who has given his life to God through baptism and is faithful in the church is a man to be trusted. That is the sort of man I want for my daughter."

Before she could stop herself, Jerusha blurted out a biting response. "Shouldn't I have something to say about who courts me?"

The blank look in her *daed*'s eyes surprised Jerusha. The question she asked hadn't even registered. "What?" he asked.

Jerusha plucked up her courage and asked the question again. "Shouldn't I be allowed some choice as to whom I may or may not marry?"

This time she saw the anger rise her *daed*'s face. "You will do as I tell you, *dochter*," he said curtly. "This is not a decision you need to concern yourself with." And with that he turned and walked out of the room.

◇◇◇

A week passed, and Jerusha had become a silent guest in a quiet house. When her father asked her do something, she answered with a simple "*Ja, Daed*," but nothing more. She did her chores and worked on her current quilt, but she withdrew herself from the family life and spent more time in her room alone. How could her *daed*, with whom she had always been so close, treat her in such a demeaning way? On the one hand she was glad she could stop thinking about Reuben and put him behind her, and yet on the other hand she was miserable because her heart ached to see him again.

Late one night she awoke to a tapping sound. Rousing herself, she went to the window. Reuben stood there with his fingers to his lips. "Come out," he mouthed silently.

She shook her head. "I can't," she mouthed back.

"Please," he said quietly, and the look in his eyes captured her heart.

Throwing on her coat and her boots, she slipped silently out of her bedroom, through the sleeping house, and out the back door. Reuben was there waiting, motioning for her to keep silent and follow him. They walked silently and quickly through the barnyard to the back of the barn. Jerusha's heart was pounding so furiously, she felt that it would wake the county.

When they were far enough from the house, Reuben spoke. "Your father has refused to let me court you."

"I know," she answered. "Actually, I think it's probably for the..."

Jerusha didn't get the words out of her mouth before Reuben took her in his arms and kissed her, softly at first and then with passion. Jerusha felt herself slipping into a vortex, surrendering and sinking into him. Then suddenly she jerked away and slapped his face.

"Stop!" she cried. "You have no right to touch me like that."

Reuben went white, and then she saw anger in his eyes. He stood staring at her, swaying for a moment in the moonlight, and then he mastered himself. He lowered his face to hide the flush of shame that suffused it.

"I'm sorry, Jerusha." It was the first time he had spoken her name, and the sound of it on his lips was like a balm to her rage.

"You're right, it's not my place to be so...so familiar with you," he said. "Forgive me. I can only excuse myself by saying that you have completely and wonderfully captured my heart, and to be away from you has tormented me. I am in love with you."

"But how can you know that you love me?" she asked. "We have only spoken two times."

"I don't know, Jerusha, but if you can tell me honestly that you do not feel the same toward me, I'll leave this town and never return."

There! It was out in the open, thrown down like a gauntlet.

She stood silently for a long moment, and then she lowered her eyes and said softly, "*Ja*, I love you also."

Everything that had happened in her life up to that moment seemed to break off and go crashing down in a heap around her. Everything she had been, everything she had planned...all of it was turned into dust in the wonder of this moment.

She wondered if she could ever turn back now from whatever should lie ahead.

◇◇◇

The wind struck Henry's car, and shook it like a rag. Jerusha jerked awake in the back, still wrapped in the thin blanket. The memory of

Reuben had been so strong that it took her a moment to realize where she was.

Then the gravity of her situation gripped her once again and the now familiar rage rose in her heart. She began to scream uncontrollably.

"God, if you mean to kill me, just kill me! I want to die! I have nothing left."

She collapsed, sobbing bitterly, on the seat. But her only answer was the howling wind and the snow piling up against the car.

Chapter Eleven

Henry

HENRY DIDN'T LIKE the looks of this storm. The temperature was below freezing, and the wind hurled the snow like needles against his skin. He was an Ohio farm boy and had been outside on many days like this, but today he was responsible for Missus Springer, and so he trudged on along Kidron Road.

She's a strange duck. Real pretty but so sad. She and Reuben used to be so friendly when Jenna was still alive.

Henry remembered the Springer family as loving, happy, and very Amish. The Plain folk had been a part of Apple Creek since before his time, and having Amish folks around seemed as natural to Henry as fleas on a dog. Reuben had built a house on the Hershberger farm after he and Jerusha were married, just across the creek from Henry's dad's place, so Henry saw them almost every day. Reuben worked the farm with Jerusha's dad and brothers, and sometimes he went to Wooster to help his own dad with his farm there.

On those days Henry kept an eye on the house even though Reuben never asked him. He liked watching Jerusha with little Jenna. She would bring the baby out onto the porch and hold her and sing to her, or set her in a small cradle Reuben had made. Then she would work on her quilts. Jerusha was the best quilt maker in all of Wayne County even though she was a young woman. Her reputation was known even among the non-Amish folks in Apple Creek, and some of her quilts were on display in the big Amish store downtown.

Reuben Springer was different from a lot of the Amish men Henry knew. The way Henry had heard it from town folk, Reuben had left Apple Creek for a long time, and nobody really knew where he had gone. The Amish folk never said anything to Henry about it, and his own folks didn't really know much. The Amish were like that—close-mouthed about their personal stuff. They were friendly enough, but they didn't much like mixing with the "English" as they called them. Reuben had come back in 1944, and after about a year he married Jerusha. He was different from the old Reuben, folks said—quieter and more stable. Rumors floated around the village that he had been in the army and was wounded in battle, that he had even won a medal, but no one ever asked, and Reuben never talked about it. Reuben just reappeared one day, was baptized, and joined the Amish church. He was faithful and worked hard on the Springer farm. After a while, Jerusha's father consented to Reuben courting her, and soon Reuben and Jerusha were married. It was as if Reuben had never been gone.

Reuben liked Henry and had taken the boy under his wing, which was unusual for the Amish to do with outsiders. But Reuben had seen more of the world than he cared to talk about. Often after school, Henry would drop by and help Reuben, as he did when Reuben was building a new shed in back of the barn.

Reuben would ask him about how he was doing with his studies and what he wanted to be when he grew up. He would talk to Henry about the Bible too, but Henry didn't mind because Reuben didn't beat him over the head with it. Henry would ask a question about something, and Reuben would tell him what the Bible said about that. Sometimes Reuben's friend Bobby Halverson would be there too. They never said much when Henry was around, but he sensed a special bond between them even though Bobby too was "English."

Those were good times. I never knew anybody as happy as them folks, especially after Jenna was born. Seems like they was always laughin', and they was real close. I guess that's why they was so friendly to me—happiness just spilled out of them.

Just then a gust of wind buffeted Henry and brought him out of his reverie. The snow was falling harder now, and he stopped and looked ahead. He could barely see six feet ahead of him. He pounded his arms against his body to take the chill off and stamped his feet to get his circulation going. The temperature had dropped since he and Jerusha had started out.

The wind began to pick up. Henry slogged forward through the falling snow and turned his thoughts back to Reuben. *Yeah, Reuben was different, but he was totally committed to the church. He didn't want any part of the world, not even...*

Henry stopped the thought. It was too painful to think about little Jenna. She had been a beautiful girl, she was curious about everything and clearly smart.

And she liked me. Still don't know what she saw in a big dumb Buckeye like me. But we sure hit it off.

Henry remembered the days he would come over after work to help Reuben and little Jenna would toddle out on the porch. "Henny, Henny," she would call, holding out her arms.

Henry would pick her up and lift her over his head. Jenna would scream with delight while Jerusha smiled at him warmly.

"Touch the roof, Jenna," Henry would say, and Jenna would reach up in the tall boy's arms and touch the porch roof with her chubby little hands.

"Up again, Henny," she would say, and Henry would lift her up to touch the roof again.

She would have kept me out there all night touchin' the roof. She was such a sweet little thing.

The memory touched a not-quite-healed place in his heart.

Mr. Hershberger, Jenna's grandfather, doted on her and made excuses to come by often after his chores were done just to sit on the Springer porch at sundown with little Jenna curled up in his arms, listening to the songbirds in the Buckeye trees.

Jenna would lay still with her hand touching her grandfather's beard and her little thumb in her mouth. Henry often found the two of them sitting still on the porch, Grandpa sound asleep with the little girl in his arms. She would smile at Henry as she cuddled against her grandfather and softly stroked his beard.

She was like a ray of sunshine even on the darkest days.

When he was at the Springer house, Henry sometimes asked Reuben why the Amish were the way they were.

"You know, Henry," Reuben would say, "I've seen both sides of life—the *Englisch* way and the Amish way, and believe me, the Amish way is best. I didn't always think so, but I've seen some pretty horrible things out there, things that are born out of love for the world and for the power the world offers. If you'd have seen what I've seen, you'd know why I believe that the way of peace is the best way."

Henry trudged on through the snow. He hadn't seen a car since he started, but the storm was fierce and Kidron was a back road, so it made sense that people wouldn't be out. This was a pretty desolate part of the county, so Henry hadn't expected to see much traffic. His had been the only car on the road when they left Apple Creek.

I sure didn't think it would take this long or that the storm would get so bad. Maybe I should have walked back to the county highway and waited for a car to pass.

Soon Henry had to force his way through drifts as the road was completely covered with snow. His eyes began playing tricks on him. Everything was so white, Henry realized he couldn't tell where he was going. He tried to see through the whiteout to find some familiar landmark but to no avail.

Suddenly he slipped and felt himself sliding into a shallow ditch.

He clambered out the other side onto what looked like a lane lined with trees. He could see the branches of the closest trees on either side of him waving wildly in the wind. He began to walk slowly down the lane.

In a few minutes a wooden post with a mailbox on it appeared out of the storm, and he saw the name Knepp on the side.

Mark Knepp's place! I must have walked straight across the meadow without even realizing I was off the pavement.

Mark Knepp was an old widower. He had a phone and could call for help. That was Henry's only hope. He was losing feeling in his hands and feet.

He stumbled to where he thought the Knepp driveway should be. *If I remember, the mailbox was out on the lane, and the driveway to the house was down a ways on the right side.*

Henry looked for a light or a shed or anything that would tell him he was close to the house. He stumbled along, panic rising in his chest.

Just then he saw something out of the corner of his eye. It was a tree limb, torn loose by the wind and falling directly at him. Before he could duck, the limb struck him squarely on the side of his head. Henry crumpled into the snow like a polled ox and slipped into darkness as the snow piled up around him.

Chapter Twelve

Summer Dreams

Jerusha was worried. Henry had been gone a long time, and it was beginning to get dark. The wind was piling snow up against the doors of the car. Jerusha rummaged around in her bag to find the old watch Reuben had given her. She pulled it out and opened the case. In the dim light she could see it was 4:30.

Jerusha tried to wrap the blanket tighter around her. It was an old blanket that said U-Haul on it in big letters, and it was speckled with large grease spots, but Jerusha folded it and pushed it down under both sides of her. That seemed to keep the cold out a little better. Then she saw a pile of old newspapers on the floorboard behind the front seat. She'd heard of homeless men covering themselves with newspaper when they slept on park benches, so she unfolded several of the papers and spread them over her. As she settled down on the backseat she felt herself begin to warm against the cold.

Jerusha picked up the box that held her quilt and started to put it on the front seat of the car. Then she paused and opened the box. The quilt lay folded and wrapped in tissue paper. Carefully she pulled it open a little so she could look at it again. Even in the dim light she could see her craftsmanship in every stitch, the beauty of the design, and the shimmer of the silken rose. Her grandmother's words came back to her.

"Every trial we have in our life is a fire that burns away the things of this world and purifies our faith, so that when Jesus returns He will find a faithful people who have placed all their trust in Him and worship nothing but Him."

Is this the trial You have for me? If it is, why is it so long? Grandmother... Jenna...Reuben...and now I'm trapped in this car—

The thought hit her like a sledgehammer.

I might die here! Is that what You are going to burn away with my trials? My life? Does my life mean nothing to You?

Sobered, she closed the box and set it on the front seat. She put her bag under her head as a pillow and stretched out on the backseat. With a little bit of shuffling and spreading the layers of paper, she found that she was fairly comfortable. She closed her eyes and tried to rest, but thoughts of Reuben and Jenna began to flood her mind. She saw her little girl snuggled in Reuben's arms as the family sat in front of a fire on a long winter night. Memories of spring days came to her, the three of them sitting together, listening in wonder to the songs of the birds in the trees and drinking in the lushness of the earth waking from a long winter's sleep. Reuben's eyes, bold and stern yet with that secret smile always hidden behind them, and Jenna's little voice whispering those precious words, "I love you, Mama..." All these things haunted Jerusha as she lay in the back of the car.

Why do You take away the people I love most?

A knot began to form in her stomach, a pain that began to swell and throb and overwhelm her. The feeling became so powerful that Jerusha wanted to scream. But then, when she was just about to lose control, she felt something rising up in her heart. It was the melody to her beloved *Loblied.* Without even thinking she took a deep breath and began to sing softly, "*Loben wir ihn von ganzem Herzen! Denn er allein ist würdig.*" A deep peace began to steal over her as she sang the hymn for the first time in almost a year. "Let us praise Him with all our hearts! For He alone is worthy."

Even as she sang she fought against Him. *No! I don't want to praise You anymore.*

And then her eyes filled with tears.

◇◇◇

The summer of 1941 had been a dark time for Jerusha. Her father had firmly refused to let Reuben come to the house. Jerusha wanted to honor her father, but the day she had confessed her feelings to Reuben, she had crossed a line. She knew without question that her love and her life belonged to Reuben forever.

She drifted through the days, trying to focus on her work, but even quilting couldn't hold her attention, and after a while she would sigh and set the work aside. Reuben filled her thoughts and her moments. He was a part of her now. She saw his face in shadowed clouds and heard his voice speaking to her. Once when she was in town she started after a man, thinking it was Reuben. The man had looked at her when he saw her following him and smiled invitingly, but he wasn't Reuben, so she had turned and walked quickly away, red faced and shamed at her boldness. She started a dozen letters to him but tore up each one because the words seemed so small compared to the enormity of her feelings.

Then had come the day when Reuben asked her to make a decision. He had waited for her as she walked along the path into town. She had gasped at first, he had approached so quietly. He stood beside her, staring at her with those deep blue eyes, her emotions raging like a storm, her face turning bright red.

"I can still make you blush, eh, Miss Hershberger?" he said, and his eyes smiled at her.

"Reuben, you mustn't do this," she said softly. "My *daed*..."

"Jerusha, don't worry about your *daed* right now," he said as he took her hand. "I just want to see you for a moment. I want to tell you that nothing has changed for me. All I think about is finding a way for us to be together."

"There is a way, Reuben. If you'll just get baptized and join the church, my father would welcome you into our family."

"I can't join the church just because I'm in love with you," Reuben said. "If I join the church, it will be because I want God and His ways more than anything, because I'm in love with Him even more than I am with you. And the truth is I want you and I want other things more than I want Him."

"What do you want so badly that it could keep you from loving Him?" Jerusha asked.

"There are so many things to do—places to see, music to hear, books to read..." Reuben's face became animated as he talked.

He took both her hands in his. "I want to go to the Metropolitan Museum of Art in New York City and devour the paintings with my eyes. I want to ride through the Rocky Mountains in the back of a pickup truck. I want to see whales swimming along the coast of California. Jerusha, I want to get out of Apple Creek, and I want you to come with me."

"*Leave* Apple Creek! But Reuben, this is my life, this is all I know. My family has lived here almost a hundred years. I don't want the things you want. I want normal things, things that will keep us here at home, where we can be happy and content with our way of life. I want you to marry me and be a farmer like our people have always been. I want the simple ways. I want an Amish husband. I want—"

"Jerusha, do you love me?" he broke in.

"More than anything, but—"

"If you loved me more than anything, you could leave this place and come with me," he said, his voice rising with emotion.

"Reuben, why would you ask me to do something you know I can't do? You're asking me to disobey my father and leave the only home

I've ever known. Is this any way to build a new life? I would be bitter because I would always feel that you manipulated me into coming with you, and I would regret hurting my father and my people so deeply. Surely you wouldn't want me to do that."

As she looked at Reuben she felt something slipping away from her, and she wanted to reach out and clutch at it, but she couldn't see it or feel it, and a nameless dread filled her heart.

"Jerusha, I'm leaving Apple Creek. Will you come with me or not?"

"Please, Reuben," she begged him, "don't ask me to go away from everything I know. What would we do for money? Where would we live?"

"I have some money, I have a car, and I have a job offer in Colorado," he answered. "I told the man I would be bringing my wife, and that's all right with him. We would have a place to stay on a ranch, and I would work with his horses. The pay is good. I could save up my money, and then we could go out to California."

"A car! But cars are forbidden! And how did you get a job offer so far away?"

"I have friends."

Jerusha looked at Reuben. His face was red, and he was breathing hard, and his hands held hers with a steel grip. Something in him suddenly frightened her, something she was just now seeing for the first time. It wasn't bad, but it was unknown. All her life she had lived in the safety of her family, her work, and her faith. But this man had stolen her heart, and now he wanted to pull her out of the shelter of her life and push her into a place she had never wanted. It was as though she had come to a crossroads with a sign that said, "Beyond this place there be dragons," and this man wanted her to walk with him into this fearsome and mysterious new land.

She tore away from him and stood trembling, staring at his face. Then she turned and ran back to her home and her family and safety. Reuben looked after her, and then he turned and walked away.

◇◇◇

The little girl was cold, very cold. Her only waking thoughts were of her mama.

"Mama, come find me...I'm so cold," she would murmur and then sink back into a dream-filled sleep.

She had been in the car for a night and another whole day. It was the end of the second day of the storm, and as she lay quiet she thought she heard a soft voice speak to her.

"Don't be afraid, little one, I'm here."

"Are you my mama in heaven?" asked the little girl.

"No, my child, I'm not your mama, but I have been sent to help you."

"Will I go to see my mama?" asked the little girl.

"Not now," said the gentle voice. "You must lay still. I will stay with you and keep you warm..."

The gentle voice faded away, and then the little girl felt the strangest sensation, as though she were being covered by thick, warm feathers.

Chapter Thirteen

The Heart of the Beast

Mark Knepp got up from his chair and walked slowly to the pile of wood by the heavy cast-iron stove. The old white and black coonhound lying on a rug by the fire didn't stir as Mark grabbed several more pieces of wood. The stove was already glowing red from the fire inside, but it wasn't keeping the chill out of the house. He opened the fire door and put in the freshly split oak. Then he went into the bedroom and rummaged in the closet until he found the wool pullover sweater hanging in the back. He put it on over his Pendleton shirt and returned to his living room. He sat down in the overstuffed chair in front of the stove and scooted it closer to the heat. An old orange tabby cat walked out of the mudroom and jumped up onto Mark's lap. It circled a couple of times and lay down, snuggling against the wool sweater.

"Yes sir, Tiger, it's cold as anything out there," Mark said as he rubbed behind its ears. "This is a humdinger for sure."

At first this storm had seemed to Mark like a normal November snowfall, but during the night the temperature had dropped significantly, and the wind and snow picked up. By Thanksgiving morning the snow was coming down thick and wet, and soon the fields and trees around Mark's place were heaped with white.

"We may be in for the long haul. What was that poem we used to read in school?" Mark searched his memory until a few stanzas came back to him.

A chill no coat, however stout,
Of homespun stuff could quite shut out,
A hard, dull bitterness of cold,
That checked, mid-vein, the circling race
Of life-blood in the sharpened face,
The coming of the snow-storm told.

Mark smiled. "Right! John Greenleaf Whittier! I may not be getting any younger, but there's still life in the old noggin."

Mark laughed at his own statement while the cat yawned and stretched and dug its claws into the sweater. The old pot-bellied stove, satisfied for the moment with the new wood, soon warmed the room enough that, while not toasty, it was at least comfortable. Outside, the snow drifted up against the house, and the wind blew mournfully around the eaves.

Mark had gone out earlier that morning and dug a path through the snow to the old shed he called a barn. Inside the door he picked up a short pitchfork and went back to the hay pile. His dog, Smitty, lay curled up in the alfalfa. When the dog saw him he jumped up and barked excitedly.

"So that's where you spent the night," Mark said as the dog pushed against him, biting gently at his hand.

Mark pulled a forkful of hay out of the pile and walked over to the sheep pen. The ancient ram glared at him and stamped its foot as Mark filled the feeder with hay and then poured in some grain. The two ewes pushed against each other as they gobbled the fodder.

"A little late for breakfast, eh, old boy," Mark said as he scattered some grain on the floor for the chickens.

The rooster had led its harem to the barn door when Mark came in, but it turned back when it saw the snow outside and began to scratch at the grain, making gentle clucking sounds to prompt the hens to eat. Mark finished his chores and headed back to the house. Smitty followed him and whined at the back door to be let in.

"Don't blame you, Smitty," he said. "It's cold out here."

Now, with his chores finished, the old man sat by the fire with the cat asleep on his lap and Smitty stretched out by the stove, offering up an occasional twitch and a whimper in his sleep.

It was Thanksgiving Day, but Mark wasn't celebrating. When Millie died two years earlier, he lost much of his zest for living. Since then, holidays came and went pretty much the same as other days. He had been married to Millie for fifty-six years, and now, without his wife around, he could feel his own life winding down. He had settled into a day-to-day routine while the sun rose and set without him paying much attention.

Until Millie passed, Mark had thought of himself as a devout Christian. He went to church with Millie every Sunday, tithed, supported missions, and did everything expected of him. But now that Millie was gone, it just seemed more like a social club than something that was of comfort to him in his grief. After a while, Mark realized he was just waiting for his own time to go. He was looking forward to seeing his beloved wife in heaven, so church just didn't seem so important anymore. He stopped attending regularly, which he knew would not make Millie happy, but somehow he just didn't have the juice to get up and around on Sunday mornings.

Soon the old man fell asleep, and the hours passed. He woke up around two that afternoon and stretched himself. He picked the cat up from off his lap and set him down beside the chair. The cat complained loudly.

Mark went over to the cupboard to see what he could find to eat. He rummaged around until he found some Ritz crackers and a jar of peanut butter. He went to the refrigerator for some milk and poured it into a pan on the stove. Then he rustled around in the cupboard until he found the plastic jar of chocolate syrup, squeezed some into the milk, and turned the burner on.

After it had warmed up, he poured the milk into a cup, turned on the radio on the kitchen counter, and set his snack on the reading table next to his chair. Then he put some more wood on the fire and settled back.

The radio was playing Glenn Miller—"Moonlight Serenade" or something like that—and Mark started eating his crackers and drinking his milk. The warm milk and the music soothed him, and soon he moved back to his overstuffed chair and fell asleep.

When Mark awoke it was already dark outside. He turned on the lamp next to his chair and sat for a minute, letting his eyes adjust to the dim light. Suddenly he heard a loud crash outside. The dog and cat both jerked awake and stared at the door.

"That sounded like a tree going over," Mark said. "Come on, boy, let's go see."

Smitty jumped to his feet and went to the door and whined. Mark went to the back porch and got a flashlight off the shelf. He slipped on his galoshes and put on the old army parka that was hanging on a hook by the door. He went to the front door, and when he opened it the cold wind and snow blew into the room.

"C'mon, Smitty, let's check it out," he called to the dog.

As he shined the flashlight around, Mark soon saw the cause of the noise. The big laurel tree out on the lane had blown over and was partially blocking the driveway. Mark pulled the face flap of the parka over his mouth, and he and Smitty walked down the driveway toward the tree. Suddenly Mark stumbled over something and sprawled headlong into the snow. The flashlight flew out of his hand and hit the ground hard, but the light stayed on.

"What was that?" Mark asked as he gingerly rubbed a bruised knee. He grabbed the flashlight and took a closer look. Smitty was whining frantically and digging at something under the snow. Mark hobbled over and started brushing the snow away as Smitty pawed at the heap. In a few seconds he realized what he had tripped over. Lying in the snow faceup with a bloody gash on the side of his head was a young man.

◇◇◇

The little girl pushed deeper into the pile of clothing and the seat cushion. She slipped in and out of consciousness, now dreaming of angels. She had never seen an angel, but her mama had told her about them. They had wings and were very kind and helped people who were in trouble. As she lay on the ceiling of the upside-down car, the fierce wind continued to blow, and the car slipped a few more inches down the bank onto the frozen pond. The ice groaned and crackled, and beneath the front of the car, the crack in the ice widened.

◇◇◇

Mark Knepp brushed the snow off the unconscious young man's face and then gasped.

"Henry Lowenstein! What in the world are you doing out here, boy?"

No answer.

"Henry, can you hear me? Wake up, Henry!"

Mark shook Henry, but he didn't stir.

"Gotta get him inside," the old man said as Smitty whined and pawed at the lad. The old man reached under Henry's arms, took hold, and began to drag him slowly toward the house. He managed to get him up on the porch and then kicked the door open and dragged Henry inside, pulling him over by the stove. The lad's lips were blue, and his face was pale white. Mark checked for a pulse. There! Henry was alive but in bad shape. The old man wrestled off the boy's coat and gloves and pulled off his boots and frozen pants.

He went into the back room and pulled some blankets and pillows from the old cedar chest. He folded up a couple of blankets and laid them beside Henry. Then he rolled the boy over onto them and got him adjusted. He slipped a pillow under Henry's head and covered him with several more blankets and a thick down comforter. Once he got Henry bundled up, he went to the phone. He picked up the receiver but heard nothing. The line was dead.

"Well, that's not good," the old man said to himself. "I'll have to take care of him here tonight and then try to get into town in the morning."

He went back to the boy and washed off the blood with a warm wet cloth. The boy groaned and stirred but didn't wake up.

"Hang in there, Henry," said Mark softly. "Just hang in there, boy."

◇◇◇

Jerusha, wrapped in the blanket, trembled on the backseat. She had screamed out her rage and fear, and now she was exhausted and numb inside. The night closed in on her, and the wind howled like a fierce beast. The cold crept into the car like a starving animal, gnawing at her weakening resolve. She was lost in her memories, lost in her heart, lost in the storm, and lost to her God.

The Third Day

FRIDAY, NOVEMBER 24, 1950

Chapter Fourteen

Missing

◇◇◇

Early Friday morning, the day after Thanksgiving, Bobby Halverson drove his tractor down Dalton's main street, clearing out a lane of traffic. He was heading for Highway 30 to make a run down to Apple Creek Road and from there into Apple Creek. There weren't any cars parked along the street, so he was able to push the snow off onto the sidewalk as he plowed. Dutch's tune-up on the engine made a big difference, and the tractor was running smoothly in spite of the fierce weather.

Bobby had been up since before dawn. He had already made one run up to Dalton from his folks' place in Apple Creek and was on the return leg, clearing the opposite side of the road.

Bobby was bundled up against the cold, but even with the heater going full blast the cab was icy. On his way out of Dalton he took a detour by Henry Lowenstein's grandparents' house. He drove by slowly, looking for Henry's old Buick, but it wasn't parked in front. Puzzled, he pulled the tractor over and left it running while he ran up to the Lowensteins' door and knocked. In a few seconds, Henry's grandmother opened the door and peered through the screen, still dressed in a bathrobe and with curlers in her hair.

"Why, Bobby Halverson, what are you doing up so early?" she asked. "Come on in here before you freeze to death."

She opened the screen door, and Bobby stepped inside.

"I can only stay a minute, Betty," he said. "I've got the tractor running outside, and I don't want her to stall. Has Henry left for home already?"

"Why, Henry never showed up," she answered. "We waited until four thirty yesterday to eat, but Henry never came. My turkey had to be reheated, and the biscuits were cold. I figured it was the weather, but even so, you'd think he would have at least called."

"He couldn't. The lines are down between here and Apple Creek," Bobby said. "My guess is that Henry turned around before he got here, and then he couldn't call. I'll stop by his dad's place to see if he's there. He had Jerusha Springer with him, so I'll stop at her place too."

"How about a cup of coffee and a hot cinnamon roll before you go? It'll help keep you warm out there. It must be freezing in that cab."

"Well, that would be nice, but I need to get going pretty quick," said Bobby.

"I just took the rolls out of the oven, and the coffee's hot. I'll pour it into a thermos, and you can bring it back later."

While Betty bustled about in the kitchen, Bobby wondered about Henry and Jerusha. He had last seen them on Carr Road below Highway 188.

They could have gone up Carr to 30 and then turned right and headed into Dalton. Or they could have turned right on 188 and come into Dalton from the south...

Henry's grandmother returned with two hot buttered cinnamon rolls in a paper bag and a cup of coffee in a thermos.

"You don't think anything happened to Henry, do you, Bobby?" Betty asked.

"I wouldn't worry. Henry's a smart boy, and if the road got bad he would have gone home," Bobby said. "It was really starting to snow when I saw him, and the roads were slick. Even though it's only ten miles over to Apple Creek, it can be rough going in the snow, and Henry's tires aren't the best. It was already about five inches deep when I plowed through there yesterday. I'll check on him when I get to the village."

"Thanks, Bobby. But how will I know if you find him?"

"Hopefully they'll get the lines back up and I can call. But in the worst case, I'll be making another run back up here this afternoon, so I'll stop by and tell you what I know."

Bobby went back out in the cold. He saw Henry's grandmother looking out the window as he climbed into the cab. He pulled off one of his gloves, opened the lid on the thermos, and took a gulp of the hot coffee.

The straightest route from Apple Creek to Dalton is up Carr Road to Highway 30 and then east into town...

Bobby throttled up the plow, turned back onto Main Street, and headed out toward Highway 30, plowing the wet, heavy snow as he went. Along the road the wind had pushed up drifts, some of them almost ten feet high. The tractor chugged along, the plow pushing the snow off to the side of the road where it piled the drifts even higher. He passed Township Highway 97 and drove on toward the junction where Lincoln Way came in from the south. This part of the county was mostly rural, and once he got out of town there wasn't much to see, especially with the snow coming down. Bobby pulled his yellow snow goggles off the visor and put them on so he could see through the white snow.

If it snows any harder it will be almost impossible to see out here. If Henry went off the road, his car is probably buried by now.

Bobby could only travel about five miles an hour, so it took him forty-five minutes to reach Carr Road. He turned south and plowed toward County Highway 188. The sun was coming up, but the storm clouds and the falling snow still made everything dark and dreary.

As he drove along he saw someone standing by the road waving his arms. It was Abel Waxman, a farmer who had a place along Carr Road. Bobby pulled over and opened the window in his cab.

"Hey, Bobby, am I glad to see you," shouted Abel. "I need to get my boy over to the hospital in Wooster. He slipped on the ice this morning, and I think he broke his arm. My driveway's full of snow and I can't get out. Can you plow it for me?"

Bobby hesitated for just a minute and then shouted back. "Okay, Abel, I'll clear the road down to your house and then you can get out. Drive back up Carr and then take Highway 30. It should be clear into Wooster. I think the county boys plowed through there this morning."

"Thanks, Bobby," shouted Abel over the wind. "You're a lifesaver."

Bobby turned into Abel's driveway and started plowing. It was almost four hundred yards to the house, and the snow was piled high. The plow bucked and bumped along the road, and it took Bobby almost half an hour to force his way through. Abel went ahead and ran back into the house to get his boy. The lad came out with his arm in a crude splint and a pained look on his face. Abel and his son climbed into their truck while Bobby turned around, and they followed him out to the road. Abel honked as he turned north and headed toward Wooster.

Bobby pushed on through the drifts toward Apple Creek. As he did he remembered the last time he had been up to the hospital in Wooster.

It had been a terrible day. Nothing he had experienced in the war, not even the Battle of the Ridge, had affected him as much as what he saw that day at the hospital. Somehow even in the trenches of war he had found a way to believe God would help him in time of need. But that day at the hospital, he decided there was no help to be found in God.

Lost in his thoughts, Bobby turned off Carr onto the lane leading to the Lowensteins' place. The Lowenstein property was across the creek from Joshua Hershberger's farm, between Carr and High Street on Dover Road. The Hershbergers had been there since the late 1800s. Bobby pulled into the farmyard at the Lowensteins' and looked for Henry's car, but he didn't see it anywhere. Leaving the tractor running, he climbed out and walked across the creek and through the trees to the Springer house. He had been here many times in the happy days when Reuben and Jenna had still been here. As Bobby walked through the cold wind and snow, he felt the dull ache in his hip.

That old piece of shrapnel doesn't like the cold. If it hadn't been for Reuben, though, I would have had more than a grenade fragment in me.

Bobby walked up the familiar path to the front door. The place was dark, and there were no signs of life.

Reuben built this place for Jerusha with his own hands when he came back to Apple Creek after the war. We had some good times here. Even though Reuben went back to the church, he never forgot our friendship. I guess when men go through what we did, they stay buddies forever.

Bobby stepped up on the porch and knocked on the door. He remembered happier days when Jerusha would open the door with a smile and Reuben would be standing behind her, holding little Jenna in his arms.

He was a handsome guy, and she looked like a movie star. Even with their simple clothes they were a good-lookin' couple. And that little girl! What a beauty. Her daddy's eyes and her mama's face. She would have been a real looker...if she had lived.

Bobby reined in his thoughts. That was a place in his memories he didn't want to visit. Little Jenna had captured his heart from the day she was born. He loved her like a daughter, and because of her and the happiness that Reuben and Jerusha shared, he had revisited his dream of becoming Amish and joining their church. But that was all water under the bridge. Jenna was gone, Reuben had disappeared, and in her continuing grief, Jerusha was drying up like summer grass without any rain. And besides, Bobby wasn't so sure about a God who would let such terrible things happen to such a lovely family.

He knocked again, but no one answered. Jerusha was not there. The house stood empty, cold, and dark. The unmarked snow was piled on the porch and it was obvious that nobody had been there for a couple of days. Bobby turned and headed over the bridge to the Lowenstein place and knocked on their door. Hank Lowenstein opened the door.

"Hey, Bobby, what are you doing here?" Hank asked. "Come on in before you freeze your tail off."

"I'm looking for Henry," said Bobby. "Is he here?"

Hank looked puzzled. "No, he's over at his grandmother's in Dalton. He went up there to have Thanksgiving."

"I was by there this morning. Betty said he never showed up. I thought he might have turned around and headed home when the storm got so bad."

"Well, that's not good," said Hank. "I haven't seen him since he left here yesterday morning. What should we do?"

"Not much you can do except wait here and see if he comes home," said Bobby. "I'm going to head up the highway to Kidron and see if he went in the back way to Dalton. If they're off the road up there, I'll find them—don't you worry."

Bobby went back to the plow and headed toward Dalton. When he got to Highway 188 he turned east and headed toward Kidron Road. It took him almost an hour, but he finally saw the road sign through the blowing snow. By now the wind was really strong, and visibility was about twenty yards. He turned north on Kidron and headed toward Nussbaum, the back way into Dalton. About three hundred yards up the road, he spotted something on the right in the ditch. He had to look really hard to see what it was. When he came up on it he saw that it was a dead cow, laying on its back, its legs sticking up, frozen solid.

Gonna be a lot of dead livestock after this storm. It's gonna look like Mother Nature's deep freeze out here.

He turned right on Nussbaum and headed on into Dalton, keeping his eyes peeled for Henry's car. By the time he got to Dalton he was shaking from the cold. He drove over to Betty Lowenstein's house, got out and rang the doorbell. Betty came to the door and started in right away. "They found Henry. Mark Knepp heard a tree crashing down on his property. He went out to see if anything was damaged, and he tripped right over Henry. The boy had been knocked cold by a falling limb. Mark dragged him inside and got him warmed up, but he's still unconscious. He took care of him until he could get into town and bring the doctor back to his place to treat him. Henry's alive, but he got a nasty knock on his head, and the doctor says it's still touch and go."

"What about Jerusha?" Bobby asked.

"No sign of her or of Henry's car..."

Chapter Fifteen

The Trouble with Reuben

◇◇◇

Bobby Halverson sat down in Betty's living room and put his head in his hands. It was midmorning on Friday. He had been up since before dawn, and he was exhausted. "No sign of Jerusha?" he asked.

"No, Mark didn't find Jerusha," Betty answered. "But of course he couldn't have known she was with Henry, and when I told him, he went right out to see if he could find her."

"I'll help him, but I don't know where to begin," said Bobby. "It looks like Henry broke down somewhere and was trying to get help. He could have wandered over to Mark's place from any direction in this whiteout. Didn't Henry say anything?"

"No," Betty answered. "He's not awake yet. He's still in danger. He's been moved over to Dr. Samuels' office on Buckeye Street. Doc said he would send someone over as soon as Henry wakes up."

"What am I going to do, Betty? Jerusha is out in this storm, and she could be anywhere between Apple Creek and the Knepp place."

"Bobby, you can't go out now. You're exhausted. Why don't you stay here and rest. When Henry regains consciousness, he can tell us where the car is."

"But that could be too late. Jerusha's in danger in this weather. It might be too late already."

"Tell you what. Just lie down on the sofa and rest for an hour. I'll wake you up in plenty of time to make another pass down to Apple Creek. Obviously Henry came up the back way into town, or he wouldn't have showed up on Knepp Lane. That should narrow down your search area."

Bobby let out a deep breath and thought for a moment. "Okay, I'll rest for a while, but I'm too wound up to sleep. I sure could use something to eat though."

"You're in the right place. I've got Henry's share of the turkey left over, plenty of gravy, and some of my famous biscuits. I'll brew you up a gallon of coffee."

"Mind if I pull the tractor into your shed and plug in the battery charger so I can get the glow plugs juiced up?" Bobby asked. "I can't just let it sit there idling or I'll run out of diesel."

"Sure thing, Bobby. You go ahead and I'll be in the kitchen."

Bobby trudged out to the tractor, climbed in, drove it around back to the Lowensteins' big shed, and shut it down. Then he pulled the battery charger out of the toolbox, plugged it in, and clamped the wires on the battery posts. He made his way back to the house through the howling wind and stepped into the kitchen.

"Sit down, Bobby," Betty said. "I got a plate all hot for you."

As he ate, Bobby thought about the years he had known Reuben and everything they had been through together. For a moment a scene captured his thoughts like an awful nightmare. Men were fighting like animals in the mud, shooting and stabbing each other and screaming insanely. Bullets whistled by, and every few seconds he heard the sickening splat as one struck human flesh. And in the forefront of the battle was Reuben Springer, wounded but still fighting like a berserker to defend his fellow Marines against the attack. Bobby shook his head and tried to shake off the vision.

What a mess! It's like all the messes you and I have gotten into. I guess we were made for trouble, buddy. Since that first day we met it's been nothin' but trouble...

◇◇◇

The first time Bobby met Reuben, there was definitely trouble. Bobby had been drinking in his favorite bar in Wooster. It was November of 1941. Bobby usually drank alone. He liked sitting at a small table in the back of the room where it was dark and he could nurse a brew while he watched the goings-on without having to put up with some stupid drunk trying to make conversation with him. At a table near the bar a bunch of construction workers had been going hot and heavy for some time and were getting noisier and more obnoxious with each pitcher of beer. One of the men, a big red-faced loudmouth named Clancy, was doing the lion's share of the talking.

"I tell you, we're going to get into it with the Japs pretty soon," he said thickly, "and when we do, we'll show 'em what it means to mess with Americans. If we go to war, I'm signing up on the first day. What about you?"

"I got a wife and kids" mumbled another worker named Smitty. "I'm not so sure I want to get all shot up so I'm no good to my family."

"What are you, yellow?" Clancy snarled. "Nothin' worse than a yellow coward. Well, we'll remember you hiding behind mama's skirts as we go off to fight."

"Aw, lay off. I ain't no slacker," the other man muttered. "And besides, you're too old to join up."

Clancy went on, ignoring Smitty's remark. "And the truth is, we got a town full of cowards walkin' around here in their fancy hats like they own the place, but they're yellow. They were yellow in the last war and they're gonna' quit on America in the next one too. Them Amish. It sticks in my craw, the way they're always talkin' about loving one another while they let real Americans who love their country die for them, and they don't lift a finger. They're cowards, plain and simple. Ain't nobody more yellow than the Amish, and if I'm wrong, well, say it ain't so."

"It ain't so," said a quiet voice.

Bobby hadn't noticed when the young man stepped up to the bar just a few feet from the table of drunks, so when the quiet voice corrected Clancy, Bobby looked up. Standing at the bar was a tall, dark-haired man in his early twenties. He had the look of someone who had seen hard work. He had broad shoulders, long arms, a handsome, symmetrical face, and piercing blue eyes.

"Whad'ya say?" asked Clancy, turning to face the newcomer.

"I said the Amish aren't cowards," said the young man.

"Sure they are," said Clancy. "Yellow-bellied stinking traitors who let the real men die while they hide out on their farms and live off the fat of the land."

"They love their country as much as you say you do. Besides, I think you're probably just a lot of talk," said the stranger.

"Whatta ya mean by that?" snarled Clancy.

"I mean that in my short life, I've observed that those that know, don't say, and those that say, don't know. From listening to you spout off, I'd say that in spite of all your brave talk, the first time a machine gun slug whispers past your ear, you'll cut and run."

"Why you!" shouted Clancy as he rose up and pushed his chair back so that it tumbled over behind him. "I'll show you who's gonna cut and run."

Clancy grabbed a beer bottle by its neck off the table and smashed it against the bar. He was stepping forward to thrust his weapon into the young man's face when a strong hand stopped the forward motion of his arm.

"Lemme go, I'm gonna kill this guy," yelled Clancy, twisting around to get a look at his restrainer. Bobby Halverson's calm face stared back.

"Fight fair, Clancy, or you'll wish you never got out of your chair," Bobby said softly.

Bobby's steel grip on his wrist made Clancy wince in pain, and the bottle dropped out of his hand. Bobby let him go.

The man named Clancey was not deterred. "I don't need nothing to show pretty boy here how to keep his mouth shut."

Clancy lurched at the stranger and took a wild swing. The man slipped out of the way of the haymaker and raised his hands with the palms facing out.

"I don't think you want to do this, mister," the tall young man said quietly.

Clancy roared a profanity and then took another swing, but the stranger ducked beneath it. Quick as a flash he let Clancy have it with a powerful right hand to the stomach and a stunning left fist to the point of his chin. Clancy stayed upright for a moment, but the light had gone out of his eyes. He swayed forward and fell like a log onto another table, scattering glasses and patrons.

Clancy's buddies started to get up, and Reuben backed up toward the bar. Just then the bartender came bustling over and got in between the men and Reuben and pointed to the door.

"That's enough! Party's over, fellas. No brawls in my place. Take your buddy and go on home," he said. "I'm not gonna serve you any more booze, so you may as well beat it."

"Aw, Jimmy," whined another one of the workers, "we're just getting started."

"You heard me," said Jimmy. "Come back tomorrow when you sober up."

The men grumbled and pulled Clancy to his feet. His eyes wandered in their sockets, and a thin trickle of blood ran down his chin.

"Anybody get the number of that truck?" he said as his buddies dragged him toward the door. He looked at the stranger as he passed by.

"Don't let me see you in here again, or you'll be sorry," he mumbled.

"Yeah, right, Clancy," Bobby said as he looked at Clancy's rapidly swelling face.

The young man watched Clancy leave and then turned to Bobby. "Thanks for stepping in, but I really didn't need your help."

"No problem," Bobby said. "I just like to see the sides even. How was I supposed to know you could punch like a mule kick?"

"Well, thanks. I guess I could be a little friendlier." The young man smiled back and stuck out his hand. "I'm Reuben Springer, and speaking of mule kicks, I noticed that Clancy didn't try to stand up to you."

"Bobby Halverson. Yeah, Clancy and I sorted out our pecking order a long time ago. Now come on and sit down and tell me where you learned to punch like that—particularly if you're friends with Amish."

The two men made their way back to Bobby's table.

"Jimmy, bring over a couple of beers," Bobby said.

"I think I'd just like a soda," said Reuben. "I'm not much of a drinker. As a matter of fact, this is my first time in a bar."

"You certainly didn't waste any time getting into the swing of things," Bobby said. "By the way, what made you decide to defend the Amish folks?"

"I am Amish," said Reuben, taking a breath, "Well, sort of Amish, I guess you'd say."

"How can you be 'sort of Amish'?" Bobby asked. "It appears to me you either are or you aren't."

"It's hard to explain, but right now I'm under the *meidung*—the Amish word for shunning. That means I have done things that violate the Amish way of life, and they've basically thrown me out until I change my ways."

"What did you do, if you don't mind my asking?" Bobby asked.

"It's not so much what I did, but what I won't do," Reuben replied. "I won't get baptized and join the church, and I'm way older than most Amish young men are when they do that. And the truth is, I don't really want to join the church. I want to see the world and find out some things on my own instead of taking the church's word for everything. The Amish live under all these rules that have been passed down for generations, but they're just rules to me, and a lot of them don't make any sense. I can't follow after something I don't believe in. So I'm hoping to leave Apple Creek to go out and find out for myself."

"My folks live in Apple Creek," said Bobby. "How come I never saw you around?"

"My dad has a farm up here in Wooster," Reuben replied. "But he married a widow in Apple Creek. She had a bigger place, so we moved there to work it."

"Well, if you want to leave, why don't you just do it?" Bobby asked.

"I have a little problem," Reuben said with a slight smile.

"Aha! Woman troubles, eh?" Bobby said. "So you came in here to drown your sorrows, but you don't drink. That's funny! You want to talk about it? I'm a good listener."

Reuben looked at Bobby intently for a few minutes. "I'm not very good at talking about myself," he said, "but if you have an hour or so, I'll unburden myself. And if I'm going to really open up," he said with a grin, "I guess I better have one of those beers after all."

Chapter Sixteen

Friends

Reuben took to that first beer like a duck to water. Within an hour—and after three Pabst Blue Ribbons—Bobby knew all about Jerusha, how beautiful she was, how much she and Reuben loved each other, and the enormous obstacles in their way.

Bobby listened, asking a few questions and occasionally offering a comment. Bobby did have some experience with the matter at hand, but he didn't want to come off like a know-it-all. Bobby had married early—at seventeen—but it hadn't worked out. His wife had wanted Bobby to take her to the big city. When Bobby wouldn't, she found someone who would, and that was that.

The experience made Bobby a good listener. The beer loosened Reuben's tongue, and soon Bobby felt as if he'd known Reuben for a long time. He had a lot more facets to his personality than most of the Amish he'd met. He was smart and funny, but he could be serious and philosophical too, and after a short while Bobby decided that he liked Reuben a lot. As the evening wore on, Reuben told Bobby about his last meeting with Jerusha and how she had refused to go with him to Colorado.

"You've got a job out there," Bobby said. "Why don't you go alone?"

"I can't leave her," said Reuben, hanging his head. "She's got such a hold on me, but she won't marry me unless I get baptized and become a member of the church, and I just can't. It would be hypocritical. There are too many rules that have no basis in reality. I want to get out and see the world and just get on with my life, but I'm afraid she'll get married to someone else, so I can't leave. I'm really stuck. What should I do?"

"Well, I'd say you're between a rock and a hard place, my friend," Bobby answered as he took another long sip of his beer. "And the truth is, I didn't do such a bang-up job with my marriage, so I'm not exactly the person you should ask for advice."

They continued talking until Jimmy leaned over the bar and hollered, "Last call!"

"You got a place to stay?" Bobby asked.

"I have some friends here in Wooster," Reuben said, "but they're visiting in Akron. So I was just going to sleep in my truck until they get back."

"It's a little cold for that," Bobby said. "Why don't you come over to my place? I have a Murphy bed in the front room of my apartment. It's pretty comfortable."

And that was the beginning of our friendship. You came over and stayed, and I needed a roommate, so you moved in. I got you a job at the construction company, and that was how it started...

It was an interesting friendship because the two men were almost exact opposites. Bobby was friendly and outgoing, and he enjoyed social gatherings. He had never been much for studies, but he had a lot of useful knowledge about life. People could come to Bobby with their personal or practical problems and find a sympathetic ear or a helping hand. Reuben, on the other hand, was quiet and liked to keep to himself. He had a quick mind and was a voracious reader who remembered almost everything he read. He read both classic and contemporary writers and could hold his own in a conversation about Shakespeare or Hemingway. He knew about Rembrandt and Picasso and had a deep love for both Beethoven and Billie Holiday.

Once Bobby asked Reuben about his almost encyclopedic knowledge of the arts.

"I thought you guys weren't allowed to read all this stuff or look at art."

"When I was a kid I had an *Englisch* friend my folks didn't know about. His name was Sammy. He was Jewish and what you might call an intellectual. We had a drop-off place in the woods behind my house where he would leave library books. I read everything from *Hamlet* to *The Maltese Falcon* by the time I was eighteen. He taught me a lot about the things of the world—history, music, and other religions, especially his. Kind of odd, don't you think? A Jewish whiz kid and an Amish misfit becoming best friends. I think hanging around with Sammy had a lot to do with my dissatisfaction with the Amish way."

"What about the music?" asked Bobby.

"Sammy was into music," said Reuben. "He had the most amazing collection of records—everything from Enrico Caruso to Gene Autry. When I could sneak away, we'd go into his room and listen to record after record. He'd fill me in on the composer, the artist, and the period when the music was written. He also taught me to box. That's where I learned to fight. When he was little, other kids always gave him a hard time for being Jewish, so he took boxing lessons and shut a few bullies up, and after that nobody bothered him. Sammy was a tough customer, and he gave me a real education in the art of self-defense."

Bobby learned a lot in their discussions, but so did Reuben. Reuben helped Bobby to expand his horizons in art and literature, and Bobby taught Reuben how to fix the carburetor in his Ford pickup and how to get along with people. The two men were compatible, so Bobby didn't mind Reuben living in his apartment. Reuben was neat and kept his clothes and personal stuff in order. They only had one argument in the whole time they roomed together, and that was over the Amish position on serving in the army. They were sitting in the kitchen discussing the Japanese occupation of French Indochina and the oil embargo the United States had placed on Japan's military.

"Reuben, I'm not much for world politics, but I know people," he said, "and I can tell you that the Japanese aren't going to stand still for this boycott."

"What do you think they'll do?" Reuben asked.

Bobby pulled a pack of Camels out of his shirt pocket and rapped them on the tabletop to pack them down. He tore open the pack, pulled out a cigarette, and lit it.

"If it were me," said Bobby, "I'd find another source of oil and take it over. The Japanese army is already in Indochina. They're well trained and battle hardened because they've been fighting in China since 1939. It's just a short boat ride over to the Dutch East Indies. The only thing that can keep them out of those oil fields is American intervention."

"But Roosevelt is trying to solve this diplomatically," Reuben said.

"That's what they say," Bobby replied, "but it didn't help the Japanese bargaining position to join up with Hitler and Mussolini. The Japanese are going to have to do something to neutralize America. They will have to get us out of the way, which means you can expect them to do something nasty, real soon."

"You think it'll come to war?" Reuben asked.

"Don't see how we can stay out of it." There was a pause in the conversation while Bobby blew out a long stream of smoke. Then he asked the question that had been unspoken but very present. "If we have to go to war, what will you do?"

"War is wrong, and it's against the Bible," Reuben replied.

"You didn't answer my question," Bobby said as he tapped the ash off his smoke and looked intently at Reuben. "So I'll ask it again. If war comes..."

"I heard the question," Reuben said, as a red flush rose in his face.

"Well, what's the answer?"

Reuben glared at Bobby. It was as though he was feeling his way through the answer in his mind, sorting out his thoughts on the matter for the first time. Finally he spoke.

"War is something the Amish detest. Violence against other human beings strikes at the very core of Amish beliefs. Our stand on violence was forged in the crucible of torture, persecution, hideous pain, and horrible death. Those who lived through it came out determined to reject every facet of war, down to the tiniest detail. That determination affects everything we do and say, how we relate to each other and to the *Englisch*, and even the way we dress and our appearance."

Bobby was silent, and Reuben continued. "Have you ever wondered why the Amish wear beards but not mustaches?"

"Yes, as a matter of fact, I have," Bobby said.

"We consider mustaches to be a sign of violent masculinity, something warriors and conquerors would wear. Jesus said we are to love our neighbor as ourselves, so it's wrong to attack weak or defenseless people," said Reuben. "We should be kind and forgiving."

"Yes, but do you really believe all that stuff, Reuben?" Bobby asked. "Be honest."

Reuben paused. "Well...I believe some of it," he said slowly.

"The way you talk, it seems to me you're really not so sure about it."

Reuben flushed and looked down at the floor.

"Here's what I'm getting at, if you don't mind me being blunt," Bobby went on. "The Amish live in a free country because American men have died in its defense. For a group of people to take advantage of this freedom and yet refuse to take any responsibility for it seems wrong to me—and to a lot of other people."

"That's not exactly what it's about," Reuben said.

"What *is* it about then, Reuben?" Bobby asked. "The Amish have looked down on the *Englisch* for years. They let us know in no uncertain terms that because we don't follow their way of life, somehow that makes us lesser people. And yet you can watch American boys go off to war to fight and die in defense of the freedom that allows you to live the way you do and practice your faith the way you do. If America hadn't invited you folks to come here back in the 1700s, there would be precious few of you left in Europe. In spite of what this nation has done for your people, you have the nerve to tell us we're wrong to live the way we do. A lot of good men and women died to preserve the freedom that allows you to feel and act the way you do toward anyone who isn't like you, and yet you won't lift a finger to defend that freedom."

"Don't keep saying 'you' to me," Reuben snapped. "I'm not Amish anymore, remember? I'm currently *persona non grata*."

"Well then, my friend," said Bobby, looking Reuben straight in the eye, "since you can't hide behind the religion anymore, I'll ask you one more time. What are you going to do if America goes to war?"

"The Constitution says the Amish don't have to fight if they sincerely object to killing other men," Reuben said, trying to redirect the conversation.

"Reuben, wake up for Pete's sake! The Constitution won't be worth the paper it's written on if Hitler or Tojo have their way in this world. The Amish will be the first to go if we lose a war and some dictator comes in here and wants everyone to join his jackbooted thug army. The Constitution won't save the Amish then. Only the blood of the men who fight and die will save them."

"The Amish won't fight," said Reuben.

"Well, if they won't fight, I suppose that's their right, but I'm not asking *them*, I'm asking you," Bobby said as he lit another Camel. "Since they won't fight, maybe the Amish should stop condemning the *Englisch* to hell since the English are good enough to fight in their defense. In the meantime, if you're really out of the club, what are you going to do if war comes?"

"I don't know," Reuben said. "All my life I've been taught that violence is wrong and that no matter what happens, we're not to lift a hand in wrath or anger. My family has a book full of the stories of martyrs who stood by as Catholic or Protestant soldiers killed their wives and children. They take it as a point of pride. Well, I don't take pride in it. If someone hurt Jerusha, I would kill that person. And I wouldn't make it an easy death. He would suffer before he died. It doesn't make me proud to say that, but I do know that some things are so precious they are worth killing or dying for. For me, that would be Jerusha. As far as what you're asking me, I just don't know what I'd do."

Bobby knew when to quit. His question had bothered Reuben more than he had expected. He took another puff on his Camel and smiled. "Let's drop it. What'll we do for dinner?"

Reuben looked at Bobby with an expression mingled with shame, hurt, and anger. "You don't have to patronize me, Bobby," said Reuben quietly. "I get the point. You think the Amish are cowards, and I think most of them are sincere believers in the way Jesus taught His disciples to live. As for me, you're right. What I'll do if America goes to war will be something I work out for myself, without hiding behind my Amish upbringing."

Well Reuben, you sure didn't have much time to make that decision, did you? We had that discussion in November. Three weeks later the Japanese bombed Pearl Harbor.

Chapter Seventeen

A Quilt for...

On Friday morning, Jerusha awakened in the back of Henry's car, covered by spread-out newspapers and the thin blanket. She lay there a long time, drifting in and out of sleep. Finally she roused herself and looked at Reuben's old watch. It was almost noon. She had tried to sleep during the night and early morning to conserve her strength but had awakened several times when she got too cold, and when that happened she started the car and let the heater run for ten minutes or so until she warmed up.

She was thankful she had put some sandwiches and fruit in her bag when she left home. More than ever she realized she must eat to keep up her strength. But the longer this dragged on, the more she realized how dangerous her situation was. Something had happened to Henry; that was for sure. He had been gone almost twenty-four hours. If help didn't come soon, she would surely die.

As these morbid thoughts played out in her mind, she heard the sound of a motor coming down the road. From the chug-chug-chug, she recognized Bobby Halverson's snowplow. She tried to open the car door, but the snow had piled against it, and it wouldn't budge. She became frantic as the sound of the tractor came closer and closer.

"Bobby, Bobby!" she began screaming, "I'm in the car, I'm in here!"

She leaned over the seat and pressed on the horn frantically, but the drifted snow muted the sound.

Jerusha tried kicking the door but then realized that she didn't dare break the window. So she put her shoulder against the door and her feet against the hump in the middle of the floor and pushed with all her strength. At last she felt the snow starting to give and the door begin to open. Jerusha pushed it open wide enough to carefully squeeze through. As she made the last push through and dug her way out of the snow, she could hear the retreat of Bobby's tractor. He hadn't seen her—the car was too far down in the ditch and was hidden by a snowdrift.

Jerusha made her way up the bank of the ditch and tried to run up the road after Bobby, but she slid and slipped and fell on the icy pavement.

"Bobby! Bobby, stop! Don't leave me," she screamed as she stumbled after the slowly disappearing plow, but the wind was so strong that it caught her voice and carried it away like drifting autumn leaves. Soon the tractor was out of sight in the windblown snow, and the chug-chug-chug slowly faded until Jerusha could no longer hear it. She collapsed to her knees on the road and wept.

"Bobby," she whispered, "please don't leave me here..."

Then the wind began to blow even more powerfully, and Jerusha knew she had to get back into the car or die on the road. For just a moment the thought crossed her mind that to be dead would mean that she would be with Jenna and that this constant sorrow would be done. But then an even stronger instinct asserted itself, and she stood and made her way back to the car. She crawled into the backseat and pulled the door shut.

This was God's fault again. He could have caused Bobby to see her, to hear her...but He hadn't. *Was it because I loved Reuben even though he was shunned? Was it because I disobeyed my father and snuck out to see Reuben, because I let him kiss me? What was it? Tell me, tell me...*

"Tell me!" she screamed aloud. "Why are You doing this to me?"

Jerusha pounded the seat with her hands and screamed out her rage and pain and agony. At last, worn out and exhausted, she lay back, closed her eyes, and drifted off into blessed sleep.

But even in her slumber she couldn't escape this trial. Strange dreams filled Jerusha's sleep. She was with her grandmother. Even though her grandmother was lying still and cold in the pine box in a bare room, her eyes were open and she was speaking to Jerusha.

"Never hurry, always pay attention, do the work as unto the Lord," she heard her grandmother say. "You have been given a way to give back to the Lord as He has given to you. It is a special gift not everyone is given. But to whom much is given, much is required. That is why we put a small mistake in the quilt before we finish. It is so that we do not make God angry with us for being too proud."

And then she felt her grandmother's hands on hers, guiding the stitches, showing the way to sew in the imperfection. But she fought against the hands and pulled away. Other voices that sounded like the women of the village began to echo in her dream. "You didn't put the mistake in your quilt, and that's why God is mad at you..."

Then it was her grandmother again. "You're too proud, Jerusha. This gift is not for you, but for those you can bless with your quilts. It is God working through you to touch others, and not to be held for yourself. You can't use this gift to bring attention or recognition to yourself. You must always stay true to our faith and our ways and not be tricked by the devil and the world."

Jerusha heard herself as a child reply to her grandmother, "I will always stay true to our family and our ways. I swear it."

And then she heard herself again, but older this time and filled with bitterness. "I'll take this quilt to the Dalton Fair and win the prize. I'll leave Apple Creek and leave this religion and leave this God who has turned His back on me. I'll make a new life among the *Englisch*, and I'll never come back."

And then she was sitting at the quilting frame, sewing the Rose of Sharon. Tiny, tiny stitches, her hand going in and out as the pattern developed before her eyes exactly as she had seen it. The beautiful silken material shimmered in the lamplight—first red, then purple, then with golden highlights, then red again like a kaleidoscope, ever changing. When she pushed the needle through for the last stitch, she pricked herself, and a bright red drop of blood fell on the rose in the heart of the quilt. And then the red rose began to bleed drops of blood. She watched, mesmerized, as the blood began to flow down the quilt. She tried to clean it off, but her hands became red with blood, and then she was holding her little girl in her arms as Jenna coughed and coughed until she spit up blood.

Like the blood of Christ, or a rose...

Then she was holding the quilt again and Jenna was gone, and Jerusha looked everywhere for her little girl but couldn't find her, and the blood still covered her hands. She rubbed her hands frantically on the quilt, but the blood wouldn't come off, and it was Jenna's blood and her blood and the blood of Christ all mixed together. Anger and grief welled up in her heart.

"I didn't kill Jenna! I didn't! Her blood is not on my hands! Why are You showing me this? You killed her, it was You! It was— "

And then she heard her grandmother's voice again. "Jerusha! Jerusha! You must wake up, girl. There is someone who needs you, someone needs your help."

In a half-waking state Jerusha answered back. "But, Grandmother, I can't help anyone. I'm the one who needs help. Someone needs to save me."

Her grandmother's voice came again. "Jerusha, *kumme* with me, *kumme* now."

Jerusha jerked awake. The dream had been so real.

And then the strangest feeling came over Jerusha. It was a feeling of absolute certainty that God was speaking to her right now, right this moment, and she must trust Him and follow Him.

"But how can I follow You when I don't trust You anymore?"

And then she could hear her grandmother's voice quoting a scripture. "*Now faith is the substance of things hoped for, the evidence of things not seen. Jerusha,* kumme*!*"

Jerusha opened the door and struggled out into the snow. The wind was howling, and she could barely see. She buttoned her coat tight around her and then grabbed the blanket off the backseat and pulled it over her head and shoulders. Slowly she began to push through the snowdrifts. When she got into the woods the wind wasn't so intense, but it was still freezing cold. The snow was deep, but as she went forward there seemed to be a path through the woods. She struggled ahead, feeling drawn—and yet not exactly that. Why was she doing this? It had been a dream...hadn't it? And yet she felt compelled to struggle ahead up over a little rise and down into a large clearing in the trees. Suddenly she realized where she was.

This is Jepsons' Pond. I came here with Reuben the day before he left...

In the blowing snow she could see something ahead that looked like an upside-down car. About half its length stuck out onto the ice from the shore. She looked up and could see where the car had torn its way through the trees and come to rest on the edge of the pond.

The county highway must be just over that rise. Someone crashed off the road and came through the trees up there and slid down to the pond! Maybe there's someone inside...

Jerusha walked toward the car, carefully stepping out onto the surface of the pond. She had skated here as a child, and she knew that with the temperature this low, it would likely be solid all the way across.

The front of the car was out on the ice, and its trunk pointed up the bank. As Jerusha carefully stepped around to the driver's side, she saw a large fracture in the ice running out from under the hood. The roof of the car had settled into the crack about six inches. The windows of the car were covered with snow and ice, so she picked up a piece of metal lying near the car and began to scrape the ice and then brush it off with her hands. Finally, she had cleared off enough to see in. She could see that some water had leaked into the car and frozen in a pool on the roof below the upside-down dashboard. As she peered in she saw something that looked like a small foot sticking out from under a seat cushion. She struggled around to the other side of the car and scraped the window off so she could make it out. Suddenly her dream of two nights ago returned to her like a knife to her heart. She had dreamed of Jenna, lost somewhere in the dark. Jenna was staring out from behind some kind of a window, her little hands pushing against the glass and her eyes wet with tears, crying out.

"Mama...Mama, come find me. Mama, where are you?"

Jerusha fell to her knees and looked in the window. There inside the car, almost completely covered by a seat cushion and old clothing, was a child—a little girl. Her face was toward the window. As Jerusha stared in amazement, the little girl's eyes opened. She looked straight at Jerusha and her mouth moved. Jerusha could tell what she was saying, and her heart jumped in her chest.

"Mama...Mama, come find me. Help me, Mama!"

Chapter Eighteen

Hard Choices

◇◇◇

Bobby Halverson sat in Betty's kitchen eating Thanksgiving leftovers. He was thinking about Reuben and the war and the strange twist of fate that had brought them together. The entwining of their lives stretched out behind, and he wondered again at the journey they had shared together.

If I hadn't been in the bar that night in Wooster, and if you hadn't stood up to Clancy, I wouldn't have met you, and we never would have become friends—and then I couldn't have challenged you about fighting for your country. If I hadn't been in your life, you might have decided to join the church and marry Jerusha way back then, and everything would have been different—and I might not be alive today. Isn't it strange how our whole life can swing on one little moment or one decision? I remember the day you made your choice, and I remember how pleased I was when you told me what you decided. What did I know about anything? What happened after that was so hard on you. You never asked for trouble, but it always seemed to find you. There was always trouble, and you always seemed to get the brunt of it. Maybe it would have been better if you had gone down another road...

◇◇◇

Three weeks after the Japanese bombed Pearl Harbor, Bobby sat with Reuben at the little chrome dinette set in the kitchen of their apartment. They had finished dinner, and Bobby was drinking a beer. Reuben sat across from him with his own beer, looking morosely down at the tabletop.

"I'm going down tomorrow to enlist," Bobby said, getting right to the point. "I went over to the Marine Corps recruiting office in Akron yesterday, and they seem to think that I'm a suitable candidate for grunthood, so I'm going in for a physical and then it's off to Parris Island. You're welcome to stay here while I'm gone. I've already talked to the landlady, and she's fine with that."

"Bobby, I—"

"Don't try to make me change my mind," Bobby cut in. "I've made it up and nobody's gonna change it. Pearl Harbor decided it for me. The Japanese have underestimated the will and anger of the American people. The guy at the recruiting station told me that hundreds of men have come in to—"

"Bobby, will you just shut up and listen for a moment?" Reuben took a deep breath and then began to talk quickly and earnestly.

"I've been thinking long and hard about what you said a few weeks ago. I still feel that killing other men isn't a good thing, and I think if everybody really did what Jesus says in the Bible, there would be no killing in the world, and everybody would get along or at least just leave each other alone.

"But I've come to see that in every group of human beings there will always be someone who tries to get it over on everyone else. And there are all kinds of ways that we do it to each other, from talking behind people's backs to crushing another country with an army. I think people are just born that way. As long as there are men like Hitler and Tojo, there will be wars because tyrants think they should be in control of everyone else and they'll do whatever it takes to achieve that.

"I know there are bad men in America too, but for the most part, this is a free nation with lots of room for everybody. And you were right—it stays that way because some men and women are brave enough and care enough to willingly lay down their lives so their neighbors can stay free. I said that I believe there are some things worth dying for, and I was talking about Jerusha. But your questions made me see things in a different light. It occurred to me that if the Germans or the Japanese got their hands on America, they would take away our rights. Then there would probably be no Reuben and Jerusha in that sort of future. So I had to make a decision.

"It was a hard choice because it went against everything I've ever known. I don't know if Jerusha will ever understand, but like you, I've decided to go and fight those who want to destroy our country. In fact, I beat you to the punch. I've already signed up. I've been accepted for the Marine Corps, so if you're going to sign up, it looks like we'll both be headed for Parris Island. I'm hoping that if I make it back alive, I can make Jerusha see why I did this."

Bobby hardly knew what to say. "Well, my friend, that's the longest speech I ever heard out of you." He leaned forward to take Reuben's hand in a grip of friendship. "I don't know what's ahead for us, but I'll do my best to make sure you make it back to that gal of yours."

That was the day your troubles really started. The war did something to you. It wounded you inside, and later you made choices that hurt Jerusha and Jenna. I wish I had kept my mouth shut and just let you stay in Apple Creek.

A sadness filled Bobby's heart as he thought about the tragedy that had broken Reuben and Jerusha's lives.

Why am I still alive, living my comfortable life in Apple Creek? I should have died in that trench on that God-forsaken island. But I'm here and Jenna is gone, Reuben is gone, and now Jerusha is gone. Why couldn't You let them be, God, and cause me trouble instead? Shoot, I don't even believe in You, except maybe as a big troublemaker in the sky. I guess I'm a perfect candidate for tragedy. So why not me? Why them?

From the front room came the sound of a knock on the door. Betty went to see who it was. Bobby heard voices, and then Betty came rushing into the kitchen.

"Bobby, Henry's awake! Mark Knepp came over to tell us. He'll give you a ride back to the doctor's office if you want to talk to Henry."

Bobby grabbed his coat and gloves and went into the front room.

"Bobby," drawled Mark. "Henry's come to and he's been asking for you. He's pretty shook up and it's hard to understand what he's saying, but it seems he wants you to come. I got my car out here and I can take you over. Boy, it's still a humdinger out there. Can't see ten feet in front of your face."

Bobby finished pulling on his coat, and the two men rushed out into the frigid air, climbed into Mark's Ford, and headed to Dr. Samuels' office. When they arrived, a nurse showed them the way to the back of the office, where Dr. Samuels was waiting.

"He's in here, Bobby, but he's not very coherent. Keeps saying the same thing over and over. He's been asking for you."

Bobby went into the room. Henry was lying on the bed covered with several blankets. He had a nasty purple bruise on the right side of his head and face. A thick white bandage was wrapped around the top of his head. His eyes were having a hard time focusing, but when he saw Bobby, he tried to pull himself together.

"Bovvy...helv her," he said.

"Where is she, Henry?" Bobby asked. "Where's Jerusha?"

"Hid a cow, Bovvy," Henry said.

Bobby turned to the doctor. "What's wrong with him, Doc?" he asked.

"He's had a terrific blow to the head. He still can't tell me how many fingers I'm holding up, but he insists he needs to tell you something."

"He does," Bobby said. "Henry was driving Jerusha Springer to the quilt fair, but when Mark found Henry, he was alone. So Jerusha is somewhere out there in this blizzard, and Henry is the only one who knows where she is."

"Bovvy...Bovvy, gid ober here," croaked Henry. "Godda gidder... godda help."

Bobby leaned over Henry's bed. "Where is she, Henry? Where's Jerusha?"

"Liddle Jenna gone, Bovvy," mumbled Henry. "So sad...so sad."

Bobby took Henry by the arm. He tried to make Henry look at him, but Henry was staring at the ceiling.

"Is he going to be all right, Doc? Is he going to be able to tell me anything?"

"I'm surprised he can even talk at all."

Bobby was growing desperate. "Henry, boy! You've got to pull it together and tell me where Jerusha is," he shouted.

Bobby felt a gentle hand on his shoulder. "Easy, Bobby," Mark said. "I know you want to find Jerusha, but you have to give Henry some time. The boy is hurt bad, but he's strong as an ox. He'll come to in a while."

"But she might die out there if she's not already dead!" cried Bobby. "I've got to find her, and Henry's the only one who knows where she is."

"Why don't we calm down and pray?" said Mark.

"You go ahead if you think it will help, Mark," Bobby said as he turned away. "I'm not sure I want to ask anything of a God who would let my friends get into such trouble."

Just then Henry mumbled a few more words. "Ony a banket, Bovvy...ony a banket. Code, so code. Godda gidder, Bovvy...too code... too code."

Bobby went back to Henry's bedside. He wanted to grab the boy and shake him, make him talk, say anything, but he knew Mark was right.

Suddenly Henry looked right at Bobby and grabbed his arm. "Godda gidder, Bovvy. Gonna die...too code...too code," he mumbled.

Henry collapsed back on the bed and closed his eyes. The doctor moved to the bedside, took Henry's wrist to check his pulse, and then opened the boy's eyelids and checked his eyes.

"He's out again, Bobby," said Dr. Samuels. "He'll probably be out for a while. Go back to Betty's place, and I'll send someone over to get you when he's awake."

"C'mon, Bobby, I'll take you," Mark said. "Then I'll come back here and wait. I got nothing else to do, and I left plenty of food for the animals out at my place. As soon as he wakes up again I'll come get you. You should get some rest."

"Okay, Mark," Bobby answered. "I guess I can't do any more until he comes to."

The two men left Dr. Samuels' office and drove back to Betty's place. Mark dropped Bobby off and headed back downtown to wait for Henry to wake up. When Betty saw Bobby's face she knew that things didn't look well for Jerusha.

"He's incoherent," Bobby said. "He keeps rambling on about the cold and little Jenna Springer, but he wasn't alert enough to give me any clue as to where Jerusha is. I have to decide whether I should just go out and comb the roads for Henry's car or wait here until he wakes up. Either way it's a long shot as far as finding her in this weather."

"It doesn't look good, does it?" Betty said.

Bobby slumped down on the couch and closed his eyes. "No, Betty, it doesn't look good at all."

Chapter Nineteen

Trials and Tests

◇◇◇

Bobby checked on the snowplow but decided to wait for Mark to come get him instead of going out again. In truth, he needed the rest and took a nap on Betty's couch after a small snack. He slept soundly for two hours until he felt someone gently shaking him. It was Betty.

"Bobby, wake up. Mark's here to take you back to Doc Samuels' office. Henry's awake again."

Bobby swung his legs over the edge of the couch and sat for a minute with his face in his hands. Then he looked up. Mark Knepp was standing by the front door. His hat and the shoulders of his coat were covered with snow, and a little pool of water was forming on the hardwood floor around his feet.

"Henry's awake, and he's asking for you again," Mark said. "He's sounding a little more coherent now."

Bobby gave a little groan and rubbed his hands through his hair.

"I don't think that nap did me any good," he said with a grimace. "I feel groggier than when I went to sleep."

Bobby stood up and went to the coatrack, grabbed his coat and hat, and pulled them on. Together the two men started out the door.

"Let me know what's happening if you have time," Betty said.

"Well, if Henry tells us where Jerusha is, I'll come back here to get my tractor and head right out, so I'll let you know then," Bobby answered.

"I'm going with you to look for Jerusha," Mark said.

"It's pretty nasty out there. It'll be tough going," Bobby said.

"If you plow ahead, I'll follow close with the car," Mark said. "That way when we find Jerusha we can get her out of the storm quicker. There's not much room for her up in that little cab of yours. I got brand-new studded tires on the Ford, so she'll be fine behind your plow."

"All right then. Just make sure you stay close behind me."

A few minutes later the two men arrived at the doctor's office, and Dr. Samuels met them at the door.

"Come on in, fellas," he said. "Henry's asking for you again, Bobby."

They went into the back room. Henry looked up at them from the bed and then focused on Bobby.

"Bovvy, godda gidder...Godda gidder."

Bobby sat down by the bed. "I know I have to get her, Henry, but you have to tell me where she is."

"Bovvy, where's Reuven? Godda gid Reuven," Henry said.

"I don't know where Reuben is. He's gone, and I don't know where to find him. No one does. Right now we can't worry about Reuben. We have to find Jerusha. Where is she, Henry?"

"Godda gid Reuven, Bovvy. Reuven will gidder."

Bobby frowned in frustration. "Henry, I told you, I don't know where Reuben is. Now just tell me where you left Jerusha."

Henry's eyes twitched and he screwed up his face as he tried to speak. Then a tear ran down his face as he slowly answered. "Don't remember, Bovvy. Don't remember..."

Bobby stared at the boy and then shook his head. "I'm with you, Henry. I wish Reuben were here," he said quietly. "I could really use his help to get through this one."

◇◇◇

After Bobby and Reuben enlisted in the Marine Corps, they shipped out for basic training. The trip to South Carolina had been an uneasy one for the two friends. They didn't talk much. Reuben was in a funk most of the way, but Bobby ignored his friend's dark mood and concentrated on controlling his own anxiety about what lay ahead. Bobby was amazed at how quickly their lives had changed. After Reuben told Bobby about his decision to sign up, they packed their gear, stored the most important stuff, and found a friend who agreed to take over the apartment.

Bobby had enlisted a few days after Reuben, and both of them were due to leave the second Monday of January 1942. On the Sunday before they left, Reuben disappeared for almost the whole day. When he returned, Bobby asked him where he had been, but Reuben didn't want to talk about it. Bobby finally got him to confess that he had met with Jerusha one more time.

"It didn't go well," was all that Bobby could coax out of him, along with a muttered imprecation toward women in general and Jerusha in particular.

Monday morning they went down to the train station with their suitcases and climbed aboard a troop train along with a large group of rambunctious recruits.

When they arrived after the two-day journey, the laughing, smiling group sauntered nonchalantly off the train at the Marine barracks at Parris Island. Within a few seconds they were running as fast as they could from place to place while being yelled at and manhandled. They ran to the chow hall, where they had their first Marine meal. After that they ran to the infirmary, where a row of Navy corpsmen and doctors gave them inoculations, checked their eyesight, and drew blood for testing.

Then it was off to Administration for paperwork, dog tags, ID cards, allotments, service record books, and issuance of the all-important service number. On the way between the meal and the dog tags they were introduced to the base barbers, who buzzed them bald and sent them on their way, minus their hair and anything else that gave uniqueness to their personalities. They received their service clothing, their rifles, and their first PX issue of personal items.

Then the new recruits were formed into platoons of between forty-eight and sixty men, and just when they thought it couldn't get any worse, Reuben and Bobby's platoon was introduced to their drill instructor, Gunnery Sergeant Edgar F. Thompkins. Thompkins lined them up in a ragged semblance of order and then silently paced to and fro in front of them, shaking his head and scowling. At six feet five inches tall, Thompkins loomed over the platoon as the recruits stood frozen in awe. After a terrifying three minutes of silence, Gunnery Sergeant Thompkins spoke with a voice like broken glass.

"Sissies and slackers," he said, his voice grating, "listen to me, you putrid maggots, and listen good. My name is Gunnery Sergeant Edgar F. Thompkins. You address me as 'sir.' Not Sergeant or Mr. Thompkins, but 'sir.' If you do not show me the respect I deserve, you will find yourself missing important parts of your anatomy. You will preface every statement you make to me with the word 'sir.' You will answer every question by saying, 'Sir, yes, sir!' or 'Sir, no, sir!'

"Because you are all stupid, I'm going to make it simple for you. I will never ask you a question you need to answer with more than those three words—'Sir, yes, sir!' or 'Sir, no, sir!' I, on the other hand, will address you as 'maggot.' My job is to turn you sissies into men. You think you're men now, but you're wrong. You don't have the faintest idea what a man is. But by the time I'm finished with you, you will be men or you will be dead. Just because you signed a piece of paper doesn't make you a Marine either. You will be a Marine when I say you are a Marine."

Gunnery Sergeant Edgar F. Thompkins began to warm to his task, and his voice got louder and pitched up just a little bit higher.

"My job is to make you into Marines in five weeks. I can guarantee you that by the end of the first two weeks you will hate me as you have hated no other, but if you make it through to the end you will love me like your mother. As I look at you pieces of human garbage today, I don't have the slightest idea how I'm going to be able to turn you into fighting men. But I can guarantee you this—you *will* become Marines or die trying. Have I made myself clear?"

"Sir, yes, sir!" the men shouted in unison.

Over the next five weeks, Bobby, Reuben, and the rest of their platoon learned how to dress the Marine Corps way, how to eat fast or go hungry, and how to march. Every day they marched for miles, forward marching, rip marching, flank marching, back and forth, up and down, across the field and back again, going nowhere on the double. Forty inches back to breast, shoulders back, chin up, cover off. Countless times, by the numbers, by the hour, without numbers, by the day...the same routine. When they weren't marching, the men ran everywhere they went and slept only a few hours each night. The forced marches and hard training began to make a change in the platoon, and by the end of the second week the hills didn't look nearly as steep and the once-flabby bodies began to take on a hardness that was unfamiliar to most of the recruits.

"Wow," Bobby said to Reuben, when they had a short break one day. "I'm using muscles I didn't even know I had."

"Me too," Reuben said. "I'm in better shape than I've ever been."

Just then Gunnery Sergeant Thompkins walked up to the two men.

"Springer!" he shouted.

"Sir, yes, sir!" shouted both men as they snapped to attention.

"Not you, Halverson," said the sergeant. "I just want to talk to Maggot Springer."

Thompkins motioned Reuben to step up close to him. Reuben stood at attention, ramrod straight, staring straight ahead. Sergeant Thompkins pushed his flat hat back on his head, put his hands on his hips, put his face within an inch of Reuben's, and stared straight into his eyes.

"It has come to my attention, Maggot Springer, that you come to us from the cowardly Amish religion. Is that right?"

"Sir, yes, sir! Sir, no, sir!" shouted Reuben.

"What was that, Maggot Springer?" Thompkins said.

"Sir, I come from the Amish, sir, but sir, the Amish aren't cowardly, sir!" shouted Reuben.

"Well, I don't see any of them joining up, Springer."

"Sir, you're looking at one, sir!" shouted Reuben.

Thompkins took Reuben by the shirt and dragged him even closer. "When you are in the trenches, Maggot Springer, and one thousand enemy soldiers are charging up the hill at you pointing their bayonets and screaming like banshees, the men on your left and on your right will be counting on you to kill as many of those little insects as you can without blinking an eye and without running away. If you're Amish, I say you'll run when that happens. I don't think you have the nerve to kill a man. The apple doesn't fall far from the tree, Springer. I don't think you'll fight when push comes to shove."

Thompkins put his hand in the middle of Reuben's chest and pushed hard. Reuben staggered back and then snapped to attention again.

"Did you hear me? I said I think you're a coward, Springer, descended from generations of cowards." Thompkins pushed him in the chest again.

"Sir, don't push me, sir," said Reuben quietly, and Bobby could see a deadly light start to blaze in his friend's eyes, the same look he had seen before the bar fight with Clancy.

"What did you say, Maggot Springer?" Thompkins pushed Reuben again.

"Sir, I respectfully request that the sergeant not push me, sir," said Reuben, a little louder. Bobby could see the muscles on Reuben's arms start to bunch up and his hands form into fists.

"Would you like to punch me, Coward Springer?" Thompkins asked quietly as he pushed Reuben again.

"Sir, yes, sir!" Reuben said.

"Do you want to go through proper channels and put in a formal request?" Thompkins asked with a wicked grin. He towered over Reuben, but there was no fear on Reuben's face.

"Sir, requesting permission to beat the brains out of the Gunnery Sergeant, sir," said Reuben quietly.

"Permission granted, Maggot Springer," Thompkins said, and quick as a flash, Reuben threw a powerful punch at Thompkins' face.

Even more quickly, Thompkins moved to the side, took Reuben's arm as it flew by, twisted his body, and tossed Reuben head over heels in a heap at Bobby's feet. Like a cat, Reuben sprang to his feet and came back at the sergeant, his fists seeking Thompkins' chest and stomach. The sergeant took the blows without flinching and then grabbed Reuben by the arms. He fell backward while bringing his feet up into Reuben's belly and tossed him into a wall. Reuben hit the wall and dropped like a rag doll.

Thompkins smiled and stepped over to Reuben, offering him his hand to get up. Reuben allowed the sergeant to pull him to his feet, and before Thompkins could react, Reuben used his forward motion to move past Thompkins. As he did, he grabbed Thompkins, rolled forward and down, and flipped Thompkins onto his back a few feet away, almost knocking the wind out of him. Sergeant Thompkins leaped to his feet and was about to jump on Reuben when a sharp voice from behind them brought them both up short.

"Sergeant Thompkins, what's going on here?" Standing before them was the company commanding officer, Colonel Robertson.

Sergeant Thompkins snapped to attention, as did Bobby and Reuben.

"Sir, the recruit, Springer, and I were going over some of the fundamentals of hand-to-hand combat. The recruit seems promising, sir, and I was hoping to give him a head start in the training, sir. The recruit was demonstrating a move I had not encountered before, and I was about to allow him to show me the move one more time, so I could... formulate an appropriate response."

The Colonel looked at Thompkins and then at Reuben and then at Thompkins again.

"Very well, Sergeant," said the Colonel, "I will be interested in seeing your response when the platoon demonstrates its skills on record day. Carry on."

The Colonel continued on his way. Thompkins and Reuben stared at each other for a moment. Then Thompkins stepped up to Reuben, stood in front of him, smiled, and stuck out his hand. Reuben took it, and the two men shook hands.

"I retract my statement, Maggot Springer," said the Sergeant. "I believe you when you say you will fight. Carry on."

And with that, the Gunnery Sergeant turned on his heel and walked away. Bobby and Reuben looked at each other in amazement.

"I think you just passed a big test, my friend," Bobby said.

Chapter Twenty

Looking Up

◇◇◇

The little girl heard a sound, like a scraping at the window. She opened her eyes and looked up. The side window of the car was in front of her, and she could see something moving outside, brushing the snow away from the glass. The movement outside the car continued, and suddenly the little girl was looking up into the most beautiful face she had ever seen. The eyes in the face stared back at her, and the mouth opened in surprise.

◇◇◇

Bobby Halverson loved the Marines. To him it was the most natural thing in the world to endure rigorous training that strengthened mind and body to achieve a goal—in this case, to defeat an enemy that threatened his country's way of life.

The five weeks of boot camp was the most gut-wrenching and painful experience most of the men in his platoon had ever endured. For Bobby, it was heaven. He loved every minute of it because he had an inbred sense of discipline and order. Bobby understood that the best way to accomplish a great task was to put yourself under the direction of those who understood it completely and whose only desire was to impart that knowledge to you. He saw clearly the necessity of learning to obey orders without question—not the orders of foolish men but of those who had established themselves as effective leaders and who led by example. Bobby flourished during boot camp and soon became a squad leader, receiving a meritorious promotion for demonstrating leadership.

The Marine experience was much more difficult for Reuben. He had grown up in a culture that taught its followers that to harm other men was wrong. He was also a free thinker whose mind grasped the sublime concepts in great writing, music, and art. The day-after-day repetitive teaching techniques of the Marine drill instructors wore him down. He didn't lag behind and was among the best in any task, but his heart wasn't in it the way Bobby's was. Not until they came to rifle training did Reuben begin to excel. From the moment he was issued his M1903 Springfield, Reuben demonstrated a skill that showed a long familiarity with rifles.

"I thought you Amish guys didn't know about guns," Bobby said one night as they lay in their bunks.

"Just because we don't kill people doesn't mean we don't know about guns," Reuben replied. "The Amish have been hunting the woods of Pennsylvania and Ohio since we came here in the seventeen hundreds. My *daed* taught me how to shoot a rifle before I was six years old. This Springfield is a thirty-aught-six. That's what I used to hunt deer almost all of my life."

"Well, you learn something every day," Bobby said with a grin.

Reuben grew to know his rifle intimately. He carried it every day, marching with it, running with it, drilling with it, and learning to handle it easily, gracefully, lovingly, and with respect. Reuben understood the power of his rifle. He knew it could be an extremely accurate and powerful extension of his mind and body by which he could inflict destruction on the enemy. He took comfort in it and soon felt naked without it.

The Corps understood that before anything else, the Marine was a rifleman. So a large part of the training at Parris Island was teaching men how to shoot. The first time their platoon went to the rifle range, Reuben and Bobby sat together to fire their rifles. Reuben had been working on his rifle every day, and it was zeroed to perfection. He had steady hands and could hold his breath indefinitely, steadying the muzzle. He had twenty-ten vision and an inherent ability to factor wind and distance into his shooting. On that day he fired sixty-six shots, all but ten of them at rapid fire, at targets two hundred, three hundred, and five hundred yards away. Each bulls-eye counted five points with a maximum score of 330. When the smoke cleared, Reuben had scored 319 points. Bobby came in second in the platoon with 298.

The next day Bobby and Reuben were taken aside and asked to shoot again. This time Bobby scored 305 and Reuben scored 314. Again on the third day, they were asked to shoot, and again they both made record high marks. On the fourth day, Reuben and Bobby were called into the base headquarters.

Their company commander was seated at his desk. Standing behind him was a thin, handsome officer with dark brown hair. Reuben and Bobby snapped to attention.

"At ease, gentlemen," said Colonel Robertson. "I want to talk with you for a moment. Halverson, you have demonstrated real leadership and are quickly becoming the kind of Marine that will be of great service to the Corps. You are to be commended."

"Sir, thank you, sir," Bobby replied.

"As for you, Springer, I must say we had our doubts. Given your background and the fact that most Amish are conscientious objectors and won't lift a finger to defend this country, we have honestly debated whether it would be simpler to send you home rather than put you out in the field where these issues might present a clear and present danger to the men fighting alongside you. However, your DI assures me that you have spunk and determination and have performed your duties well, if not quite masterfully.

"This was enough for us to concede to letting you finish your training and be assigned with the rest of your platoon to the First Division, which—and I say this in strictest confidence—will be seeing action soon. Now, it has also come to our attention that you're not only a competent marksman, but that your scores have earned you the rating of Expert Rifleman, a ranking that your friend Halverson here also carries.

"Gentlemen, this officer behind me is Lieutenant Colonel Whaling, affectionately known to his troops as Wild Bill. Colonel Whaling has been placed in charge of the newly formed scout and sniper unit and will be moving some of the top marksmen in this company and others to an elite school, where they will receive additional training.

"If they pass the training, they will be placed into special scout and sniper platoons within each company. Their duty will be to reconnoiter ahead of the advancing troops and scout out enemy troop concentrations and strongholds. The duty will be hazardous, the life miserable, and the rewards few. But only the best will be picked. I am asking if you men would like to volunteer for this duty."

Reuben looked at Bobby for only a moment. The two men responded in one voice.

"Sir, yes, sir!"

"Another thing you need to know is that having basic familiarity with the outdoors is a plus," said Colonel Whaling. "Do you?"

"Sir, we come from rural Ohio and have been hunting and fishing all of our lives. I don't know about Reuben, but I was in the scouting movement and spent many days tramping the woods and camping, sir," Bobby answered.

"Sir, my father introduced me to camping when I was barely old enough to walk. He loved the outdoors and so do I, sir," Reuben said.

"That's good, gentlemen," Colonel Whaling said. "Once you have completed your basic training, you will be transferred to the scout and sniper school. There your M1903 rifles will be fitted with Winchester

A-five scopes, and you will receive intensive training in their use. I can't say more than this, but it is my belief that you will be seeing action by the middle of this year. Thank you for your devotion to duty. Your country is proud to have men like you."

Reuben and Bobby saluted Colonel Whaling, and he returned the salute.

"Thank you, gentlemen," said Colonel Robertson. "You may return to your duties."

Bobby and Reuben left the CO's office and walked toward the mess hall.

"So where did you learn to shoot?" asked Reuben.

"Same place you did," Bobby said. "Hunting with my dad. I had a Winchester 94 that loaded thirty-thirty shells. I could hit a deer in the eye at three hundred yards with that rifle. A real beauty."

Just then Gunnery Sergeant Thompkins walked up. Both men stopped and saluted.

"At ease, men," said Thompkins. "I understand you've been assigned to Wild Bill's scout school."

"Sir, yes, sir."

"I said 'at ease,' " Thompkins said. "I just wanted you to know that I'll be going along as your instructor. It just so happens that my last score on the range was 324. I look forward to punishing you two for a few more weeks. You're not done with me yet, boys, and the truth is, we'll probably be shipping out together. So get used to this plug-ugly face because you'll be seeing a lot of me. Now get back to the barracks. I noticed that you 'expert marksmen' are on latrine duty tonight, and I'll be wearing my white gloves for inspection." He flashed a wicked grin and sent them on their way with an explosive, "On the double!"

◇◇◇

The rest of boot camp flew by quickly. Things were looking up. Gunnery Sergeant Thompkins, while still a strict disciplinarian, directed his most critical comments to the men who were just struggling to get by. Bobby and Reuben, having earned a spot in the elite scout and sniper unit, weren't exactly treated with deference, but at least they were no longer regarded with disdain.

Finally, after completing their training, the brand-new Marines gathered around their drill instructor to receive their orders for further training or assignment directly to the Fleet Marine Force. Then the recruit platoons formed one last time for their graduation parade. Down the huge parade ground they marched, feeling the thrill of the title they had earned with hard work—United States Marine. As they passed the reviewing stand the command rang out: "Eyes right!" and battalion banners and sabers dipped and flashed in salute. The band struck up the "Marine's Hymn" as the colonel returned the salute.

Reuben felt a strange thrill run throughout his body as he marched. He was a soldier! Not only was he a soldier, he was a member of an elite fighting unit in the United States military. For an Amish boy from rural Ohio, Reuben had certainly come a long way. Even though everything he had learned as a youth spoke against it, pride welled up in Reuben's heart.

If only Jerusha could see me now, he thought, and then a flash of sorrow knifed through his heart. *She would hate everything I've become.*

Chapter Twenty-One

Into the Storm

Bobby and Mark sat at Henry's bedside, hoping for Henry's scrambled brain to organize itself long enough to allow Henry to tell them where he had left Jerusha. Henry continued to mumble about Jenna and Reuben, and then he said something that didn't make much sense.

"Hid a cow, Bovvy...hid a cow."

"You hid a cow, Henry?" Bobby asked. "You said that before."

"Inna car...hid a cow inna car." Henry was trying to push himself up.

"Easy, Henry," said Dr. Samuels. "Go slow and think it through. You've got to help Bobby understand."

"Okay, Henry, you hid a cow in the car," Bobby said. "You seem to think that's important, but what does it mean?"

"Hid a cow inna car, slid a ditch," Henry said.

Suddenly Henry reached up and jerked Bobby down close. Gathering himself up, he spoke as loudly as he could. "Hid a cow inna car... slid a ditch! Bovvy! Hid a cow inna car...slid a ditch!"

Bobby stared at Henry.

What is he trying to tell me? Suddenly a picture of a frozen cow in a ditch with its legs sticking up popped into Bobby's mind. *Mother Nature's deep freeze!*

"Henry! Did you hit a cow on Kidron Road?" Bobby asked excitedly.

Henry sighed and fell back on the bed and offered a lopsided smile. "Hid a cow...slid a ditch, Kidron..."

Henry closed his eyes. He had delivered his message, and now he could rest.

"I know where the car is!" Bobby shouted. "I must have driven right past it while I was looking at that cow. It's on the other side of the road right up from the county highway. Mark, take me back to my tractor!"

"Sure, Bobby," Mark said. "Let's go get 'er."

They drove back to Betty's house and around back to the shed. Bobby turned the glow plugs on. The battery had a good charge, so they began to heat up right away. They went inside to tell Betty about Henry and to wait for the plugs to heat up.

"He's okay, Betty," said Bobby. "The doctor says he just needs to rest. And he was able to give me a pretty good idea where the car is."

"Oh, thank the Lord," whispered Betty.

They waited ten minutes, and then Bobby went out to the tractor, jumped in the cab, and cranked her over. After a momentary hesitation, the old diesel motor fired up and started running.

Bobby backed out of the shed and swung out onto the street. Mark followed in the Ford.

The wind had picked up to near gale force, and the light was failing as Bobby and Mark headed down the township highway toward Kidron Road.

◇◇◇

The battering of the rough seas beneath the hull of the decrepit troop transport played havoc with Bobby Halverson's churning stomach. A true landlubber, Bobby had never seen the ocean before April of 1942. When he finally stood on the shore of the Pacific after the First Division landed in San Diego, he stared in awe at the vast blue expanse. The sound of the gulls wheeling in the air above his head was as plaintive and mournful as if they were lamenting the loss of something that was never to be found again, and the cries called to something deep in his spirit that was unnamable and sublime.

It's like my old life is gone and nothing will ever be the same again, he thought.

◇◇◇

Since Pearl Harbor, the Japanese army had battered Wake Island into submission, captured Bataan and Corregidor, set the British troops on the run in Burma and Singapore, and easily taken the Dutch East Indies. Their dominion stretched in a two-thousand-mile-long arc that was now dangerously close to Australia and New Zealand. It seemed that nothing could stop the swarming millions of battle-hardened Japanese soldiers. The US fighting forces received a momentary respite when the American Navy defeated the Japanese invasion fleet at Midway Island. Now the powers in Washington desperately needed to do something to stop the rising tide of Japanese Imperialism, and the Marines were ready to go.

Unfortunately, there was another front, and the consensus was that Europe was where the most crucial battles would be fought. Much of the supplies and manpower had therefore been allocated to the European theater, leaving only two divisions of Marines totaling 40,000 men for use in the Pacific. After much discussion it was decided that the attack would come somewhere in the southern part of the Japanese area of control.

The First Marine Division, which included the scout and sniper platoons, had been sent to San Diego, from there to Hawaii, and then on to a beautiful South Sea harbor called Nuku'alofa. There the Marines waited while the top brass made the final decision, which they did in July of 1942.

Thus it was that Bobby and Reuben found themselves on an ancient transport, tossing on rough seas beneath a concealing cover of clouds somewhere in the South Pacific, steaming toward their first engagement with the Japanese army.

Although it normally took more than a year to earn rapid promotion, Bobby had been promoted to lance corporal because of his outstanding leadership qualities and because of the shortage of ranking leaders. Reuben had been promoted to private first class. The two men were assigned to Gunnery Sergeant Thompkins' platoon of snipers, and after basic training, the three men had become close friends.

On Monday, July 27, Ed Thompkins came over to Bobby and Reuben and motioned them aside.

"I just sat in on a briefing session in Colonel Hunt's cabin," he said quietly. "We're headed for the island of Guadalcanal. It's a strategic objective because the enemy has just finished building an airfield on the island, and they plan to use it to disrupt our supply lines to northern Australia. We have to take the island and hold it until we get reinforced."

"How many Japanese are on the island?" asked Bobby.

"The word is that we have them outnumbered, but they can bring more men in from a dozen locations."

"When are we going in?" Bobby asked.

"A week to ten days. It's a big island, so our platoon is going to see a lot of action."

Reuben felt uncertainty begin to rise up in him. He had been so confident while he was being trained for the very purpose ahead of him—killing the enemy. Could he really do this? It's one thing to shoot at an outline of a man on a target range, but it's something entirely different to shoot another human being or thrust a bayonet through him. What would Jerusha say if she knew?

Bobby saw the troubled look on his face, and when Thompkins left he drew Reuben aside.

"Okay, what's going on in that complicated brain of yours?" Bobby asked.

Reuben hesitated but then said, "I don't know really how to describe this except to say that it's like I'm fighting a constant battle inside my head. I honestly don't know how I'm going to respond when the bullets are zipping around me or when I put a man in the sights of my rifle for the first time." He looked down at the deck.

"If it's any consolation, you're not the only one who goes through these struggles," Bobby said. "We all wonder how we'll respond when the moment finally comes. It seems to me that courage isn't something you carry around in your pocket like a silver dollar. My guess is that nobody finds out what he'll really do until the moment he has to do it."

When Reuben didn't say anything, Bobby continued. "When I was a kid, I went hunting one time with my dad. I had shot plenty of deer in my life and didn't expect to have any problems that day. My dad and I spent three hours slow-crawling up on this big buck. He was in a stand of trees scratching the ground to attract some females, and he didn't see us. We got around on the downwind side of him so he couldn't get our scent. We would crawl a foot or two and then lie still. We worked our way through a thick stand of pine that had all kinds of elderberry and scrub brush, so we couldn't see him until we got right up on him. One minute he was completely hidden, and then I crawled forward one more time and there he was, not more than fifteen feet away. I had my gun cradled in my arms so it was easy to bring it up to firing position. Just as I was ready to shoot, he turned his head and looked straight into my eyes. I froze. My mouth went dry and my skin got cold. It was like someone turned the sun down about twenty degrees. There I was with my dad behind me giving me little nudges on the sole of my boot. I couldn't pull the trigger. It was as simple as that. I just couldn't do it.

"I think the deer didn't see me at first, or he didn't recognize me. It was probably only five or ten seconds, but it seemed like an hour. Then he saw me, and with a big bound he was gone, just vanished. And I'm lying there feeling like an idiot, and my dad stands up and says, 'It's okay, son, just a little buck fever. It happens to all of us. Boy, we sure got close to that son of a gun before he saw us, didn't we? He was a beauty.'

"When we got home, my dad didn't say anything about it to my mom, and the next week we bagged two deer without any trouble. So I don't know, Reuben. It will all play itself out in the moment, so there's no sense in worrying or wondering. I'm betting you'll do the right thing."

Reuben offered a smile, but a nagging doubt lingered in the back of his mind.

It's like a rat inside my head, gnawing away in the darkness. Lord, help me to be a good Marine.

The spontaneous prayer surprised Reuben. He hadn't thought about God in a long time.

◇◇◇

On Monday, August 3, Colonel Hunt, the commanding officer, put out a notice to his troops. Bobby read it aloud to his platoon.

"The coming offensive in the Guadalcanal area marks the first offensive of the war against the enemy involving ground forces of the United States. The Marines have been selected to facilitate this action, which will prove to be the forerunner of successive offensive actions that will end in ultimate victory for our cause. Our country expects nothing but victory from us, and it shall have just that. The word 'failure' is no longer in our vocabulary.

"We have worked hard and trained faithfully for this action, and I have every confidence in our ability and desire to force our will upon the enemy. We are meeting a tough and wily opponent, but he is not able to overcome us because we are United States Marines.

"Our commanding general and staff are counting on us and will give us wholehearted support and assistance. Our contemporaries of the other task organizations are red-blooded Marines like ourselves, and they are ably led. They, too, will be there at the final downfall of the enemy.

"Each of us has his assigned task. Let each vow to perform it to the utmost of his ability, with added effort for good measure.

"Good luck and God bless you."

There You are again, thought Reuben as Bobby folded the paper and put it in his pocket. *I haven't even thought about You in a long time, and now I'm praying for Your blessing. I hope You're real, I really do. And if You are, I want to ask You two things. Let me be a good Marine and do my duty, and let me get home to Jerusha in one piece. That's all. Oh, and please keep Bobby safe too. He's all I have out here.*

◇◇◇

On Friday, August 7, 1942, at 0400 hours, the Marines watched from the deck of their transport as the convoy of ships moved close in to the shore of Guadalcanal. The sky was still dark with no pre-dawn glow, but ahead of them the even darker mass of the mountains of Guadalcanal stood in relief against the sky. The men were silent. Only the sweeping of the water past the bow of their ship could be heard. They couldn't see in the darkness, but they knew that all around them, other ships, battlewagons and cruisers, were creeping closer to the shore. No shots had been fired from the island, and one lieutenant was heard to mutter, "I can't believe it. Either the Japanese are very dumb or it's a trick."

The light began to grow in the east, and off to the left they could see the outline of Tulagi Island, where more Marines would be going ashore. Suddenly, the night was split by a brilliant green flash from the cruiser to their left, followed by the roar of artillery rounds headed for the beach. At that signal a huge barrage of fire from the gathered ships lit up the sky. Overhead the fighters and bombers streaked toward the shore. Bobby and Reuben were standing by the rail of the ship. They watched tracers stream from the fighters as they strafed the beach. In the growing light they heard the rumble of bomb clusters striking home as huge clouds of smoke billowed up from the shore and toward the mountains. Bobby looked at Reuben, and then the order was given to climb into their landing boats. Reuben grabbed Bobby's hand.

"This is it, Bobby," he said. "Good luck and God be with you." He noted the surprised look on Bobby's face and then the smile.

"Thanks, buddy. Stay close."

And then Bobby was gone over the side, and Reuben clambered down the net after him. The invasion of Guadalcanal had begun.

Chapter Twenty-Two

Contact

◇◇◇

It was late Friday afternoon, November 24, and still the Great Thanksgiving Storm had not let up. The freezing wind and blinding snow made it hard to see, but Jerusha's eyes had not deceived her. A little girl was in this car, and the color of her skin indicated that she was likely hypothermic.

The wind was tearing at Jerusha, and she clutched the thin blanket tighter around her shoulders. She knew that she had to get out of the storm, so she tried to open the car door, but it was jammed. She jerked at it a few times and then slowly made her way around to the driver's side and pulled at the back door. It opened, and Jerusha crawled inside. She pulled the door shut and moved to the little girl's side. She pushed some of the loose clothing aside and touched the face of the little girl. It was icy cold, but she was alive. The girl opened her eyes and looked at Jerusha.

"Are you an angel?" she asked.

Jerusha felt a sob catch in her throat. "No, dear, I'm not an angel," she answered. "I'm lost in the storm, just like you."

◇◇◇

Reuben and Bobby were bivouacked with their sniper platoon under the cover of a palm grove about a mile inland from the landing zone on Guadalcanal's Red Beach. It was the afternoon of August 7, 1942, and the men had worked their way into the jungle ahead of the main force to scout out enemy positions. The landing on Guadalcanal had gone off without a hitch. The enemy had offered almost no resistance as the First Division came ashore, and the officers were puzzled. Their commander, Colonel Hunt, had immediately moved his assault troops off the beach into the surrounding jungle, wading the steep-banked Ilu River, headed for the enemy airfield that was the focus of the invasion.

As the evening came on, the Marines set up a defensive perimeter and were waiting until morning to continue their attack. The Japanese had retaliated late in the afternoon with an air raid from neighboring islands but had done little damage and flown off. Now the silence was eerie, and the absence of opposition was worrisome to the riflemen. The men had come upon hastily abandoned tents and dormitories. The Japanese troops, most of whom were actually Korean laborers, had obviously fled to the west, leaving huge stores of their supplies and food. Bobby was smoking one of the Japanese cigarettes.

"These things are terrible," he said, spitting bits of tobacco from his mouth. "You have to put this dumb paper filter on the smoke to keep the tobacco from scorching your mouth, and then there's no taste. What good is that?"

"If the Japanese don't kill you, their cigarettes probably will," Reuben said with a smile. "During my *rumspringa*, I smoked a cigarette. I took two puffs, turned as white as a sheet, broke out in a sweat, and threw up. It became very clear to me in that moment that tobacco is a deadly poison."

"Well, I'll die happy then," Bobby said with a laugh.

One of the men stood up to look around, and suddenly there was the sharp crack of a rifle. The Marine spun around and fell beside the tree where he had been standing.

"Sniper!" Bobby yelled, and the rest of the patrol dove for cover.

Reuben glanced over at the fallen soldier. It was clear he was dead.

"Where is he?" whispered someone to Reuben's left.

Another sharp crack sounded, and a bullet glanced off a palm tree above Reuben's head and went zipping into the jungle.

"He's up there in that clump of palms, about a hundred yards ahead," Bobby whispered. "I saw the puff of smoke. Reuben, you should be able to get a shot at him."

Reuben wiggled forward on his belly and took a look where Bobby was pointing. Another crack came from the trees, and this time Reuben saw the smoke from the rifle.

"He's about twenty feet up that tree on the left where the palm crowns," Bobby said. "Take a shot, Reuben."

Reuben pulled the stock of his rifle into his shoulder and sighted through the Winchester scope. He slowly scanned the tree Bobby indicated but saw nothing. Then suddenly there was a tiny movement, and Reuben saw a face begin to take shape out of the foliage surrounding it. The Japanese soldier had opened his mouth and showed his teeth. It was probably an unconscious habit, but it sealed his doom. Reuben now had the man square in his sight. His finger started to tighten on the trigger.

Suddenly the face in his sniper scope seemed to change into his father's face. "*Thou shalt not kill, Reuben*," his father said to him.

Reuben pulled back slightly and then put his eye to the sight again. Again he saw his father's face in the crosshairs.

His father's voice spoke to him again. "*Love the Lord thy God with all thy heart and mind and strength, and love thy neighbor as thyself.*"

Reuben broke into a cold sweat. His mouth became dry, and he felt the muscles in his right leg start to twitch. As he peered through the scope at the figure in the tree, unable to move, he heard the report of a rifle hammering his left eardrum. The face of the enemy soldier in his sights suddenly erupted in a bright red fountain. The shock made him jerk, and he reflexively pulled the trigger. His bullet caught the man square in the chest as he jerked backward from the impact of the first bullet. There was a violent thrashing in the top of the tree, and then the sniper slowly toppled out and fell straight down through the branches, hitting the ground with a thud. Reuben looked to his left. Gunnery Sergeant Thompkins was grinning at him.

"Buck fever, boy?" he asked. "He's not going to wait for you to shoot him, you know."

Reuben quickly changed the subject. "Should we search him?"

"Sure thing, Springer," Thompkins said. "We'll cover you. Keep low. There may be other snipers out there."

Reuben worked his way around through the low brush until he came to the tree where the sniper had been hidden. He dropped to his hands and knees and crawled up to the body.

There were no official documents, but in the breast pocket of his shirt there was a small wallet. Reuben pulled it out and looked through it. There were a few slips of paper with Japanese writing on them. A small picture slipped out and fell to the ground. Reuben picked it up. It was a family photo of the man with a woman and a baby. The man was not handsome but was clean cut and well groomed in his dress uniform. The young woman was quite lovely, with dark, almond eyes and delicate features. The baby in her arms was probably about six months old. Reuben stared at the picture. Then he looked at the body of the husband and father who would never return home.

Reuben stuffed the picture into his pocket and made his way back to the patrol.

"No papers," he said to Thompkins. "Just a guy with a rifle trying to kill some Marines."

"Let's move to a different position then," Thompkins said. "But keep down and stay sharp. We may have drawn some attention with that little fracas."

"What about Raymond?" asked one of the men, pointing to the body of the Marine who had been killed.

"We'll mark his body and send the evac guys back to pick it up," Thompkins said. "Now let's move out. Spread out and keep down."

One of the men quickly snapped the fallen Marine's bayonet onto his rifle and stuck it in the ground by the body. Sergeant Thompkins grabbed the Marine's dogtag, pulled it off with a quick jerk and shoved it in his pocket. Then the patrol moved silently into the brush and headed toward the airfield. After marching half an hour under their heavy packs, they had seen no more sign of the enemy. They came out into a grove of coconut palms. Thompkins set sentries at either end of the grove, and the patrol settled in for the night. Bobby settled down next to Reuben and pulled a smoke out of his pocket.

"The smoking lamp is not lit, Halverson," the sergeant said. "Put that away. I want everyone quiet. If we are fired on in the night, do not, I repeat, do not use your tracer bullets. They will give away your position. Stay alert. This is not a picnic."

Bobby and Reuben settled behind a fallen palmetto log. As darkness fell, the two men stared out into the jungle.

"What happened back there, Reuben?" Bobby asked quietly.

"It was really strange," Reuben said. "I had the sniper lined up in my sights and was ready to shoot, and then I saw my *daed*'s face in the crosshairs. He was telling me that to kill is wrong. I couldn't pull the trigger. I thought I could, but I'm not certain anymore. I sure don't want to let everybody down if we get into a real firefight."

Bobby was silent for a moment and then said, "Like I've said before, I'm believing that when push comes to shove, you'll do what needs to be done. Let's get some shut-eye."

Sleeping was not as easy as Bobby thought. The jungle was not still. The night was full of the sound of creatures rustling in the leaves. Every few minutes there was a sound like two blocks of wood banging together and another sound like a dog barking. The sounds left the men jumpy and unable to sleep. From time to time they could hear rifle shots in the distance. At one point, a submachine gun started rattling away off to the left, followed by the sharp crack of a Japanese rifle and then a volley of shots from the heavier Marine rifles. The sentries were nervous and jittery.

Finally the firing died away, and the men fell into restless sleep. All too soon the first light of dawn broke over the jungle. One of the sentries slipped silently back to the bivouac area and conferred with Sergeant Thompkins in a whisper. Thompkins woke the men up and called them in around him.

"A patrol of about a hundred enemy troops passed near us over by that swampy area and then took off into the jungle toward the airfield. Johnson, get on the radio and call Edson. Be sure to use the code name Red Mike. Tell him what we saw and ask for orders."

Johnson got on the radio and talked quietly with headquarters for a minute. Then he turned to Thompkins.

"The main force of Marines is moving toward the airfield. Red Mike wants us to reconnoiter the south side and report."

"Okay men, let's grab some chow, break camp, and get going," Thompkins said. "And when we're moving through the jungle I want you men to remember your training and walk quiet, like an Indian in the woods. The man who can walk the quietest will live the longest. And when you come to a clearing, either move around it or, if you have to cross it, move quickly and quietly and stay low. Dump your mess kits except for the cup and the spoon. They make too much noise. Keep your eyes on the trees, move to an objective point a hundred yards at a time, and then wait for the rest of the men. That's all. Now let's move."

The men quickly ate some of their C rations, packed their gear, and moved out. As Reuben slipped through the jungle with his patrol, he thought about the picture of the Japanese family in his pocket. Once again he found himself offering up a silent prayer.

Lord, let me get home to Jerusha. A wry grin crossed his face. *I guess there really aren't any atheists in foxholes, Lord.*

Chapter Twenty-Three

The Battle of the Ridge

The month after the invasion hadn't gone well for the Americans. On the second day after they landed, the Japanese sent a fleet of cruisers and destroyers to attack the landing fleet off Guadalcanal. In the naval battle that followed, five American cruisers were sunk or disabled. The outcome of the sea battle wasn't good news to the Marines. Rumors began to circulate that the troops were now cut off, that the whole invasion was going to turn into another Bataan. All the men were gloomy about the reports. And to top it all off, it began to rain. Soon the Marine scouts were slogging through mud and swamps, searching for the enemy. The Japanese had many trenches and foxholes where they hid until a patrol passed, and then the concealed enemy would open up on them. Casualties were not yet high among the Marines, but they were mounting.

For Reuben and Bobby, August was a long nightmare of marching, scouting, hiding in the jungle, and staying away from any real fighting. The first episode with the sniper had been their only face-to-face confrontation with the enemy. During that time, however, they had scouted out several detachments of Japanese soldiers, called in artillery and air strikes on their positions, and then slipped back into the jungle without contact. The men were tired, hungry, wet, and miserable.

But by September, much of Guadalcanal had fallen into American hands, though the Japanese continued to put up fierce resistance. On September 8, Bobby and Reuben's platoon was ordered to accompany Colonel "Red Mike" Edson up the coast to attack the Japanese positions on the Taivu Point and capture the village of Tasimboko. They boarded some small transports equipped with landing craft for a quick trip up the coast.

Fortunately, just before they arrived at their destination, a small convoy of American cargo ships escorted by destroyers passed by them. Their mission was a completely different one, but when the Japanese at Tasimboko saw all the ships together, they assumed a large invasion force was landing, so most of them ran away. The Marines landed with very little resistance, and once again Reuben and Bobby were out of the fighting. They mopped up a few stragglers and some snipers and then headed back for the main camp on the Tenaru River.

On Sunday, September 13, after returning from Tasimboko, Reuben and Bobby's platoon had gone to bed. Shortly after that they were awakened and told to move out and up to the top of the ridge that formed the main line of defense for Henderson Field. During the day there had been many skirmishes with Japanese patrols, and a major attack was expected that night. The ridge was fifteen hundred yards from the airfield and was defended by Marines from the engineer battalion and the First Marine Division.

Gunnery Sergeant Thompkins got his men into the trenches along the top of the ridge, where they waited for the enemy. They didn't wait long. Several flares lit up the night sky. By the flickering light Reuben could see a wave of Japanese soldiers running up the hill toward the American positions. They began screaming, "Banzai!" and firing their weapons.

The main force began to converge on the knoll where Reuben and Bobby's platoon was positioned alongside Red Mike Edson's men. They were obviously trying to push the Marines off the ridge and open the way to recapture the airfield. Reuben sighted down the hill at the oncoming horde and as he did, a strange and new feeling began to rise up from deep within him. It wasn't fear; it was more than that. It was primitive and raw, a consuming rage and terror that overwhelmed him. Suddenly Reuben was firing his rifle into the massed men below. One, two, three Japanese went down under the chilling accuracy of his shooting.

To the left and right of him Bobby and Sergeant Thompkins were firing into the mass of charging men with terrifying effect. Twenty or more Japanese were dead or dying on the hill in front of them. The line coming at them wavered and broke, and they turned and ran back down the hill. At the bottom of the hill, Reuben could see officers with swords screaming at their men and pointing back up the hill.

A large detachment of Japanese soldiers appeared out of the jungle and joined the group that had retreated. They all turned and once more began advancing up the hill. Red flares lit the night sky again, and the scene reminded Reuben of what he had always thought hell might look like. The Japanese began firing their submachine guns with great effect. Up and down the line Marines were going down.

The sniper patrol responded with withering fire, making every shot count. Once again they turned and ran down the hill, leaving more than a hundred of their dead behind.

During the lull, Reuben felt a hand on his shoulder. He turned to look into the eyes of his friend.

"I knew you'd come through, Reuben, I just knew it," Bobby said. He had a bloody furrow along the side of his head where a submachine gun bullet had barely missed him, and his eyes looked the way Reuben felt inside.

Sergeant Thompkins moved quietly along the line, checking his men.

"Check your ammo, keep down, and keep concentrating your fire on the main group as they come along the ridge. If they can push us off this knoll, there's nothing between them and the airfield. We have to hold."

Just then Colonel Edson came along the lines. He was dirty and sweating, and his uniform shirt looked as if it had been cut with a knife, but he was unharmed.

"We got into a little hand-to-hand down the line there," he said, "but we ran them off. You boys are doing an incredible job. Keep up the great shooting. They'll be coming back. You have to hold here, boys." The colonel moved down the line to rally his men.

Suddenly the red flares lit the sky again. "Here they come," someone shouted, and another wave of Japanese began moving up the hill.

"Marine, you die!" someone screamed from the Japanese ranks.

"Come and get it, Tojo, we're up here waiting for you," someone yelled back, and once again the roar of gunfire rose to a horrible pitch. Shells from American artillery flew over the top of the ridge with a horrible humanlike scream and landed among the Japanese. Grenades flew up the hill, some to explode harmlessly outside the trenches, some landing among the Marines with deadly effect. Throughout the night, wave after wave of Japanese climbed the hill and broke like the rising tide, higher and higher on the ridge. Slowly the Marines farther down the hill were pushed back until most of the men were gathered in the trenches and foxholes around the last knoll on the hill.

At around four in the morning, red flares lit the sky again, and the Japanese came on once more. The men around Reuben were running out of ammunition. Some had pulled out their pistols or grabbed ammunition off the body of a fallen comrade. Reuben fired until the barrel of his rifle was too hot to touch. All around him was the screaming and moaning of wounded and dying men and the battle cries of men fighting to the death. Suddenly a live grenade bounced into the trench where Bobby and Reuben were fighting.

"Grenade!" yelled a voice behind them, and then the hulking body of Gunnery Sergeant Edgar Thompkins flew through the air and landed on the grenade. There was an explosion, and the sergeant was blown into the air. When he landed, he was writhing in agony, half of his arm blown away. Bobby also went down in a heap, and from the way he fell, Reuben figured he must be dead.

The Japanese soldiers advanced again with more screams. "Banzai! Banzai! Banzai!"

Suddenly Reuben was looking at the battle as though from above, detached and analytical. He heard himself begin to scream like an animal, a horrible, growling, gurgling sound torn from the very center of his being. He grabbed his bayonet and leaped on the first soldier, pulled it out and whirled away from a thrusting bayonet. He snatched up a rifle and clubbed the next soldier trying to come into the trench. He sensed another soldier behind him and then felt a sharp pain shoot through his upper arm. He had been stabbed, but he didn't stop. He grabbed his K-Bar knife out of his belt as he pulled himself off the bayonet stuck in his arm. He leaped forward and struck the man in front of him with it.

Then Reuben began striking out at anything that moved. One of the men was able to raise his rifle part way and get off a round. Reuben felt a blow to his side but it didn't stop him. He leaped forward and jumped on the man. Frenzied Japanese tried to pull him off their comrade. Suddenly there was a terrific explosion as an artillery round went off close by. The concussion blew the enraged group of men into the air. They landed in a jumbled mass in the trench. Reuben was at the bottom underneath four Japanese soldiers. He tried to push them off but they were all dead. He could feel blood seeping out of his wounds.

So this is how it ends. Goodbye, Jerusha...

And then he slipped into darkness.

◇◇◇

Jerusha crawled up next to the little girl, who instinctively held out her arms.

"Where's your mama, honey?" Jerusha asked as she pulled the little body close to her.

"My mama's asleep. The bad man gave her something and she went to sleep."

"The bad man?" asked Jerusha. "Where is the bad man now?"

The little girl snuggled closer to Jerusha. "He fell in the water and then he was gone...out there," she said as she pointed to the pond. "I thought you were an angel."

Jerusha pushed her way under the seat cushion and clothing and tried to get warm. Suddenly the struggles of the last few days overwhelmed her. She felt a great weakness come over her, and she knew she was passing out. She pulled the little girl close to her.

Is this how it ends, Lord?

And then the darkness closed in.

Chapter Twenty-Four

The Journey Home

Reuben awakened to the steady roll of waves under a ship. He opened his eyes slowly and looked around. Sun was shining through a round window in the wall. It was cracked open, and outside he could hear the cries of gulls. Everything in the small room was white, the bed he was lying in was soft and warm, and the sheets smelled fresh and clean.

I'm in heaven...

A picture came to Reuben's mind of a man in a berserk rage, killing and killing again, a man screaming and laughing at the same time. The man's face was covered in blood, his teeth bared and his mouth slavering. He was the man. He threw his arm over his face and groaned aloud. A sharp pain shot through his shoulder and his back. Then a hand touched him, and a familiar voice spoke to him.

"Easy, buddy, easy." It was Bobby.

"Bobby," said Reuben faintly as he looked around. "Are we in heaven? I saw you die."

Bobby was sitting on a chair next to Reuben's bed. He was in a robe and pajamas, and a crutch was leaning against the wall next to him.

"No, we're not dead, though you were closer than I was," Bobby said.

"You took a real beating up there. I've never seen anything like that in my life. You were shot, stabbed, beaten, and shot again. I just got a big hunk of shrapnel in my leg."

"But when the grenade exploded, I saw you go down. I was sure you were dead."

"You know, I thought I was dead too. Most of the blast came right at me. Sergeant Thompkins stopped most of the pieces, but a big one hit me right in the hip. I guess the concussion knocked me out for a minute. When I came to you were faced off with about ten guys. It was a good thing we were in the trench because there were even more of them coming down the trench toward you but they got backed up. They couldn't all get at you at once, and I think that saved you. And Sarge and I were blocking the way.

"What about the Sarge?"

Bobby hesitated for a moment. "He didn't make it."

"He didn't make it? You mean he's...he's gone?"

"Yeah...he is," said Bobby. "A doctor made a mistake in the operating tent and Ed died because of it."

Reuben lay back on his pillow. He didn't say anything for a long time. Bobby was surprised to see a few tears course down Reuben's cheek. The tears made him uncomfortable, but he didn't say anything. Finally Reuben spoke. "Where are we?"

"We are on a hospital ship headed for Pearl," Bobby said. "We both got million-dollar wounds, and we're going home. The brass has awarded us Purple Hearts, although scuttlebutt has it that you're in line for something more. Colonel Edson has recommended you for at least a Silver Star. When they found you up on the knoll, there were forty dead Japanese soldiers in the trench with you and on the slope in front of us. I watched you kill most of them by yourself. You kept the platoon from being overrun."

"What about you?" asked Reuben. "You and Sarge were right there with me. We did it together."

"I think he put me in for something too," Bobby said. "And I think Sarge will be awarded something posthumously. I guess if we didn't make that stand on the top of the ridge, they would have swept right over our lines and recaptured the airfield."

"Red Mike put us in for medals?"

"Yeah, and I hear he's up for one himself. He held the whole show together up there, running up and down the line, getting in to some nasty hand-to-hand himself, and keeping the guys facing forward and on the line. It was quite a battle. The corpsman at the hospital tent told me that the last charge took place at dawn, and when we beat them back again, the Japanese called it quits. One of the guys in the hospital with me said that at the end of the battle, the ridge was littered with bodies."

Reuben looked away, back to the porthole.

Sensing his friend's uneasiness, Bobby said, "We're going home. That's the good news. We'll be in rehab for a while, but we'll be stationed in Hawaii, so it won't be such a hard life while we recover. The doctor said I would limp a little the rest of my life. The shrapnel is in there too deep to dig out, so they're leaving it. Now you—you got shot twice, stabbed in the arm and the leg, pounded with fists and guns and generally whupped on good. When they dug you out from under that pile of dead bodies, I could have sworn you were dead. I thought—"

"I don't want to talk about it," Reuben said, turning back to his friend.

"Okay, we'll leave it alone for now, but at some point you're going to have to talk it through," said Bobby softly. "That was pretty horrible for all of us, and I don't think bottling it all up inside will help you to get through it."

"I don't want to bottle it up, I just want to forget it," Reuben said.

"Whatever you say. Now why don't you get some more sleep. I could use some shut-eye myself." Bobby grabbed his crutch and used it to leverage himself up out of the chair. He gave a deep groan and Reuben saw a row of sweat beads pop out on his forehead.

"Pretty bad?" he asked.

"Only when I move it," Bobby said through the pain. "When it happened, it was like getting hit on the hip bone with a baseball bat with knives strapped on it. It was agonizing. That's why I passed out. I didn't think anything could hurt that bad. But it's improving a little every day. I finally got up on it yesterday, but it still feels like I've got an ice pick jammed in my thigh. I'm just next door, so that was the only reason I made it over here. I've been waiting for you to wake up for the last hour so I could tell the nurse to give you a sleeping pill." He smiled and took Reuben's hand. "It'll be okay. Thank you for saving my life up there."

"How did I save your life?" Reuben asked.

"The Japanese soldiers don't leave any wounded when they can't take prisoners. They figure we'll get well and come back to fight them again. If you hadn't kept them busy until the cavalry arrived, they would have bayoneted us all. That's how you saved my life."

Bobby started a slow shuffle across the stateroom floor as he headed for the door. He stopped before he walked out and turned slowly on his crutch.

"Get some rest," he said. "I'll pop in soon."

◇◇◇

The next few days were quiet. Reuben was heavily medicated for his pain, and he slipped in and out of drug-induced sleep. Whether it was the drugs, the pain, or the memories that brought the dreams, Reuben couldn't tell. He only knew he dreaded sleep.

In one dream, he was in a forest. A low-lying mist clung to the ground. The leafless oaks were hung with moss, and the branches twisted like gnarled arms in the half-light. Ahead of him a slight figure slipped through the scrub growth under the trees. It was a girl, and he could just catch a glimpse of her as she darted ahead of him. Blonde wisps of hair showed from under a prayer *kappe*, and once when the girl stopped beside a tree and looked back, he recognized her. Jerusha.

He ran after her, the thorn-covered branches scratching his face and arms. One of the thorns jammed into his back, and he nearly fainted from the pain. The girl stayed just ahead of him as they ran over rough, rocky ground, always up toward the top of a hill. He was wearing a black, broad-brimmed hat and a black coat. He looked down at his arm, where blood was running out of the sleeve. He ran into a low-hanging branch that knocked his hat off, but his hat was now a helmet and his coat was battle fatigues. He broke out into the open at the top of the hill and saw the figure turned away from him. He ran up behind her and took her in his arms.

"Jerusha, why did you run?" he asked.

He turned the figure toward him, but the face wasn't Jerusha's. It was the hideous face of the Japanese soldier he had killed with his knife. The man stared at Reuben through eyes of icy death. He whispered, "Marine, you die!"

Reuben tried to lift his arms to defend himself, but he couldn't move. The man's hands tightened on his throat. He wanted to cry out, but he couldn't move a muscle. Finally, with a tremendous act of his will he forced a deep groan out of his gut. It broke the spell, and Reuben jerked awake dripping with sweat. He cried out in agony and remorse, screaming Jerusha's name over and over. The nurse stationed down the hall heard his cries and ran in to help him. He was lying on his side and he felt something warm seeping down his back.

"PFC Springer, you've torn your bandage loose. My goodness, you're bleeding. Hold still while I get some help."

The nurse left as Reuben lay weeping on his bed.

"Jerusha, Jerusha, I'm sorry. Please forgive me," he sobbed.

As he lay there, the days and months he had endured since he left Jerusha came flooding back. He remembered taking her in his arms the night he asked her to go away with him. He felt again the passion that swept over him as he looked down into her lovely face. He felt her surrender to him as he kissed her, and for just that moment she belonged to him completely and without reservation. He remembered her breaking away from him and running away, weeping. He remembered enlisting and wondering whether he could ever be a good Marine. He remembered the picture of the young sniper he had shot, and he saw the face of the man standing with his wife and child, looking so happy before he ended his life on a moldy jungle floor thousands of miles from home.

I'm coming home to Apple Creek, my love. I'll come back to you and to the church. I'll be everything you want me to be. I'll never go out into the world again. It's too evil, too horrible.

In that moment, Reuben closed a door in his mind and shut out the war, the battles, the men who had been his comrades, and the horrible memories of the men who had died by his hand.

The elders were right; it's wrong to kill. Jesus was right. God, You were right. If You let me live, I'll go home and do everything You ask me to do. I'll take back the old ways, and I'll make You pleased with me. I'll never leave Apple Creek again. I'll turn my back on the world and all its ways.

Chapter Twenty-Five

The Decision

◇◇◇

The wind howled around the upside-down car as Jerusha lay under a seat cushion and a pile of clothes with the little girl next to her. The cold metal of the roof of the car felt as if it were gradually sucking the life out of her. She had to do something. But what?

Suddenly she heard her grandmother's voice. "*Jerusha,* kumme*! Get up! You must help this little girl or she will die here. You must get her out of the storm.*"

"But *Grossmudder*, I don't know what to do," she cried aloud. "I'm so tired. I can't help her. I just want to go to sleep. It's the easiest way."

"*Jerusha, you must not sleep. This little girl has a life to live, and you have been sent to help her. You must get her to safety. Think, girl, think!*"

Then Jerusha remembered. *The cabin—the Jepsons' cabin! Reuben and I came here that Sunday before he left. He wanted to explain to me, he tried to make me see...*

If she had her bearings right, the Jepsons' cabin was just through the woods about a quarter of a mile. They had homesteaded the property years before but lost their money in the crash of 1929. They had abandoned the place and moved away, and the old cabin had remained empty in the woods, a testament to broken dreams and hope deferred.

Jerusha and the other children of the village had often come to Jepsons' Pond when they were young. She knew this place. Some of the youngsters had used the cabin from time to time as a trysting place or a hangout, but mostly it stood alone, falling slowly into disrepair, boarded up and empty.

If I can get this child to the cabin we might survive, but she looks so cold. I must find a way to keep her warm. Then she remembered her grandmother's words.

"*You're too proud, Jerusha. This gift is not for you, but for those you can bless with your quilts. It's God working through you to touch others. It's not to be held for yourself.*"

Suddenly she found a battle raging inside her, like two different voices—one arrogant, one gentle.

"*You can't use the quilt. That's Jenna's quilt, and it's your ticket out of this miserable life,*" said the arrogant voice.

"*It's the only way to save this child!*" said the gentle voice. "*You must use it.*"

"*If you do you'll remain in Apple Creek forever. You'll never get out,*" said the arrogant voice.

"*Jerusha, this gift you've been given is to bless others. You can't bring Jenna back, and you can't run away from who you are. You must face your pain and go on with your life,*" said the gentle voice.

Suddenly a picture came to Jerusha's mind. She was ten years old, lying in the hayloft and singing the *Loblied* with all her heart. She heard her father's voice call up to her; like the voice of God speaking to her.

"*Kumme, dochter*, there is work to be done."

Then she knew who the two voices were.

The arrogant voice is what I've become, shriveled up and bitter inside my heart. I've let what's happened to me plant a seed inside me that has borne terrible fruit in my life. The gentle voice is who I was, praising God and listening to the voice of my father. What have I become? I'm lost, lost like this little girl, alone in the storm with no one to save me.

Then Jerusha knew what she must do. She shook the little girl awake and spoke to her clearly and slowly so she would understand.

"I have to go for a while, little one," she said softly.

The little girl's eyes opened wide in fear. "Don't leave me," she cried. "The bad man will get me! Please don't go!"

"I have to go, my darling," said Jerusha. "I must get you out of the storm, but I need something warmer to wrap you in. I have to go back to my car to get it. I won't be long. I'll wrap you up as best as I can with these clothes, and I'll come back soon. Don't be afraid."

The little girl looked into Jerusha's eyes, and the fear went out of her face. Her little hand reached up and softly stroked Jerusha's cheek.

Jerusha looked at the little girl. Reddish blonde hair framed a strong forehead and a determined chin. The girl's eyes were a deep, violet. Like Jenna's.

She pushed the thoughts aside and began to wrap the little girl with the loose clothing that was scattered about the car. She put some of the clothes under her to keep her away from the metal roof and then piled the cushion and the remaining clothes around her until only her face was peeking out.

Jerusha felt something leap in her heart as she looked down at the little face. She pushed the car door open and crawled out into the storm. She glanced back once and saw a little hand waving goodbye to her. She quickly turned and retraced her steps toward Henry's car. The wind was howling around her, and the snow was blinding. She staggered on, the cold wind stabbing through her clothing like sharp knives. She pushed on through the snow, over the rise, through the woods, and back to Henry's car. She wrenched open the passenger door and grabbed the box that held the quilt. She felt the cold slowly draining the life out of her.

"Lord, help me!" she screamed into the teeth of the storm. The shrieking wind and horrific cold were almost more than she could bear. But then suddenly a strange warmth began to steal through her body. Again she heard a voice.

"*Kumme, dochter! There is work to be done.*"

This time the voice was not her father's voice. It was deeper, gentler, so peaceful, and in that moment she felt as though someone took her hand and began to lead her through the storm.

◇◇◇

Bobby and Mark made their way slowly down Kidron Road. Bobby was in front, plowing the way, and Mark followed close behind in the Ford. Bobby kept his eyes peeled for the dead cow.

It was right along here somewhere. Boy, it's hard to see out here! Got to keep my eyes open...There it is!

The dead cow lay on its back in the ditch with its legs pointing grotesquely up in the air. Bobby leaned out of the cab and waved to Mark. Mark pulled up, got out, and made his way to the tractor.

"The car must be along here on the other side of the road," Bobby yelled. "Henry said he hit the cow and slid into the ditch. I'll go on toward the highway, and you head back the other way toward town. We should find it within a hundred yards either way. Don't go farther than that, and meet me back here in ten minutes. If you find anything, honk your horn and flash your lights. If I find her I'll turn on my red flashers."

Mark turned the Ford around and slowly moved away into the storm. Bobby began to head south on Kidron Road. He had gone no more than fifty feet when he saw the car. It was off the road in the ditch with the front end pointed toward him. A snowdrift nearly covered it, and it was easy to see how he had missed it when he came by earlier.

Bobby switched on his red flashers, hoping Mark could see them in the storm. He climbed down out of the cab and into the violent, howling wind, barely able to stand up. Bobby made his way down the bank and peered into the car. There was a pile of unfolded newspapers on the backseat, but the car was empty! Just then Mark pulled up alongside the tractor. Bobby struggled back up to the road, made his way to Mark's car, and opened the door.

"Jerusha's gone," he yelled. "The car is empty. She was there. Henry said she had a blanket, and it looks like she piled up newspapers to keep warm, but now it's empty and she's gone."

"What do you want to do?" yelled Mark.

"Let me see if I can tell where she went or if there are any signs leading away from the car," Bobby shouted.

Bobby struggled through the drifted snow back down to the car and searched all around it. Beside the car, where the wind wasn't so fierce, Bobby saw what remained of footprints, now blurred by the snow. He was unable to tell which direction the tracks led. His heart sank. He turned and pushed his way back up to the Ford.

"I don't know what to do, Mark. I see footprints, but they're no help," Bobby said.

"You're just going to have to put this all in the Lord's hands," said Mark.

"What?" shouted Bobby.

Mark raised his voice to a shout. "I said you're going to have to put this in God's hands. She's gone, and there's no way to find her now in this storm. You can't stay out here. It's getting dark. You've got to give it up for today and get some rest. You can start again in the morning."

"In the Lord's hands." That's what Reuben said the last time I saw him. He said he was going to put his life in the Lord's hands—his relationship with Jerusha, his past, his future...The war sure changed Reuben. It took something away from who he was. He was never afraid before he went to Guadalcanal. Sure, he worried about whether he would measure up in battle, we all did, but he was never afraid. He took life day by day, and I never saw him really troubled by anything that came his way...until that last battle and then when Sarge died. Something closed up inside him after that. When he left he told me he was going home, back to the church and the old ways, and he was leaving the world behind him and never looking back. He wouldn't talk about it. That's all he would say about it.

"Bobby, did you hear me?" shouted Mark.

"What? Oh yeah, in the Lord's hands. Okay, Mark, you're right," Bobby shouted. "We can't do anything more tonight. If the Lord is the only one who can sort this out, I'm going to have to let your faith do the job because I sure don't have any. I wish Reuben were here. I could sure use his help. Come on, Mark. Follow me back to Dalton. We'll try again in the morning."

"Let's pray," said Mark.

"What?" shouted Bobby.

"I said let's pray!" shouted Mark.

"Oh...uh, okay, Mark, but I don't know what to say."

"Okay," said Mark. "Then just shut up and listen, and when I get done, say amen."

Mark grabbed Bobby's hand, and in the middle of the raging storm, he knelt down on the road. Bobby awkwardly followed his lead.

"Lord..." Strangely, Bobby could hear every word as Mark began to pray. "Lord, You know where Jerusha is. She may already be with You, and if she is, she's better for it. But if she's still alive and out in this storm, we ask that You would set Your mighty angels round about her to guard and protect her. Lead her to safety and keep her until we can find her. We trust You for it in Jesus' mighty name. Amen."

Mark looked at Bobby.

"Oh...uh, amen," Bobby said.

◇◇◇

Jerusha struggled back to the upside-down car and the little girl. She opened the door and crawled inside, out of the wind. She opened the collar of the little girl's thin coat and felt her skin. It was icy to the touch, but she was alive. *I've got to get her to the cabin. I need just a little more strength to do this.*

Jerusha stopped for a minute and then spoke out loud. "Lord, I've turned from You and denounced You, and I know I don't deserve anything from You. But this little girl will die unless I get her out of the storm. I don't know if You'll help me after what I've said to You, but would You give me the strength to help this little girl?"

Then Jerusha opened the box and took out the Rose of Sharon quilt. She pulled the tiny body out from under the pile of clothing, gently wrapped the little girl in the quilt, and lifted the bundle into her arms.

Chapter Twenty-Six

The Shadow of His Wings

Jerusha crawled out of the overturned car, carrying the little girl wrapped in the Rose of Sharon quilt. The wind had reached cyclone force, and the snow was blinding. Jerusha stood up and oriented herself. She could see the flat, frozen surface of the pond and on the far side, barely discernible through the blizzard, the forest.

I'm on the highway side of the pond. The cabin is across the pond and through those trees. There's a path by the big pine and through the gorse bushes. It's only about a quarter of a mile. I've got to find the path.

Jerusha stepped onto the ice. It was firm under her step. She leaned into the wind and started across the pond. Every step was nightmarish, every breath almost impossible to take. The wind seemed to be trying to snatch the air out of her lungs. Bitter cold clutched at her like hands of death. The ice was treacherous and slippery beneath her feet. Though it was frozen, she knew that there could be thin spots, and with the added weight of the little girl...no, she would not think about it.

Step-by-step she continued across. Once she heard a crack and stood in her tracks, holding her breath. Then she began again slowly.

Finally, after what seemed an eternity, she neared the opposite bank. The pond made a small inlet where the creek ran down to it. A dead tree had fallen into the inlet, and the ice had formed around it. The branches stuck up like dead fingers clutching at her from the grave.

As she made her way past the partially protruding log, she felt the ice give beneath her feet. The log had kept the water from freezing solid, and there was an unfrozen pocket of water just under the surface. With a loud crack the ice broke, and Jerusha plunged into the freezing water up to her knees. Carefully she laid the little girl on the ice and pushed her toward the bank. It was solid there, and the ice held. Then Jerusha stretched her upper body out flat on the ice and slowly lifted her right knee up over the edge. At first the edge of the ice broke off, but as she moved closer to the bank, it became thicker and stronger. When she could finally stretch her leg out on solid ice, she rolled over and lifted the other leg out of the water. She lay on the ice gasping for breath, soaked to her knees and numbed by the cold. She sat up, pulled off her galoshes, and emptied the water out. She pulled them back on, slowly stood up, took hold of the quilt, and dragged the unconscious girl to the bank. When she had the child out of danger, she picked her up and looked toward the forest ahead. But where was the path?

Please help me, Lord, or I will die right here. Give me the strength to save this little girl.

She began to walk toward the trees. She could feel the bottom of her coat and her dress beginning to freeze solid, making it difficult for her to move her legs. Ahead...surely the path was ahead among the trees. It just had to be.

At last she stepped through the trees marking the entrance to the forest. As she trudged ahead, an occasional branch whipped at her face. One branch caught on the quilt and tore it, sending a piece of the red silk to the snow. The wind whipped it away.

Another step. She looked ahead. *The gorse thicket. It's through here and down into the meadow, and beyond that...the cabin.*

The thicket stood like an enemy, the branches bent by the wind like a row of bayonets. She forced her way through. The brush grabbed at the quilt and snagged it. Jerusha had to jerk the fabric to pull it free, and as she did she felt the material rip.

Exhausted, she lumbered on. The little girl lay still, a dead weight in her weary arms. Minutes later, Jerusha came out the other side of the thicket. The wind, howling like a banshee, tried to knock her down, but she gathered herself for one last push.

Then called I upon the name of the Lord; O Lord, I beseech thee, save me.

Step-by-step she crossed the meadow. There was the creek! And there, beyond the creek, the cabin. Jerusha held the little girl tightly and forced her way through the drifts of snow.

The back door...that's the way in. There is a broken latch and you just jiggle it...

She climbed up on the porch and made her way around to the side of the cabin, through a little covered walkway between the cabin and a small shed, and to the back door. She grasped the handle and shook it up and down while she pushed against it with all her weight. There was a click, and the door creaked open. She stumbled inside and closed the door behind her.

Jerusha collapsed on the floor, exhausted. It was wonderful to just be out of the wind and the snow, and she lay there for a moment breathing deeply. Then she felt a slight movement in her arms. The little girl. Jerusha roused herself.

I've got to find something that I can use to build a fire.

Jerusha gently laid the child down and then stood up and looked around. A couple of empty beer cans were lying in the corner. The inside walls of the old cabin were made of pine boards, and some pieces were torn off. A few of them were nailed together into a rough wooden table that stood by the front door. There were a few cracks in the floor, and any carpet or linoleum that had been in the house had long since disappeared. The day's last light was filtering through some small windows above the door, and it was rapidly growing dark. The rest of the windows were boarded over.

An old potbellied stove stood against the far wall, and next to it was a pile of sticks and pieces of wood. Someone had been here and left some dry firewood. Next to the stove was a low shelf made of two milk crates and one of the pine boards. On the shelf was a small candle in a saucer. Jerusha looked along the shelf. There, at the end of the board, she saw a book of matches.

Thank You! Thank You! Now what do I have to do? Think, Jerusha, fight the cold! Oh, Reuben, I wish you were here. You would start a fire so quickly. You made one for me the day we came here, before you left for the war. That day started out so beautifully and ended so badly. We lay by the fire on blankets, and you held me. You wanted me to marry you, to be yours forever... but I said no. I couldn't marry a man who wasn't baptized in the church. When you took me home that night I realized I might never see you again.

Jerusha put her face in her hands and wept.

I'm so sorry, Reuben, for everything...

"Jerusha! Wake up!"

Jerusha pulled herself together as much as she could. She was so cold she was shaking, and her feet and hands were numb. Her thoughts were wandering.

I'm going into shock. I've got to stop dreaming and start a fire. I've got to stay focused here, or we will both die!

Jerusha picked up some of the wood. There were some dry kindling-sized pieces, but there was no paper. There were only three or four matches left in the packet, so she had to find something that would catch and burn.

The quilt! I can use the padding to start the fire.

She started to tear the quilt open when she heard a voice in her head. It was angry and bitter and arrogant.

"What are you doing? This quilt is your masterpiece. You're throwing away your only chance to get away, to start a new life. Are you insane?"

And then the gentle voice...

"This little girl's life is at stake. You must do whatever it takes to save her."

Jerusha remembered watching her father shape the boards for her grandmother's coffin and what he had said to her that day.

"*You have become well known for your skill, but you must always remember that Jesus is the vine and you are only the branch. Without Him you can do nothing. There may come a day when you must give all back to Him.*"

Is this the day that I give all back to You? But when You took Jenna, You took all I had. You gave me a beautiful child, and then You took her from me. I had a wonderful husband, and he's gone too. You stripped me of everything. I have nothing left except the quilt. Are You taking that from me too?

And then she heard the same voice that had spoken to her in the storm—deep, peaceful, and kind.

"*You still have Me*, dochter."

Do I, Lord? Do I still have You?

"Jerusha! Start a fire—now!"

Jerusha struggled against the overwhelming drowsiness, her shivering, and her wandering thoughts and roused herself. She knew what she had to do. She pulled a corner of the quilt from around the little girl, grasped it firmly with both hands, and ripped it open. The thick padding layer was now exposed. She tore a piece from the padding and pulled it apart into strips. She opened the woodstove and laid the strips in a heap. Then she stacked a small pile of the kindling over the padding.

Why do I feel as if I'm killing something instead of saving someone?

She picked up the matches and held them close to the stove. There were only three left in the book. She pulled one out and struck it. It flared and then fizzled and went out. She took the second match and struck it. This one didn't even flare before the tip crumbled and dropped off. Jerusha could feel herself succumbing to the freezing cold from her wet clothing.

Please, help me!

She struck the last match, and it flared into life. Carefully she reached into the stove and lit the padding. It caught! As the small flame began to grow, Jerusha added more of the wood until the fire began to crackle and the light from the open stove door was dancing on the wall.

Quickly she pulled off her coat and her wet dress. She dragged the makeshift table in front of the fire and draped the dress over it to dry. Then she opened the remainder of the quilt and checked the little girl.

She looks about four years old. The same age as Jenna when…when she left me.

The girl's hair was damp and plastered to her face. Her skin was pale, and she was thin, almost emaciated. Jerusha checked her pulse. It was faint but beating.

I remember your pulse beating in your throat as I sat by the hospital bed, my darling Jenna. So faint, just a little tiny beat, and then I felt you go…

The little girl gave a slight cough, but she didn't awaken.

I've got to warm her up. She's going to die if she doesn't get warm.

Quickly Jerusha opened the little girl's coat and took off her damp dress and undergarments. The fire was beginning to give a little heat into the room, and she put one of the bigger pieces of wood on the fire. She could see the sides of the stove begin to turn red as it heated up. Then she pulled Henry's old blanket around her shoulders, opened her blouse and pulled the little girl next to her bare skin. She wrapped the blanket and quilt around them and sat down close to the stove. She felt the child's icy-cold body against hers, and her skin shrank from the cold. As fire generated more heat, she felt the warmth of her body begin to transfer to the little girl.

Just like when I held my baby Jenna in my arms, my life flowing into hers, my love pouring into my Jenna. Oh, my blessed girl…

As she held the little girl against her body and her life began to bring life to this lost little one, something in her heart that had been frozen and dead began to thaw. As the storm raged outside the old cabin, a spring of tears that had been held in check by the bitter walls of her self-imposed prison began to flow from her inner being and then from her eyes, and Jerusha cried and cried.

◇◇◇

The Jepsons' cabin wasn't that far from Dalton, but with the storm raging it might as well have been a hundred miles away. Temperatures continued to plunge, and much of Ohio suffered power outages and road closures.

After finding Henry's deserted car, Bobby Halverson quit searching and drove home to his parents' house in Apple Creek. He pulled the tractor around to the back and put it into the barn. Then he walked wearily inside and slumped down at the kitchen table. His mother brought him some hot coffee and led him into the front room to sit by the fire.

Mark Knepp had returned to his house on the way back from Kidron Road and checked on the animals. Now he was sitting in front of his fire, but he wasn't sleeping. He was praying deeply and fervently for Jerusha, for Bobby, and for others who might be lost in the storm.

◇◇◇

Inside the Jepson's cabin, the terrible cold circled like a starving wolf slinking outside the circle of heat, kept at bay by the glowing stove but waiting for the fire to die down so it could move in and make its kill. Jerusha lay next to the stove and held the little girl next to her heart, wrapped in the remainder of her Rose of Sharon quilt.

The Fourth Day

Saturday, November 25, 1950

Chapter Twenty-Seven

Die Heilberührung

Early Saturday morning, November 25, Bobby Halverson was asleep at his parents' house in Apple Creek. After he and Mark found Henry's abandoned car, Mark persuaded Bobby to go home and get some rest. Bobby slept fitfully through the night as the storm raged on outside. He dreamed chaotic and frightening dreams.

He was wandering through the snow, searching for Jerusha. But then he wasn't looking for Jerusha anymore, he was searching for Reuben or Jenna—which one was it? In his dream, their faces kept changing. He saw them just up ahead through the blinding snow, and he ran up to where they were. But just before he caught up to them, they ran away. Bobby tried to follow, but the snow kept getting deeper and deeper, and he was up to his waist and could hardly move, and his legs felt like cement blocks.

"Wait, wait for me!" he called after the fleeing figures. "I have to save you!" But Jerusha or Reuben or Jenna—who was he trying to find?—scurried away, leaving Bobby trapped in the deepening snow.

Then everything changed, and he was in the steaming jungles of Guadalcanal, crawling through the mud, hiding from the enemy, silently searching for Jerusha and Jenna. What was he supposed to do when he found them? Shoot them? Then he was sitting in a chow tent with Reuben, but Reuben was wearing a broad-brimmed black hat and overalls. He had a beard but no mustache.

"Hey, Reuben, you're out of uniform."

In his dream, Reuben looked at him strangely and said, "Not anymore," and then a messenger ran into the tent.

"Reuben, they found Jenna and Jerusha. They're both dead."

"Dead! But how did they die?" Bobby asked.

"They froze to death in the jungle," replied the messenger. And then Reuben went berserk in the tent and came at Bobby with a knife.

"You didn't try to save them," he screamed at Bobby as he tried to stab him.

Bobby grabbed Reuben's arm as he stared into savage eyes burning with hate. He tried to hold Reuben's arm back, but Reuben was too strong, and the knife came closer as they struggled together...

"Bobby! Bobby! Son, wake up!"

Bobby felt a hand shake him, and he jerked awake. His mother's concerned face stared down at him. Even though the room was cold, Bobby dripped with sweat.

"Another war dream, son?" his mother asked gently.

"Sort of. I was searching for Jerusha or Jenna, and I didn't know which one I had to find. Then I was with Reuben in the war, and we were fighting and Reuben tried to kill me because I let Jerusha die..."

"Well, it was just a dream, and you're awake now. Would you like some coffee?"

"Sure. Thanks." Bobby swung his legs over the edge of the bed and sat with his head in his hands.

Maybe it was a dream and maybe not. I've got to keep looking for Jerusha. If Reuben ever comes back and finds out I gave up trying to find her, it would kill him...or maybe he would kill me.

"What's it like outside, Mom?" he called out to the kitchen. "And what time is it?"

"It's six o'clock. Been blowing a gale all night," she called back. "It's worse today than it was yesterday. Coffee's ready."

Bobby grabbed some dry long johns, two pairs of heavy wool socks, denim coveralls, several layers of turtlenecks, and his heavy Pendleton wool shirt and started getting dressed. He was still pulling on his shirt when he walked out to the kitchen. He glanced out the window to see the tree branches flapping sideways in the wind and the heavy snow falling. The kitchen lights flickered off and then back on.

"It's been doing that for a while," his mother said. Noticing his heavy clothes, she asked, "Are you going out again?"

"I have to, Mom. Jerusha's out there somewhere."

"But what if she's already dead?" his mother asked. "It's been below zero all night, and unless she got in somewhere, I'm afraid there's not much hope for her."

"I know. But for her sake and Reuben's I've got to keep looking until I know."

"I understand you wanting to find Jerusha, but why are you so worried about helping Reuben? He's a no-account if you ask me. Running off like that and leaving his little wife to suffer through that tragedy all by herself."

"He's a good man. He's just had some hard times. He earned the Congressional Medal of Honor. If it weren't for that no-account, your boy wouldn't be standing here today. Reuben saved me and a bunch of other Marines and kept the enemy from breaking through our line. He even—"

Bobby's mother raised her hands. "Okay, Bobby, you're right. He's a hero, and he saved my boy, and I'll always be grateful for that. It seems odd, though, that an Amish boy is the one who got that medal out of all the boys on that island."

"There were at least ten Congressional Medals awarded after that campaign. And don't forget, I got a medal too. Reuben was just in the right place at the wrong time. I don't think he ever knew war would be like that. None of us did. That's probably why Reuben is so troubled. He thought he could be a good Marine. He was a sniper who shot Japanese soldiers from a long way off...all very impersonal, just routine stuff. But when it came down to fighting and killing the enemy with his bare hands, something broke inside him.

"That's why he came back and buried himself in the church. He just couldn't take the world and all the bad things going on in it. He thought by becoming a good churchgoing Amish man, he could forget the war. But he went too far the other way, and that's why Jenna died.

"Reuben didn't want any part of the world, so he put all his trust in his church. Then when she died...well, her death broke him. First the world betrayed him, and then his religion betrayed him too. He had nothing left to hold on to. I don't hold it against him for running away. I just wish I knew where he was. I do know this—wherever he is, he's a hurtin' pup if he's even still alive. I owe him my life, and I've got to repay him. And if that means going out in this storm and finding Jerusha..."

Just then the back door banged open from the force of the wind as Bobby's dad came in. Snow blew in on the linoleum floor as Fred Halverson stomped his boots on the mat in the mudroom and brushed his coat off.

"Got the glow plugs warming up," he said. "Figured you'd be going out after Jerusha again today. The tractor will be ready to go in about ten minutes. Can you get any diesel?"

"Thanks, Pop. I'm going to grab a bite and get some of Mom's coffee in me, and then I'm going out. I'll stop by Dutch's place before I head out and get some fuel."

Bobby's mom took hold of his arm. "Promise me you'll check in when you come back through town. We need to know where you are if you get in trouble. And you should probably throw some blankets in the tractor, just in case you find her out there."

"Okay. And don't worry. If I can make it through the Battle of the Ridge, I can make it through this storm. I'll try to keep you posted."

Bobby sat down at the table as his mom bustled about the kitchen. In a few minutes she flopped some steaming pancakes on a plate, laid some fried eggs and bacon on top, and handed it to Bobby with a big mug of coffee.

I'll do the best I can, Reuben. If she's alive out there, I'll find her. I promise.

◇◇◇

Dawn crept slowly in through the cracks around the boarded-up window of the old shack. Jerusha lay in front of the stove, wrapped in the quilt with the little girl snuggled against her. She had gotten up several times during the night to tend the fire, and the wood supply was running low. She looked at the little girl lying beside her.

So much like Jenna. That strong face, the reddish blonde hair, the deep violet eyes. It's so strange how much she resembles my girl.

The heat from Jerusha's body had warmed the girl, and the bluish tinge was gone from her skin. A faint flush of pink tinted her cheeks, and her breathing had become deeper and stronger. As Jerusha held her, she couldn't keep thoughts of Jenna from her mind. And this time, something was different.

It doesn't hurt so much anymore! I can think about Jenna without having a knife in my heart. What has happened?

Jerusha felt different emotions take hold of her—surprise, thankfulness, and surprisingly, down deep, a kind of fear and bitterness.

What is that? And then she knew.

I've been so bitter and hurt that I became the hurt. Hurt and pain have been my identity since Jenna died. And now part of me wants to hold on to the bitterness because it's who I've become. That bitterness is what drove Reuben away, and it's what made me hate God and revel in that hatred. I feel like I've been ill for a long time and I'm finally starting to get well. Only now, part of me still wants to stay sick.

Just then the little girl stirred. She didn't awaken, but she snuggled closer to Jerusha. Jerusha held her tightly and softly stroked her forehead and cheeks. Having the little girl's body pressed against her skin during the night had rekindled something in Jerusha, something she hadn't felt in a long time—the pure unfettered joy of a mother's love. There had been something in their skin-to-skin connection that had opened a hidden place in Jerusha's heart. She remembered weeping uncontrollably and unashamedly until she had fallen asleep.

I haven't even held a baby since Jenna died. My heart is so drawn to this little girl. Who is she? Why was she alone in the car? Who could have left such a precious child out there to die?

Jerusha noticed it was getting cold again. The fire was dying down, and she had just a few pieces of wood left. She started to get up, but the little girl clutched at her and spoke for the first time that day.

"Mama...Mama, don't leave me."

"*Mama, Mama!*" The words pierced Jerusha's heart. She looked at the little girl's face, but she wasn't awake yet; she had cried out in her sleep. Jerusha pulled the little one close to her and wrapped her arms around the tiny body. Instinctively she began brushing back the matted hair and softly kissing the little one's face.

"I'm here, baby, and I won't leave. Don't be afraid, darling girl. I'm with you now, and nothing can hurt you."

She felt the girl relax and slip deeper into sleep. Softly she unclasped the tiny hands from around her neck, laid the girl down, and wrapped the quilt closely around her. She pulled her dress off the table and felt it. It had dried completely during the night, as had the girl's underwear and dress. Jerusha buttoned up her blouse and put on her dress.

I need more wood. I've got to keep the fire going until the storm passes or someone finds us.

Jerusha put on her coat and buttoned it against the cold. She went to the back door and opened it a crack. The wind howled, and the powdery snow blew in through the gap. She opened the door a bit more and looked out. The landscape had completely changed. At least twenty inches of snow covered the ground, and in some places across the meadow the wind had piled the snow into huge drifts. Jerusha decided to see what was in the storage shed next to the house. She braced herself against the wind and made her way around to the covered archway. The shed door was closed and latched, but instead of a padlock someone had used a tree twig to hold the door shut. She pulled it out and went inside. As her eyes adjusted to the dark, she could see that someone had brought some wood in and piled it there. A pile of split pine logs was stacked against the wall, and several large branches were broken into stove-sized pieces.

Enough for a few more hours...

She gathered up what she could and made her way back inside the cabin. The little girl was lying still by the stove, sleeping in the quilt. Jerusha put the wood down and made another trip back to the shed. When she had accumulated a good-sized pile, she put some pieces in the stove and got the fire blazing again. Then she opened the quilt and quickly put the child's dry clothing back on her. She took off her own boots, crawled back under the quilt beside the little girl, and pulled Henry's old blanket over them. As soon as she wrapped herself in the quilt, the little girl put her arms around Jerusha and, without fully waking, spoke again.

"Mama...Mama, where are you?"

"I'm here, my darling, I'm here."

Jerusha felt such tenderness come over her as she spoke the words that she almost broke. It was as though the love she had bottled up inside her for so long had somehow found its way into the old dry channels of her heart and started to flow like a stream seeking its way to the ocean, and wherever the water touched, healing came to that place. She pulled the little girl up close, and as she lay there with the child, she thought of Reuben. For a moment she wondered what was different, and then she realized that the anger she had felt toward Reuben for the last year was gone. Something had happened in the night, and all bitterness toward him wasn't there anymore. It had changed into...what, pity? Compassion? Understanding?

Forgiveness? No, not forgiveness! Not after what he did. I'm not ready to forgive.

But as she thought of him, for the first time she saw through the pain and the heartache and past all the bitterness. And there it was before her as clear as day—the root of the disaster that had come upon them.

When Reuben came home from the war he was different, and You tried to show me. I should have listened...

Chapter Twenty-Eight

When Johnny Comes Marching Home

◇◇◇

Reuben *was* different after the war. He had been home four months before he came to Jerusha's house one evening in June of 1943. He looked the same; he had the same flashing smile, the same strong, symmetrical face framed in dark hair, the same deep violet eyes. But something about him puzzled Jerusha. It wasn't on the outside, like his physical wounds. No, this was something else. And whatever it was, he had seemed to build a wall around it as if to hide it. But Jerusha saw it—not clearly at first, but later, when they were together more often—and she began to be troubled by it.

When Reuben had first come home, he went straight to his father's house and asked forgiveness for the things he had done to offend the community. He said he wanted to come back to the faith. After consultation with the elders, the family decided that Reuben would have a probation period to see if his heart was really true. Because he had deviated so fully from the *ordnung*, they had come to consider him as an outsider. The elders told Reuben he was to live among the Amish for an extended period and demonstrate a genuine conversion and faith that resulted in a changed lifestyle before he could be baptized. He meekly submitted.

She heard from his friends that he had been terribly wounded in battle and that he had been in the hospital in Hawaii for five months before the Marines discharged him and sent him home in February of 1943. That he made no effort to contact her for several months was hurtful to her, and she said so to her father.

"*Was er tut, ist gut,*" said her father. "He has returned to the fold, but he has seen much. It will take him time to come back to our ways. He is forgiven of course, but before he can enter into the community, we must be sure of him. Even if he were to come today and ask, I would not let him court you. *Aber er hat verstand.* He is wise. He will come at the right time and in the proper way."

So Jerusha waited patiently for Reuben to come to her even though she longed to see him, to hold him and show him that she loved him as deeply as ever. The days went by so slowly as she waited. For the first time in her life she had to force herself to sit down at the quilting frame and work, and her heart wasn't in it. At night she would lay on her bed and stare at the ceiling until finally she drifted off, exhausted.

Eventually Reuben did contact Jerusha, but not directly. He sent a *schteekliman*, one of the deacons, who came secretly to the Hershberger home to obtain the consent of her parents for Reuben to court her. It pleased Jerusha's father that Reuben was following the *ordnung* so faithfully, but it puzzled Jerusha.

He was so independent when we met. That was one of the qualities that drew me to him. He used to say that following the rules and regulations was hypocritical if you thought they were old-fashioned and meaningless. And now he's going along with all of them.

The day that Reuben finally came to the Hershberger home, he didn't see Jerusha alone. Her parents were there as well as two of her brothers. Reuben was formal, even somewhat distant, though he was charming and seemed pleased to be there.

This is not like we were before he went to the war, Jerusha thought as she sat across the table from him.

She remembered the night she lay in Reuben's arms in front of the fire in the old Jepson place. Reuben had left a note for her, begging her to meet him. She had slipped out of the house and met him at the head of the lane that led to her house. He was driving an old pickup truck. She had been shocked to see how different he looked. His hair was shorter, and he was not wearing traditional Amish garb. They had driven toward Dalton and then turned off on a lane that Jerusha realized led out past Jepsons' Pond to the old cabin. When they got there, he built a fire with some wood that had been left there, and then he had taken her in his arms and kissed her. And then he told her that he had decided to enlist in the Marines and go to war.

She could see that he had gone far away from the faith, that he had set his life on a path that would probably take him out of her life forever. And yet as she looked at him while he talked, the deep love she had for him almost broke her. He had begged her again to leave Apple Creek and go with him. And truth be told, she desperately wanted to go with him and be his wife and never be apart from him again. It was only the deep roots of her faith and her love for a God who had walked by her side all her life that held her back. As she listened to him pour out his heart, she knew she was in danger of leaving all that she loved behind to follow this man.

But she could not, and she told Reuben so. Then they had gathered their things, and he drove her home in his forbidden truck. Then he was gone.

And now he was back, sitting across from her, smiling, charming her parents, and being the old Reuben—almost. It took everything in Jerusha to keep from leaping up and throwing herself into his arms. Instead she sat and drank in his face. He was so handsome with his dark hair and strong features. Above his forehead, just under the hairline, she could see a scar, still red and healing. He moved his arm stiffly as though it caused him pain. But the biggest change was in his eyes.

When she looked into his eyes, past the violet and into the soul, she saw a dark pit of sorrow so deep that it sucked up and swallowed all joy. The smile that had lived behind his eyes was gone. In that moment she could see how terribly he had changed. Still, her love for him allowed her to overlook the pain. This was Reuben. He was back, and he was going to join the church and court her. That was all that mattered.

Their courtship was to stay a secret to the rest of the community, but in a short while, word had spread that Jerusha and Reuben were a couple, especially after Jerusha's mother planted a large bed of celery. Celery was an important part of Amish weddings, and this was an open announcement to the Amish in Apple Creek that Jerusha's family was planning one.

Reuben kept everything formal and followed the rules of courtship. They met at the Sunday evening singings or after church meetings and talked, and then they agreed to meet at another event or at her parents' home. Because they were both in their twenties and had never been married, they often found themselves in the company of the younger members of the community. Reuben was so much older in all his ways, and the issues that seemed so important to the young people were often so trivial to him and Jerusha that they both felt awkward. While the teenagers chattered on about *rumspringa* or their part-time jobs or which of them were serious about one of the others in the group, Jerusha and Reuben sat quietly and smiled awkwardly at each other. Jerusha found herself secretly longing for the days when they had met together without all the ritual and formality, when Reuben would open his heart and share the things he knew about the world, about music and art and history.

She remembered sitting at his feet while he spoke of such things, and the power of his speech and the depth of his understanding would overmaster her, and she would be drawn into the strange, wonderful, and yet terrifying world that existed outside the confines of Apple Creek. She had come away from those times together in awe of him, and even though part of her told her that it was wrong to listen to him and by doing so, involve herself in the world, his wisdom and knowledge were a great part of who he was, and knowing that about him somehow bound her more closely to him.

Once she had asked him about the war, and he looked at her with a cold fire in his eyes and forbade her to ever ask him about it again. Rumors floated about that Reuben had gotten a medal for bravery in the war, but Reuben never said a word about it.

The courtship continued for three months. One day Jerusha's father came to her and told her that Reuben had asked formal permission to marry her.

"I have watched him," he told her, "and I would be pleased to have him for a son. His life reflects the change he has made, and the elders have agreed to baptize him. After that, we will publish your agreement to the community."

Jerusha listened quietly with mixed emotions. She felt joy, but also something else—a gnawing uneasiness about Reuben. He was simply a different man now.

"You do not seem as joyful as I would expect, *dochter*."

"It's nothing, *Daed*, " she said. "I love Reuben, and I will be glad to be his wife. I'm only thinking about the things he's suffered, and I hope my love will bring healing to his heart."

"*Ja, das ist gut, meine dochter*," said her father. "Reuben has been where we Amish fear to go, for it stands in the face of everything we hold to be true. I have never been in a situation that forced me to choose my faith over my family's safety, or that of a friend, so I cannot see into his heart, but this I know. Jesus commanded us not to kill because it leaves a scar on the very soul of a man. Reuben carries those scars, and they will change him, maybe for good, maybe not. The best thing is that he has returned to our ways, and there is healing for him in that. Be a good wife to him, Jerusha. Give him children and be his helpmeet. He may never forget what he has been through, but with your help, perhaps he can put it aside and get on with his life."

Jerusha hesitated for a moment and then said, "*Daed*, you don't know Reuben as well as I do, so you can't see how much he's changed. But I see it. I do want to be his wife, and yet sometimes I think he's not the man I fell in love with. It's as though a stranger came home from the war."

"I'm not sure I understand."

"Always before, there was a part of Reuben that took joy in life. Even when he looked stern there was a smile behind his eyes. That smile is gone. And so is the joy, and that frightens me. It's as though the piece of Reuben that makes him whole and happy died in the war. And now he's built a wall to hide the empty place where his heart used to be. I'm afraid that I may use my love to help him break down that wall and find that the darkness there kills my love too."

Jerusha looked at her father.

"That's why I may not seem so joyful when you tell me we can marry. It's that I'm afraid. Afraid I may not have enough love in me to heal him, afraid that I may not be strong enough to be his helpmeet when the trials come. A little voice inside me says, 'Wait, wait,' and I tremble when I hear it. And yet I'm so desperately in love with him. I just want to be with him forever."

Suddenly Jerusha burst into tears. Her father looked at her for a moment and then gently took her into his arms.

"My beloved *dochter*," he said quietly. "I have watched you grow from a precocious child into a woman of strength and faith. I don't know what lies before you in this union, but I do know this. I trust that you are strong enough and loving enough to walk through any trial as long as you continue to place your trust in the Lord and follow Him. We can't control the things that happen to us in our lives. We just trust that all things work together for our good. Reuben has returned to the fold, and he has placed himself under the *ordnung* again. You are a strong woman. With these things to help him, I believe Reuben can be a good husband and, with God's blessing, a good father. I am not a woman, but I know that every woman must work through such questions when she is to be married. Trust me in this, Jerusha, trust the Lord, and be a wife to this good man."

Jerusha stood in the strong circle of her father's arms and felt a peace flood her soul. Surely God had spoken to her through her *daed.*

"I will marry him, *Daed*, and I'll help him to live in the present and put the war and all the terrible things he saw behind him," she said quietly.

"*Gut,*" he said. "Then you may marry in November, after the harvest."

◇◇◇

Jerusha's heart sank within her as she lay in the dark cabin.

I should have listened to my heart and waited. Reuben was so bound up, but I just ignored the warning signs. I should never have married him.

And then Jerusha heard the voice, the one that reminded her of her *daed,* but deeper and more peaceful.

"*But then you never would have known Jenna, dochter.*"

"What good did it do me to give birth to Jenna!" she cried aloud. "The pain of losing her was too much to bear. If I had not married Reuben, I would be happy now, and I wouldn't have these scars on my heart. There would be no Jenna to long for, no Reuben to be bound to."

Jerusha began to cry again.

Just then the little girl woke up. She looked up at Jerusha, and then her little arms stole around Jerusha's neck and she pulled Jerusha close. In her half-sleep she spoke.

"Don't be sad, Mama. Please don't cry."

Jerusha looked down at the little face, and her heart melted.

What's happening to me? Why did you send me this little one?

"*To comfort you, dochter, to comfort you.*"

Chapter Twenty-Nine

Reunion

Bobby Halverson went out to the shed behind his parents' house. His dad had fired up a kerosene heater, and the shed was much warmer inside than it was outside.

He checked the electrical connections to the glow plugs to make sure they were seated properly and then got into the cab and fired up the diesel engine. He let it run for a few minutes until it was warm and the heater had taken the chill off the inside of the cab.

While he was sitting there waiting, he did something that both surprised him and made him a bit uncomfortable. He bowed his head and prayed out loud.

"Lord, if Jerusha is still alive out there somewhere, will You please help me to find her? Give me strength for this day and a clear head so I can do what I need to do. Thank you...uh, amen."

Bobby looked around to see if anyone had seen him praying and then thought better of it.

So what if I prayed? I need all the help I can get.

He pulled the flaps on his woolen cap down over his ears and headed out. The wind was howling, and the snow was piled two feet high around the Halverson house. As he pulled out of the shed, he saw his dad coming across the yard. He leaned out of the cab as his dad called up to him.

"Do you know where you're going to start?" he hollered over the wind.

"I think I'll go by the Springer house again to see if she got home somehow," Bobby yelled. "If she's not there, I'm going to run by the sheriff's office and let him know what's going on and see if he's got any extra men who can help me look. Then I'll go back out to Kidron and see what I can find, maybe go by Mark's and see if he's seen or heard anything. I'll stop by Dutch's place before I head out toward Dalton and get some fuel."

"Okay, son," his dad yelled. "Get number one fuel, not number two. It's more volatile and burns hotter. Be safe out there. Your mother and I will be praying for you."

"Thanks, Dad. I appreciate that."

For some strange reason, the fact that his parents would be praying made him feel better. Then he had a thought that he spoke aloud.

"God, I forgot. Would You please let Reuben know somehow that Jerusha's in trouble and send him home? Thanks."

This must be what they call shotgun prayers. I'm just firing them off and hoping someone hears me.

Fifteen minutes later, Bobby pulled into the lane that led down to the Springer home. It was just beginning to get light. The snow had drifted across the road, and there were no car tracks leading to the house. He pulled up in front, idled the engine, and got down to look around. The house was dreary and dark, and snow was heaped on the front porch. The windows, dark and blank, stared back at him like dead eyes. Whatever life had once been in this house was gone.

Just as he was ready to turn back, he noticed something. Prints in the snow. But whose? He could see a recent single set of tracks lead up from the side of the porch and to the front door. Then they turned and went back toward the Lowensteins' next door.

Bobby jumped down and hurried across the bridge to the Lowenstein's place and banged on the door. After a few minutes Hank came to the door.

"Bobby!" he exclaimed. "Come in, come in!"

"Thanks. I guess you heard about Henry. He's at Doc Samuels'."

"Yes, we did hear. He's going to be all right," Hank said.

"Then you know his story? He crashed the car on Kidron Road and was walking into town to get help when a windblown tree limb hit him and knocked him cold."

"We heard. We're hoping the weather clears enough for us to get over there. But what about Jerusha?" asked Hank.

"She's still missing. By the time I got Henry to tell me where the car was and Mark and I got over there, Jerusha was gone. Either she tried to walk out or someone came by to help her. The wind had blown any tracks away, so that didn't help. I came by here hoping she might have made it home somehow."

"No, we haven't seen any sign of life over there."

"I saw a set of footprints leading here and I wondered whose they might be. I was hoping maybe Reuben came home."

"Those were my tracks," Hank said. "I couldn't sleep, so I got up an hour ago and went over to the Springer's to see if Jerusha was back. The house was dark, and no one has been there."

"Okay, Hank, thanks. I'll be on my way. As my dad says, 'I'm wasting daylight.'"

"You be extra careful out there today, Bobby. I've never seen a storm like this one, and it's going to get worse today before it gets better. Martha and I will be praying for you."

Bobby turned and walked back to the tractor.

Why is everyone praying for me all of a sudden? Even I'm praying. I thought I didn't believe in God. At least that's what I told Reuben.

◇◇◇

Bobby was mustered out of the Marines with a medical discharge, a Purple Heart, and a Silver Star for his part in the Battle of the Ridge. He left Hawaii about a month before Reuben and arrived in Apple Creek at a loss as to what to do with his life.

Of course there was a flurry of activity when he came home. He was made over and welcomed back by his friends, and clucked over by his folks. The local VFW even put on a dinner for the returning hero, but within a few weeks all the attention died down, and he was just plain old Bobby Halverson again. He got hired to work at his old job, moved in with his folks, and even started going back to his favorite bar in Wooster, but somehow his life wasn't the same as he had left it. His dad saw him moping about the house one weekend afternoon and took him aside.

"When I got back from the big war, there was a song that was real popular. It went something like, 'How ya gonna keep 'em down on the farm after they seen Paree?' It looks to me like you're going through something like that, eh, son?"

"That's kind of what I'm feeling, I guess," Bobby said. "But that's not all there is to it. It's just that I never really knew what I was getting into when I went to the Pacific. I mean, it's one thing to talk about killing the enemy and saving the world for democracy, but it's different when you're in hand-to-hand combat in a trench and you know that the only way to live through it is to kill the guy you're fighting. It gets a lot more personal. Staring down a sniper scope at a slight movement in a tree two hundred yards away is one thing, but it's completely different when you have a man skewered on your bayonet and you see the life go out of his eyes. When you've been through an experience like that, it kind of makes you feel disconnected from ordinary life. I can't seem to get a grip on things since I got back."

Bobby hesitated for a minute and then went on.

"Pop, there were times out there I should have died but I didn't, especially in that last battle. When I think about it, it makes me ask the big question. You know, like why did I live when the guy standing right next to me caught a bullet or got blown to bits? What reason in all this great big universe could there be for Bobby Halverson to still be walking the earth?"

His dad smiled and put his arm around his son's shoulder.

"Bobby, I know you're not real big on religion, and the truth is neither am I. Your mother and I go to church, but I'm pretty much a back pew kind of guy. I'm not a fan of bake sales and all the rest of the folderol, but I have found comfort in some of the things the pastor talks about. Why don't you come to church with us on Sunday and maybe talk to the pastor?"

"I appreciate the offer, Pop," Bobby said, "and I'm glad you and Mom have found something that works for you. I'm just not ready to go that route."

His dad let it drop, much to Bobby's relief. Before he left Hawaii he had gotten caught up in a conversation about religion with Reuben, but Reuben's dogmatic approach to the subject grated on Bobby and only reinforced Bobby's negativity toward religion.

So life in Apple Creek for Bobby went on, and he just stayed in his funk. The days rolled by, and soon it was almost fall. Then one day the phone rang, and when he answered it, Reuben was on the other end of the line.

"Hello, Bobby," said the familiar voice.

"Well, buddy…I was wondering if you were ever going to get around to calling me. I heard you've been back for a while."

"Yeah, and I'm sorry it's taken so long. I've been getting some things in order in my life, and it's taken a lot of my attention."

"Oh? Like what?" Bobby asked. "It sure must have been important if you didn't have time to call your best buddy."

Reuben caught the tension in Bobby's voice and said, "Look, I'm sorry, okay? I really have been seriously involved in some things at the church, and it would have been awkward for me to start calling on my

Englisch friends. I'm on probation, and the elders are keeping an eye on me. I don't want to mess this up, so I've had to be very judicious about what I do and where I go. Just lately I seemed to have passed a milestone in my journey, so I have permission to see you."

"Permission?" snorted Bobby. "What happened to old freethinking Reuben?"

There was an awkward pause, and then Bobby jumped back in.

"Look, Reuben, I'm sorry. I didn't mean to get nasty with you. The truth is I've been out of sorts ever since I got back. Since I mustered out, I haven't seemed to be able to get things back in focus. So don't pay any attention to my grouchiness. When can we get together? It would be good to see you."

"That's why I called," said Reuben. "I've got something important to tell you and something to ask you, but I want to do it in person. Can you meet me today at the General Store? That's where I'm calling from."

"Not at the bar in Wooster, old beer buddy?" laughed Bobby.

Reuben chuckled, and then his voice softened a little, and he sounded more like the old Reuben. "Not today, Bobby. I've pretty much put that life behind me. Just come over to the General Store if you can. I'll be waiting out front."

Bobby drove over right away and pulled up in front of the store. Reuben was standing outside by the front door. He had changed a lot—especially the way he looked in traditional Amish clothing.

Bobby climbed out and walked up to Reuben. There was an awkward moment, and then Reuben embraced Bobby and Bobby returned the hug. Then Reuben stepped back and looked Bobby directly in the eyes.

"It's good to see you, Bobby," he said. "I mean it—it's *really* good to see you. I'm glad we both got back from that hellhole mostly in one piece."

Bobby smiled, and for the first time in months he felt some of the tension drain out of him. It was as though the two of them shared something that no one else would understand, and the knowledge that there was someone who knew just how he felt was comforting to Bobby.

"So, what have you got to tell me that's so important?" he asked.

"I'm marrying Jerusha in November."

"That's wonderful! So you got it worked out with her parents and the church?"

"Well, that's part of why I've had to be careful. I really wanted Jerusha's father to know that I'm serious about my decision to get baptized and return to the church. A month ago he gave me permission to court Jerusha, and now it's pretty much settled."

"So what is it you want to ask me?"

"I want you to come to the wedding," Reuben said. "I'd really like you to be one of my attendants, and so I'm asking you so you'll know how much your friendship means to me. On the other hand, I know you'd probably feel awkward, so I'll understand if you say no."

"You're right," Bobby said. "I'd feel about as out of place as a fish in a tree if I had to stand up front at an Amish wedding. I'll come, of course, but I'd rather just blend in with the crowd if you don't mind."

"Sure thing. It'll mean a lot just to have you there. And, hey, now that I have my life back on an even keel, I'd really like to sit down and talk to you about what's been happening with me."

There was an awkward moment, and then Bobby said, "I want to be frank with you. We've already had that conversation, and I'm glad you found your faith again. I really am. I'm glad that the war helped to draw you closer to God. But as for me...well, if anything, the war pushed me farther away. After seeing men in combat, it puzzles me that a God who is supposed to love mankind could let something like war happen. I can only come to one of two conclusions. Either He hates human beings or He doesn't exist, and my money's on the latter."

Reuben looked at Bobby. "I'm sorry to hear that, Bobby. Really sorry."

I'm sure you were, Reuben, I'm sure you were.

Chapter Thirty

Wedding Day

◇◇◇

Jerusha awoke before dawn that Tuesday in November of 1943 knowing that in just a few hours she would be married to Reuben Springer.

She slowly got out of bed, dressed, threw on her heavy coat and some boots, and slipped out of the house in the dark. There were a few inches of snow on the ground, and the air was crisp. She wandered out to the barn and climbed the ladder to the loft. She found her place in the hay and lay down on the soft cushion, letting her perplexing thoughts have their say.

I should be completely happy this morning, and I almost am. I still have a troubled place in me, an uncertainty. I want my daed *to be right that this is the right thing to do, but I'm still not sure about Reuben. He is so serious these days. Oh, I've seen him laugh and be charming, but when we're alone there's a place in him that is closed off to me—forbidden—something he keeps only for himself. He has become so...so Amish! And that is something I never expected. Lord, what am I to do? All of my heart wants him, and yet I keep hearing the tiny voice somewhere in me that says, "Wait, wait."*

As she lay mulling over her thoughts, she heard footsteps crunching across the yard, and then her *daed's* voice came up to her as it had so many times in her childhood.

"*Kumme, dochter*, there are things to be done."

Jerusha stood and took a deep breath. Then she spoke the prayer of her heart aloud.

"I will go now and marry Reuben. I am trusting You in all my ways and leaning not on my own understanding. Be with me this day, my God, for I must depend on You completely."

◇◇◇

By 8:30 that morning, most of the community had arrived at the Hershberger home. Guests packed the house, and many more gathered in the farmyard. Jerusha and Reuben wore plain clothing and sat apart while the *Armendiener* gave a sermon.

The people sang wedding hymns from the *Ausbund*, and then it was time for the vows. Jerusha and Reuben came forward. The minister asked whether they would remain together until death and be loyal and care for each other during adversity, affliction, sickness, and weakness. He then took their hands in his and, wishing them the blessing and mercy of God, told them, "Go forth in the Lord's name. You are now man and wife."

There were no rings or kisses exchanged, but as Jerusha held Reuben's hands, looked into his eyes, and heard him swear his undying love and devotion to her, the uncertainty in her heart slipped away. In spite of her fears, she knew Reuben loved her deeply, and this knowledge gave her great comfort. So she put aside the nagging doubts, shut out the still, small voice that was telling her to wait, and entered into her marriage with a full commitment.

The two made a beautiful couple. Reuben, tall and dark, with his strong face and dazzling smile; Jerusha, blonde and lovely with a sweet disposition and obviously gifted with the qualities that would make a good wife and homemaker. The attendees couldn't help but remark that this was a marriage seemingly wrought in heaven. Everyone knew that Reuben had more than earned his place in the community since his return. He had forsaken the things of the world, received baptism, and been faithful in every way required of him. He was strong in the *ordnung*, and the elders spoke openly of his leadership abilities.

As they were making their way to the reception, Jerusha saw a man in a dark *Englisch* suit among the guests. "Who is that man, Reuben?" she whispered.

Reuben looked over, and a smile broke over his stern features. "That's my friend Bobby. I've mentioned him to you before. He is... *was* my best friend." With that, Reuben rushed over to greet Bobby.

"You came!" he said, reaching out to embrace Bobby. He took him by the arm and led him to Jerusha. "I may have forsaken the world, but I have not forsaken my friend. Jerusha, this is Bobby Halverson." Reuben paused and then went on. "We...we served in the Marines together."

Bobby took Jerusha's hand and said, "I'm so pleased that Reuben invited me to your wedding."

Seeing his warm smile, Jerusha immediately knew why this man was her husband's friend. Bobby went on. "I feel as if I already know you—Reuben has told me all about you. He said you were pretty, but he didn't say the half of it."

Jerusha blushed and lowered her eyes. "Were you with Reuben...in the war?" she asked. She felt Reuben's body stiffen slightly as he stood next to her, and a look passed between them.

"Well, Mrs. Springer, I don't want to go into all that," Bobby said slowly. "I will say this. Reuben saved my life, and I will be eternally grateful for that. This puts me permanently in his debt and in yours. So if there is ever anything you need or any help that a friend can give, please call on me. It's my wedding gift to you both."

Jerusha was surprised to see a tear glisten in Reuben's eye. Then she realized that Bobby had been the first one to call her Mrs. Springer. She felt her heart open to this man. *Englisch* or not, he was a good man for Reuben.

"Thank you for coming, Bobby," Reuben said softly.

"I wouldn't have missed it for the world."

They stood and looked at each other, and again Jerusha saw a look pass between them, a message that conveyed both a shared joy and an unspoken sorrow. She knew instinctively that the look held the key to Reuben's unhappiness, and it occurred to her that it would be good to cultivate Bobby's friendship if she were to help Reuben come back to himself.

"Will you be staying for the reception, Mr. Halverson?" she asked.

Bobby laughed out loud. "Mrs. Springer, no one has called me Mr. Halverson since I got in trouble in high school. If you would be so kind as to never call me that again, I would be most grateful. It's Bobby."

Jerusha liked this Bobby Halverson. "Agreed, Bobby," she said, "and you must call me Jerusha."

"It's a deal," said Bobby. "As for the reception, I really can't stay. I have another obligation. I'll be taking my leave, but not before I wish you my most heartfelt congratulations."

Bobby took Reuben's hand in his and shook it again and then turned to Jerusha.

"I noticed that there wasn't a lot of huggin' and kissin' going on," he whispered, "so I'll just follow protocol and wish you the best with a handshake."

"Our door is always open to you, Bobby Halverson," she said as she took his hand.

For the second time that day she saw a tear start in a man's eye, and then Bobby released her hand, turned, and was gone.

"Why won't he stay, Reuben?" she asked, turning to her husband.

"Bobby isn't a religious man," Reuben said. "I'm sure it was hard enough for him to come and hear the sermon and listen to the hymns. But he's a good man, and I hope that someday he will come to God. I'm sure he feels awkward among total strangers—especially so many Amish strangers. It's enough for me that he came today, and I'm glad you opened our home to him. He's been as close as a brother to me. We..."

Reuben paused just as Jerusha's parents came to lead them to the reception, where the celebration continued. Jerusha's family moved the tables to seat the guests, and Jerusha's mother and her relatives brought out the feast.

Reuben and Jerusha sat in the front corner of the room at the *Eck* table and were the first ones served. There were so many people that they filled the reception room three times to eat in shifts. After the noon meal, there was singing. Then Jerusha's mother reminded her that it was time for "going to the table." She appointed two married couples to oversee the tradition. They went to the unmarried women between sixteen and thirty and invited them to sit in one of the large upstairs bedrooms. The men went out to the barn, where they stood around joking and visiting. Reuben and Jerusha went out to the barn and talked to the young men, trying to convince them to go into the house and upstairs where the girls were waiting.

"You must go in now," Jerusha said. "The girls are waiting, and you will spoil my wedding if you don't go in."

The young men hemmed and hawed and shuffled their feet. Many of the older boys had cast an appreciative eye on Jerusha in the past, and so in the end it was easy for her to convince them. One by one they went upstairs and asked their favorite girl to "go to the table."

The couples held hands as they came down the stairs and sat at the long table. Meanwhile the older folks sat on benches throughout the house. From time to time the group would break into a hymn. While they were singing, Jerusha's parents passed around candies, fruits, cookies, and small pieces of cake. The singing went on until finally Jerusha and Reuben left the table. Then the unmarried couples left the table and went into the barn and talked.

Jerusha and Reuben saw to it that every unmarried person over the age of sixteen had a partner for the evening table. Tradition allowed anyone who didn't wish to take part to go home, and then the bride and groom led the couples in a procession into the house. Gaslights gave off their soft glow as the Hershberger home resonated with the laughter and songs of the guests.

Jerusha sat with Reuben, and the wonder of the moment filled her heart. Reuben held her hand, and from time to time he would look into her eyes and smile. It was in one of these unguarded moments that Jerusha felt bold enough to ask, "Reuben, you said that you and Bobby shared some things during the war, and then you stopped. Will you tell me someday?"

Reuben set his face in a curious way. He tried to be gentle as he spoke to her, but there was an unaccustomed edge that frightened her. "I'll say this once, and then I wish never to speak of it again. In the war I learned that God was right all along. To kill another man is the most horrible act that one human being can do. I did things in battle that only an animal would do. I'm ashamed to the depths of my soul that I ever violated God's Word. I have returned home to a way of life that will keep me from the world and from all the horror that men do to one another. I will not speak of it again. If you love me, Jerusha, you will let this matter be."

Jerusha flinched as though he had struck her. The tone in his voice and the look in his eyes let her know without question that she had struck a deep and dark area in her husband's soul. The small voice in her heart spoke again.

Reuben is not a well man. You must stand with him in his sorrow.

She refused the thought and fought back. *No. Reuben and I will be happy...forever.*

"You're right, my husband," she said quietly. "I will not ask again."

The tenseness went out of Reuben's face. "Thank you, Jerusha," he said. "Thank you."

◇◇◇

The weeks after the wedding sped along. Winter set in, and Reuben and Jerusha Springer made visits to their friends and neighbors, who gave them gifts. With the help of their families and the community,

Reuben spent many days working on a house situated on the creek that ran through her father's property.

By spring they were ready to move. On a day in early April, when flowers were blossoming and songbirds had returned to make their nests in the willow trees, Reuben took her from her father's house to their new home. As he took her in his arms to carry her across the threshold, Jerusha asked him to wait.

"Before we go in, my darling," she whispered in his ear, "I have something to tell you."

"At a moment like this? What can you possibly tell me now?" he asked in surprise.

"Reuben...we're going to have a baby."

Reuben's eyes opened wide, and a huge smile broke across his face. His arms tightened close around her, and he buried his face in her shoulder. She could feel quiet sobs shake his shoulders, and then he looked up with tears lining his face.

"Thank you, my darling wife," was all he said, and then he carried her across the threshold. And Reuben and Jerusha entered into a season of their lives filled with great joy.

Chapter Thirty-One

To Every Thing There Is a Season

Summer is a lovely time of year in Apple Creek. Long, languid days are followed by clear, warm evenings. The night sky is brilliant with stars. The fields and orchards around the village are bursting with life. And for Reuben and Jerusha, even after all the summers they had experienced in Apple Creek, the summer of 1944 held a special splendor.

A great part of their happiness was focused on the child growing within Jerusha, and even more, God seemed to reach down from His throne and mark each day with an overpowering sense of wonder and destiny. The war raged on in the Pacific and Europe, but it didn't seem to touch Apple Creek. Instead, peace and joy filled the village.

Reuben spent most of his time in the fields, cultivating the potatoes and vegetables and watching as the heads of wheat and the ears of corn began to fill and grow heavy, portending a bumper crop. Sometimes he paused in amazement at the richness all around him, and the words of a Hebrew blessing he had learned from his childhood friend, Sammy, often came to his memory.

"*Barukh ata Adonai Eloheinu Melekh ha-olam, bo're p'ri ha-adama.*"

"*Blessed are You, Lord our God, King of the universe, who creates the fruit of the ground.*"

Each morning Jerusha rose early to milk the cows and goats and churn some of the rich cream into butter, leaving the rest for Reuben to bottle and sell in town. Jerusha loved those early mornings. The cool stillness was a mantle of tranquility that sheltered her world and her baby with serenity. Even the songbirds seemed to speak of God's loving-kindness. Often, at the end of a sweltering day, Reuben and Jerusha sat on their porch as the cool evening air brought them relief and stillness settled over their land, bringing peace.

Sometimes Reuben sat quietly, not speaking, but smiling while Jerusha fanned herself and chatted about the events of her day. Or Jerusha listened to Reuben speak about the crops or expected weather patterns. Sometimes she thought about the times before their marriage when she sat enthralled as Reuben poured out his dreams and ambitions and shared his knowledge of music and art and even other faiths—but those times were now locked away in Reuben's heart, and he spoke of them no more.

Eventually that wonderful summer drew to a close, and the leaves began to turn gold and red. The fields groaned with the richness of the harvest, and the Amish brought their horses and their combines and began to reap the fruit of their labors.

As at no other time, the reality and necessity of their decision to remain separate from the world came upon the Amish men. Life was work, and work was with their hands and animals and simple machines. They became one with the land, moving on it in unison, pushing their strong bodies to the limits of endurance. Yet even as they struggled, they rejoiced in the power they had together in a world given to them by a loving God.

Reuben worked dawn to dusk beside the other men as they moved from field to field, harvesting corn, wheat, potatoes, and barley in such abundance that more buildings were quickly constructed to contain it all. Often the men stopped at the end of a day and stood with their hats in their hands while the sun set in the west, and they sang together of God's goodness and blessing.

As the fall turned toward winter and the mornings began with a chill, Jerusha began to look forward more and more to the birth of their baby. The harvest was in, the fall weddings had taken place, and now Jerusha was in the last days of her pregnancy. She had put on weight and felt awkward and unlovely, but Reuben paid more attention to her and saw to it that she was comfortable and cared for. Most of all, he expressed his love for her in a hundred simple ways, from helping with housework to bringing her small gifts. One day she found a wonderful handcrafted cradle beside the bed. It was made of clear pine and detailed beautifully, and she realized that Reuben must have worked on it for months.

From time to time, Bobby came by to visit. Those were good times, for Reuben loved Bobby like a brother, and because her husband did, Jerusha grew to love Bobby as well. He was a gentle man, very solicitous of her condition and always ready with a kind word or a smile. They would have dinner together, and then he and Reuben would sit and talk while Jerusha worked on a quilt or sewed clothing for the baby.

Of course, Bobby and Reuben didn't speak of the war except in general terms, but Jerusha knew they shared an unspoken bond of suffering.

Bobby was in awe of Jerusha's quilts and always asked to see them. This caused Jerusha no little embarrassment, for she didn't want Bobby to think of her as proud or ambitious. But she would bring out some of the quilts and let Bobby admire them. Reuben would grumble about "pride going before a fall," but Jerusha noticed he beamed as he spoke.

Jerusha looked forward to Bobby's visits because they were the only times she caught glimpses into the hidden part of her husband. As he and Bobby talked, sometimes they slipped into a discussion about the world outside Apple Creek, and from time to time the talk developed into a disagreement. Bobby would take the side of technology and science and wonder aloud how the Amish could do without so many modern conveniences. Reuben would stand for the ways of his people.

In those times Jerusha would see both how deeply her husband understood the world and how much he had placed his life under the laws of their order. She saw that in many ways he had become legalistic in his approach to their life. If there was a rule or a dictate of their faith governing any circumstance or issue, they followed that rule without hesitation. Once Bobby challenged him directly when they were talking about whether Jerusha would go to the hospital to have the baby. Reuben had told Bobby that she would have her baby at home in the old way.

"We don't need an *Englisch* doctor to deliver our baby," Reuben said. "We've been delivering babies at home for at least three hundred years."

Jerusha added, "Not only that, but we have a wonderful midwife here in the village who has delivered dozens of babies. I'm strong and in good health, and my baby will be perfect in every way. And he or she will be born at home."

Bobby started to say something but then thought better of it when he saw Reuben's face signaling an end to the discussion.

"Well, you folks know what's best for you," he said and then deftly turned the talk in another direction. "So, are you hoping the baby will be born on Christmas day?"

Jerusha blushed. "It's very possible, although that's in the Lord's hands."

In the Lord's hands, thought Bobby. *Reuben used that expression when I left him in the hospital and came home. And now it seems that the Lord he trusted has come through for him in a big way.*

"Well, that would be a great Christmas gift for everyone, especially Uncle Bobby," he said.

"We want you to be more than the baby's uncle," said Reuben. "We would be honored if you would be a godparent. It means that you would become more closely associated with our family and would help with our baby's future if anything happened to us."

Bobby's mouth dropped open. "But Reuben, I'm not of your faith. How would your community feel about that?"

"You're family to me, and I believe it is so with my wife," said Reuben quietly. "It's our prayer that eventually you'll come to a relationship with God, but that's your choice. We know you're a good man. You've been a brother to me. So if you will consider it, we would be honored if you agreed."

Reuben looked at Jerusha, who nodded her agreement.

"I'm the honored one," said Bobby. "And yes, I will accept that responsibility. As I told you on your wedding day, if there is ever anything you need, or any help that a friend can give, please call on me."

Chapter Thirty-Two

Jenna

◇◇◇

The great Thanksgiving storm had entered its most ferocious stage. Friday had been bad, but the worst of the tempest occurred on Saturday as blizzard conditions prevailed throughout Ohio. By late in the day, snow depths reached twenty inches in eastern Ohio, and in some locations, drifts were piling up more than twenty-five feet deep. Winds as high as sixty miles per hour blew down wires and trees. Many buildings collapsed under the weight of the snow. A state of emergency was declared, and the Ohio National Guard used Jeeps to transport people to hospitals and to deliver food to rural homes. Apple Creek was an out-of-the-way village, and most of the people were fending for themselves, so the sight of Bobby Halverson's plow out on the road was comforting and let people know they were not alone. But most of Apple Creek simply stayed indoors and prayed that the storm would soon pass.

◇◇◇

Bobby left the Springer place and headed over to Dutch's garage. Dutch saw the plow pull up in front and came outside, wiping some oil off his hands with a dirty rag.

"Hey, Bobby, the old hunk-a-junk is still running, I see," he shouted up.

"Don't talk so loud, Dutch. She'll hear you, and you'll hurt her feelings. She's been running good, and I don't want you upsetting her!"

Dutch laughed and said, "What can I do for you today, Hoss?"

"Fill 'er up with number one diesel, please. And you didn't happen to come by any glow plugs, did you?"

"Not in this storm. Everything is shut down tight. I won't be getting up to Wooster until the middle of next week. That is, if this monster ever blows over. Pull her inside and I'll gas her up in the garage. And I'll give those plugs the once-over."

Dutch went inside and rolled up the garage door. Bobby pulled the tractor inside, and Dutch rolled the door back down with a bang.

"You're lucky I'm here. I got bored at home and came over to work on that forty-one Merc I got stashed in the back. But it's too blasted cold, and I was just about to pack up and leave."

"Should I leave her running?" Bobby asked.

"Nope. She's warmed up pretty good, and I got plenty of starter if she stalls."

Bobby shut off the engine and climbed down while Dutch pulled the hood open and began to check the plugs. After a few minutes he looked over and made a wry comment.

"She's doin' pretty good for a rust bucket. These plugs are still pretty beat, but they seem to be working. I'll gas her up. By the way, shouldn't you be letting the county boys do the plowin'? It's gettin' pretty stiff out there."

"I'm looking for Jerusha Springer. She and Henry Lowenstein got in a wreck, and Henry had to walk into town to get help. It's kind of a long story, but before we could get back to help, Jerusha was gone. She either tried to walk out herself and she's lost in the snow, or someone came by and found her. I'm driving up to Wooster to check the hospital, and then I'll let the sheriff know what's going on. After that I'm going to go up to Kidron Road and see if I can find any trace of her. It was pretty dark when Mark Knepp and I got there last night."

"Well, that's a real kerfuffle, Bobby. Anything I can do to help?" Dutch asked.

"I can't ask you to follow me around in this storm, but you could drop by the Springer place and check with Hank Lowenstein in a while."

"Will do," Dutch said as he pulled a hose out from beside a drum and stuck it into the fuel tank. He pumped the handle on the barrel and started filling the tractor with diesel. In a few minutes the plow was topped off, and Dutch closed up the hood.

"Just keep 'er runnin'," he said. "The plugs are almost shot, and if she sits too long in this cold and you lose power in your battery, she won't start." Dutch reached up on a shelf and grabbed a spray can. "If you do get stalled, spray this ether in the port. It just might get her goin'."

"Thanks, Dutch," Bobby said as he stuck the can behind the seat.

"You're welcome. Just stay outta' trouble and don't stall her. I'll see you later."

Dutch grabbed the door chain and rolled up the metal door. Bobby reached out of the cab and grabbed Dutch's outstretched hand. He shook it and then headed out into the storm.

◇◇◇

Bobby turned onto Dover Road. Wooster was only eight miles, and the road had been kept pretty clear, but it took him about half an hour to get there. His first stop was at the Wooster Hospital. He left the tractor running by the door and popped inside to see if anyone had brought Jerusha in. The admittance nurse checked the records, but there were no Amish women in the hospital. He left his dad's phone number in case anyone brought Jerusha in and then headed over to the Wayne County Sheriff's Office. The sheriff, a gruff old World War I vet, commiserated with Bobby but let him know that the sheriff's office was stretched pretty thin already and really didn't have any spare people to send with Bobby.

"I'm afraid you're on your own, son," he said as he spit a wad of chew into a pot beside his desk. "Just let me know what happens. She could have been picked up by someone who got her indoors and we haven't heard, or in this storm..." He paused when he saw the grim look on Bobby's face. "Well, let's hope for the best. Thanks for helpin' out with your plow. I know a lot of folks down in Apple Creek speak pretty highly of you."

"Thanks, sheriff. I'll keep you informed."

Bobby climbed back up on the tractor and headed toward Kidron Road. The old tractor chugged along, but every few minutes the wind gusts pushed it toward the ditch, and Bobby had to hang on to the wheel with all his strength to keep it on the road.

After about an hour he arrived back at the scene of the crash. The car was almost completely covered by snow, but Bobby dug down, pulled the door open, and looked for any clue as to Jerusha's whereabouts. He found nothing except a large empty cardboard box with "Rose of Sharon—quilt by Jerusha Springer" on the side. As he held the box, his hands began to shake. He felt short of breath and dizzy. Suddenly the tension and stress of the previous two days overcame him. He began to sob uncontrollably. He pushed his way out of the car, staggered a few feet, and fell to his knees in the snow.

"Jerusha, where are you?" he screamed into the howling wind.

Bobby knelt in the snow and wept. He managed a prayer but felt as if there was no answer. The wind only increased in its fury, and the snow continued to fall out of a baleful sky.

◇◇◇

Jerusha was beginning to worry. She had used up more of the wood since dawn, and the pile was shrinking. The little girl remained quiet in her arms as she slept. Jerusha realized the girl was thirsty and hungry. She gently laid the little girl down. There were a couple of empty beer cans in the corner, and she picked one up and went to the door. She opened it just a crack, packed the can full of snow, and brought it over to the stove. She put the can on the flat plate above the firebox, and in a few minutes the snow had melted into water. She took a swallow and almost retched at the stale taste of old beer and dirt.

Ugh! Good thing I didn't just give that to Jenna—

She caught herself.

◇◇◇

Bobby Halverson's off-the-cuff prophecy came true. Jerusha's baby was born on Christmas Day 1944. The labor was short and the delivery easy, and Reuben and Jerusha's little girl was born early in the morning at home in the Springers' big bed. She was strong and healthy, and when the midwife slapped her little bottom, the lusty cry was like an angel's voice to Jerusha. Reuben took her in his strong arms and blessed her.

"Loving God, thank You for the gift of life and for bringing our little girl safely into this world. May You bless her and keep her and help her to grow loving, strong, and healthy in Your love, now and always. Amen." Then he placed her in his wife's arms. Tears started in Jerusha's eyes as an overpowering love for the little girl swept over her.

"She's so white and lovely," she whispered. "What shall we call her, Reuben?"

"Well, the Celtic name Gwynwhyhar means white, fair, and smooth. That's a mouthful, so we could use the short version. Gwynwhyhar became Guenivere and then Jennifer and finally Jenny or Jenna. Shall we call her Jenna?"

"Jenna...Jenna," Jerusha repeated, letting the name roll off her tongue. "It's perfect. She'll be Jenna Springer, fair and lovely all her days."

As the days passed, Jerusha and Reuben felt as if they had never been without this beautiful child. She was so easy to care for and so sweet in all her ways from her first day, the Springers could only take joy in caring for her. She loved being held and cooed and gurgled softly when her *daed* picked her up. She nursed easily and then fell quietly asleep in Jerusha's arms.

Even at night when it was time to feed her, the soft little voice called out to them instead of jerking them abruptly from sleep. Jerusha sat with her and stared at her features, running her finger over the soft bow of her lips or smelling the sweetness of her skin. Occasionally Uncle Bobby dropped by with some vague reason why he had to talk to Reuben, but Jerusha knew he came for Jenna. She would smile and admonish him as he stood expectantly, shifting from one foot to the other.

"You don't need to make up excuses to come here, Bobby. We know you're here to see Jenna."

And Bobby would blush and then smile and nod. "Can you blame me?"

And Jerusha could not, for she wanted her little girl to grow up surrounded by people who loved the child deeply. And then she would pass the little girl into Bobby's arms and watch with glee while the normally reserved Bobby Halverson made a lovable fool of himself with baby talk and silliness as Jenna cooed in appreciation.

During the first year of her life, Jenna grew strong and precocious. She began to form words early and seemed to have an insatiable curiosity about everything, especially language. She would sit for a long time trying out sounds, repeating interesting or amusing syllables over and over. Sometimes when she said something new or made a sound that felt strange to her mouth, she giggled and waved her arms.

"She's just like you, Reuben," Jerusha said. "She's obviously a deep thinker, and she's sharing some arcane wisdom with herself."

Reuben would take the baby in his arms and hold her. Sometimes a serious look would come over his face as he beheld his daughter.

"I've made so many mistakes," he said one day. "I won't let our girl make the same errors I made. I'll keep the world and its evil from her as long as I can."

"At some point in her life, she's going to have to find out these things for herself."

Suddenly Reuben was up out of his chair, pacing, agitated. "No she won't. We will see to it that she follows the Amish ways all her life. We have the means within our faith to remain unstained from the world. We will make sure that she follows the rules of the *ordnung*."

Jerusha stared at Reuben. "I wasn't meaning to upset you," she said quietly. "You're right, of course. I know that there's safety in the way we live. Now calm yourself and sit. We have plenty of time before we have to worry about such things."

Reuben turned to Jerusha as though he was going to say something and then thought better of it. He controlled himself and sat back down in his chair. The outburst seemed to have drained him completely. His shoulders slumped, and his features looked drawn. He took a moment and then spoke.

"Jerusha, I am the way I am for a reason. I've been to hell and back. I once said I wouldn't speak of it, but there is part of it you must hear to understand me. When I was in the Pacific fighting the Japanese, I saw the very depths of man's corruption. Man is hopelessly lost, and each one of us is fully capable of the most horrifying, depraved behavior. I know because that is how I behaved when I was on Guadalcanal. After the war, I swore I would never set foot out in the world again. So I returned home and to the church because it's the only way I know to live a righteous life. The *ordnung* is like a fortress I can take refuge in. I need not ever worry, for when I have questions, our faith has the answer. That's what saves me, guides me, and keeps me sane...and that's how our family will live."

Jerusha sat silently, her emotions churning within her. *He has come back to the church to hide, but somehow in his fear he has kept the Lord out of his fortress.*

Chapter Thirty-Three

A Test of Faith

Four years passed swiftly in Reuben and Jerusha's home. Jenna grew, and soon everyone could see she was a special girl. She somehow avoided most of the pitfalls of early childhood. She was not self-centered or challenging in any way. Indeed, she was turning into a compassionate and caring little girl. An injured bird would bring her to tears; a hungry kitten would be brought to Mama for attention.

Jenna learned obedience and respect at an early age, much to the admiration of the adults who knew her. Her love for her parents was seen in how quietly she would sit and play as her mother worked around the house or quilted. And when she heard the latch lift on the door in the evening, would run to her *daed*'s arms.

"It's almost as though she already knows *der Heilige Geist*," Jerusha's father said one day. "I've never known a child so gentle and kind."

"*Ja, Vater, sie ist ein spezielles Kind*," replied Jerusha. "She is a special child."

One day when Jenna was four years old, some of Jerusha's friends and their children came to visit. After the women visited for a while, Jenna came into the house from playing in the yard with tears in her eyes.

"*Was ist los, dochter*?" asked Jerusha.

"Jonas hit me, Mama."

Jonas' mother got up to fetch her child. "I will make sure to spank him, Jerusha," she said.

"No, please don't spank him," said Jenna. "I forgive Jonas."

"But Jonas did a bad thing, Jenna," Jerusha explained. "He deserves a spanking."

"We all deserve a spanking," said Jenna, "but mostly God forgives us. So I forgive Jonas."

The women stared at Jenna with surprise, and then Jerusha took her little girl into her lap and held her. "You are kind, my darling, and you are right. We all do deserve a spanking, but God in His mercy has forgiven us."

◇◇◇

One day in the fall of 1949, without warning, the lives of the Springer family suddenly changed. Jenna came in from playing and said she didn't feel well.

Jerusha felt her forehead and, sensing no fever, offered Jenna a snack. But the girl replied, "I'm not hungry, Mama. I want to take a nap."

That in itself was unusual, but Jerusha chalked it up to Jenna having simply played too hard with the other children. Still, she put Jenna to bed and went about her work. When she went to wake Jenna later, the child was still drowsy and difficult to rouse. Jerusha let her stay in bed, and she slept through dinner.

"Where's Jenna?" Reuben asked when he came in after work.

"She didn't feel well, and she's in bed," Jerusha said.

They had dinner, and as they sat together afterward, Jerusha heard Jenna crying in her room. She went in and lit the gaslight.

"Please turn it off, Mama. It hurts my eyes."

"What's wrong, child?" Jerusha asked.

"My head hurts, Mama. It hurts bad."

Jerusha sat on the edge of the bed and felt Jenna's forehead again. This time she felt very warm.

"Mama, I said turn the light down," said Jenna irritably. "It hurts my eyes."

"*Ja*, Jenna," replied Jerusha in surprise as she stood and turned down the light. Her daughter had never spoken to her that way before.

"My neck hurts, Mama. It's hard to move."

"I'll fix you something," Jerusha said. "Just try to rest, and I'll be right back."

Jerusha went out into the living room. She had a troubled look on her face, and Reuben noticed it right away.

"What's wrong?" he asked.

"Jenna has a fever and a bad headache. I'm going to boil honey and apple cider vinegar and have her inhale it. That should help her headache."

Jerusha went into the kitchen and prepared the remedy. She took it into Jenna's room in a bowl and had her daughter put a towel over her head and inhale the steam. The girl lay back down in the bed.

That night Jerusha heard Jenna crying again. She went in to her room and was dismayed to find a reddish rash on Jenna's face and arms. She brought a cool damp cloth from the kitchen and placed it on Jenna's feverish brow. Suddenly the little girl vomited.

"Mama, I feel bad and I can't move my neck," Jenna said weakly.

Jerusha began to feel real alarm as she cleaned the girl up. She went in and awakened Reuben. "Jenna is very sick," she said. "We must do something. She has a rash and a high fever, and she just vomited."

"We should go for the healer," Reuben said. "I will go fetch her."

Reuben got dressed and left while Jerusha stayed at Jenna's side and placed cold cloths on her brow to bring the fever down. Jerusha had been healthy all her life and had never needed the healer, but she had witnessed the woman's abilities when her grandmother was diagnosed with cancer. Her grandmother had rallied and lived for several more months as the healer offered her natural remedies that compared favorably with the doctors' more expensive prescriptions. When her grandmother's cancer returned, the healer was called in a second time, and this time the grandmother died. The healer simply accepted her death as God's will, as did the family.

Now Jerusha sat by her little girl, and a great fear rose up in her heart. *What if it is Your will that my little girl does not get well? Do I have enough faith for my little girl's healing?*

The questions began to flood her mind, and she began to weep as she prayed, "Please, God, don't take my little girl. She is everything to me."

After about half an hour, Reuben returned with Anita Bausher, the healer who had treated her grandmother. Anita was highly respected in the community.

As she came to Jenna's bedside, she opened a cloth satchel she carried with her. "She has vomited?"

"Yes," replied Jerusha, "and she has a terrible headache. Her eyes are sensitive to light."

"Do you believe that God can heal your child?"

"Yes," said Reuben without waiting for Jerusha's reply. "We will trust God and follow the *ordnung.* God will heal our daughter."

Anita opened Jenna's nightgown and began to massage her, all the while whispering words or perhaps prayers that Jerusha couldn't make out. She worked her way down Jenna's body and then returned to her head and started again. After repeating the ritual three times, she reached in her bag and pulled out some small paper bags with herbs in them.

"Steep these as tea after mixing them together in equal parts," she said. "Give them to her every hour. Now let's pray."

Anita took Reuben and Jerusha's hands and began to pray aloud, asking God to heal Jenna. The three of them agreed together, and then Anita packed her bag and left.

Reuben placed his arm around Jerusha's shoulders. "God will heal our daughter. We are faithful to His laws and have always done what He has told us to do."

"But what if she needs something more than these herbs and a massage?" Jerusha asked. "What if she needs a doctor?"

"I don't trust worldly knowledge," Reuben said. "I saw what *Englisch* doctors can do during the war. We will not go to the world for what our God can provide. We have kept God's ways. He will keep us."

"But—"

"Don't you see, Jerusha? The world is filled with death and madness. Here we have goodness and holiness. The *Englisch* take their science to be an absolute. We turn to God, the church, and our faith before making medical decisions. He is our absolute. We will not turn to *Englisch* medicine."

"But, Reuben, she is so sick," Jerusha said, fairly pleading.

"That's enough!" Reuben snapped. "We will do as the healer has said."

Jerusha stared at Reuben and saw the same angry, anxious look she had seen before. She also saw that Reuben was wrong. He had become so afraid of life, so protected by his obedience to the *ordnung*, that he would risk his daughter's life to be right.

Jerusha didn't know what to do. There must be something. She had to get help for Jenna. She prayed, "God, if You love Jenna as we do, You must bring help!"

Jerusha sat up with Jenna the rest of the night. The small pinprick rash began to turn into reddish blotches on Jenna's skin. At one point the little girl awoke and looked at Jerusha.

"Where are we, Mama?" she asked. "Are we still at home? Is it time to get up?"

Jerusha held her hand and brushed the wet hair away from her forehead. All through the night she stayed with Jenna, praying and bathing her feverish brow. By dawn Jenna had become listless and unresponsive.

Reuben rose early and left to tend the animals. Jerusha had become desperate. Just then she heard the sound of a car pulling up in front of the house. Bobby! Jerusha ran to the door and pulled Bobby inside before he could even knock. He saw her face and immediately knew something was wrong.

"What is it, Jerusha?"

"It's Jenna!" she cried. "She's so sick, and Reuben won't let me take her to a doctor. He says that our ways will heal her, but she's getting worse."

"Let me see her," Bobby said.

Jerusha led the way to Jenna's room. Bobby looked at the reddish blotches on Jenna's skin and felt her forehead. It was burning with fever. Jenna lay still and unresponsive in the bed.

"Has she vomited? Does she have a stiff neck? Were these blotches like pinpricks before they got this big?"

Jerusha nodded.

Bobby got up from beside the bed. "Jerusha, listen to me and listen good. Jenna probably has meningitis. I've seen it before. My cousin died from this. The red patches mean she has septicemia—blood poisoning caused by the same bacteria. The only thing that can help her is massive doses of antibiotics. We've got to get her to the hospital."

Without waiting for an answer, Bobby rolled Jenna up in her blanket, picked her up, and started for the door. Suddenly the door opened, and Reuben walked in. He stopped and stared in surprise at Bobby.

"Bobby! I saw your car and...what are you doing with Jenna?"

"Reuben, your little girl is desperately sick. She has to get to a hospital *now*."

"You will not take Jenna to the *Englisch* doctor. If anything will kill her, that will."

"Reuben, I'm taking this child to the hospital," said Bobby. "She's dying. If you want to stop me, you will have to kill me."

Reuben recoiled from Bobby as though he had been kicked. A look of sheer terror came across his face. "But God will heal her. He must—we've been faithful..."

"Reuben, get out of my way."

Reuben stepped aside, and Bobby pushed through the door with Jenna in his arms. Jerusha stared at Reuben and then grabbed her coat and boots and went after Bobby.

Reuben stood in the middle of the room and stared after them. His lips worked soundlessly and his body began to tremble. The night of the battle in the jungle began to replay in his mind. He saw the terrified faces of the Japanese soldiers as he raged among them. He saw Sarge writhing in agony, his arm blown off. He felt the pain of the bayonets and the shock of a bullet hitting him. Suddenly he collapsed to the floor wailing.

"But, God, I've been faithful..."

Chapter Thirty-Four

Goodbye, My Darling Girl

The fire was dying down, and the wood was nearly gone. Instinctively, Jerusha pulled the girl close to her.

I held my Jenna close to me, just like this, on the day Bobby took us to the hospital. I could feel her burning with fever. I prayed so hard, but You didn't answer my prayers.

"*I sent Bobby.*"

Jerusha spoke out loud.

"*Ja*, but you didn't save Jenna!"

"*She is safe with Me and saved from a broken world. That is enough. Jenna is Mine. She has always been Mine. I gave her to you for a season to bless you and to teach you. Now there is more to learn. But there is still a root of bitterness that keeps your heart locked against Me. I have healed your pain and your anger. Now I want you to forgive as I have forgiven you. I want you to look deep into your heart. I want you to see.*"

Jerusha cried out, "Please, please don't make me remember! I can't bear it! Oh, Jenna!"

As she sobbed, the little girl awoke. Her tiny hand stole to Jerusha's face. "Don't cry," she said softly. "Please don't cry."

A feeling of peace crept over Jerusha like warmth from a fire, and she felt herself relax. A strange but familiar sensation came over her as if she were falling off a high precipice, and then, in the midst of the fall, she felt herself lifted up on wings of eagles.

Jerusha surrendered. "Do what You must," she said aloud.

And then the memory of that day came to her.

◇◇◇

Bobby drove like a madman down the highway into Wooster. He pulled up in front of the hospital and grabbed Jenna.

"Come on, Jerusha," he cried.

Jerusha jumped out of the car and followed Bobby. He was already through the doors when Jerusha caught up with him. A nurse met them and started to explain hospital protocol.

Bobby interrupted her, "Get me a doctor, quick! This little girl is dying!"

The nurse quickly ran to the desk and summoned a doctor on the intercom. Quickly, a white-haired man with a puzzled expression on his face ran down the hall.

"I'm Dr. Schaeffer," he said. "What seems to be the trouble?"

Bobby opened the blanket and showed Jenna to the doctor and said, "I think she has meningitis."

The doctor's eyes took in the reddish blotches and he said, "Vomiting? Stiff neck? High fever?"

Jerusha nodded to each question.

"Nurse," the doctor bellowed, "get this girl into the ICU immediately. Put a drip of benzylpenicillin in her and prep her. Get her ready to do a lumbar puncture. I need a sample of cerebrospinal fluid as quickly as possible."

"Doctor, is she going to be all right?" asked Jerusha.

"I can't tell you, ma'am," the doctor said bluntly. "She's a very sick child. She should have been here two days ago." He turned on his heel and followed the nurse and Jenna into the intensive care unit.

The hours that followed were a blur. The staff rushed Jenna into the critical care unit and put a penicillin drip into her arm.

"This child is very, very sick," Dr. Schaeffer told her sternly. "I'm doing all I can for her, but I could have done more had she been here sooner. Why you Amish don't trust in modern medicine I'll never know."

"Can I see her, Doctor?" Jerusha asked.

"Yes, but she's not conscious," said the doctor. "If she doesn't improve, we will most likely have to ventilate her."

"What's that?" asked Jerusha.

"They help her to breathe with a tube in her throat," Bobby said.

"Oh, Bobby!" Jerusha cried, bursting into tears. "Is my little girl going to die?"

"I don't know, Jerusha," Bobby said as he put his arm around her shoulder. "I just don't know. We have to wait and hope we got her here in time..."

...and leave her in the Lord's hands.

The staff nurse led Jerusha into the ICU and pointed her to a chair by Jenna's bed. Jenna lay still beneath a sheet, her face wet with perspiration. Her head and neck were arched slightly back and her breathing was shallow and quick. Tubes ran from both arms to a jumble of bottles hanging on racks above her.

"You just sit here, Mrs. Springer," the nurse said. "We have her on a monitor in the nurses' station, and if anything changes we'll be right in." The nurse left Jerusha sitting next to Jenna's bed.

How can this be happening? Where is Reuben?

Her thoughts whirled like a flock of blackbirds, and a deep despair crept over her. She slipped to her knees beside the bed and began to pray.

"Please, God, don't take my little girl away. Please, please, please let her live."

All day and through the night, Jerusha stayed by Jenna, praying to

God and talking quietly to her little girl. At times Jenna became agitated in her sleep, and Jerusha spoke soothingly to her and caressed her brow. Jenna would calm and sink back into sleep. From time to time a nurse would come in and check Jenna's vital signs. Early the next morning the doctor came in with the nurse. He spoke more gently to Jerusha this time.

"We have the results of the tests we ran. The Gram's stain definitely shows Jenna has meningitis caused by meningococcic bacteria. Along with that, she has a blood infection. I'm having the nurse switch her off the benzylpenicillin to ampicillin and vancomycin. I must warn you that even if these drugs are effective, the disease was quite advanced when she was admitted, and there may be serious complications if she survives. There could be deafness, swelling of the brain, and possibly cognitive impairment. If we get her through this stage, she might be a very different little girl than the one you know." He paused and then added, "I'm sorry."

"Mr. Halverson is still in the waiting room," said the nurse. "He's been there all night."

Jerusha went out to the waiting room. Bobby was sitting with his hands together, looking at the floor. When he heard Jerusha, he looked up. His face was pale, and his eyes were red from lack of sleep.

"Bobby, I'm sorry I left you out here," she said. "I—"

"It's all right, Jerusha." He smiled weakly. "I understand. How's she doing?"

Jerusha put her hands to her face and began to cry. Bobby stepped to her side and clumsily tried to comfort her.

"It's okay, Jerusha," he said quietly. "You've just got...to trust..."

"In the Lord?" snapped Jerusha. "I have prayed and prayed and begged Him to spare her and she's only gotten worse. The doctor says that even if she lives she will probably be...different. Where is Reuben?"

Bobby stared at her as though seeing a side of her he had never known. "Reuben hasn't come yet," he said. "If you want me to go get him, I will."

"You can't make Reuben overcome his fear of the world," Jerusha said. "I should have listened to my intuition when he came home from the war. He came back changed. He wasn't the man I fell in love with. You can do what you want, Bobby. I'm going to go sit with our daughter."

Jerusha turned on her heel and went back to the ICU. Bobby stared after her, the hurt from her words in his eyes.

Jerusha sat with Jenna through the rest of the morning and into the afternoon. The day had been foggy and overcast with a gloom that the weak November sun couldn't pierce. Finally in late afternoon, the overcast sky began to clear up, and the sun broke through. A shaft of light came through the window and fell on Jenna's face. The little girl opened her eyes. Jerusha leaned forward, but Jenna was looking beyond her. She opened her mouth and spoke clearly and quietly.

"I can't come now. Who will take care of my mama?"

Then she closed her eyes. Jerusha sat still. Jenna's head was still turned toward the window. Jerusha took her daughter's hand in hers and watched the slow pulse beating in Jenna's neck—once, twice...She watched it beat one more time and then stop.

Jerusha sat still, not comprehending what had just happened. She became aware of a bell ringing somewhere, and nurses filled the room. A gentle hand took her arm and led her out into the hall. She saw Dr. Schaeffer rush past as the nurse led her out into the waiting room.

Reuben was standing there with Bobby. She stared at him and then slowly walked to him. She raised her fists together and struck him on the chest.

"It's your fault!" she cried.

She raised her fists again and began to strike him slowly on the chest. Reuben stood still with a lost look on his face. He did not defend himself.

Bobby came between them then and gently stopped her arms. Reuben remained silent.

"She's dead. The doctor said if we had gotten her here earlier..."

And then Jerusha's face hardened into a mask. "I want to go home, Bobby, but I don't want Reuben there." She didn't look at Reuben or acknowledge him.

"Jerusha, think of what you're doing," Bobby said. "Don't make a decision like that now." And then the enormity of what had happened came to Bobby, and he began to weep.

Reuben remained still, his face unreadable.

"Bobby, if you don't take me home, I'll call a cab and go home myself." Jerusha walked out the door into the cold.

Bobby followed after her. "All right, Jerusha, I'll take you home. Wait here for a minute."

Bobby went back inside and spoke to Reuben. Jerusha could see them through the glass door. Bobby was animated, his arms moving. Reuben stood still and answered in monosyllables. Finally Bobby came out.

"Jerusha, Reuben's going to stay with me for a few days until we get this sorted out. He needs some things from the house. Maybe you should stay with your parents tonight while he collects them."

The bitter cold chilled Jerusha to the bone. Numbly, she agreed to Bobby's suggestion. The last light of the sun spiked in pale rays above the western horizon. The wind began to pick up, blowing snow. Darkness closed in on Jerusha's heart.

It was winter in Apple Creek.

Chapter Thirty-Five

Flight into Darkness

It was freezing cold in the cabin, but Jerusha was drenched in sweat. Tears poured down her face.

I saw her little heart stop beating, and then she was gone. O God, this is too much to bear.

And then the voice spoke to her heart. "*I did not say that you would have no pain in this world. I did say that I would never leave you or forsake you. Let not your heart be troubled. Jenna is with Me, but Reuben is still with you, and he needs you.*"

Jerusha had watched Reuben through the big glass door at the hospital while Bobby talked to him. He had looked like a deer caught in the headlights. His face was white, his hands shook, and he could only answer Bobby's questions with monosyllables.

"*It was not Reuben's fault that Jenna became sick. I did not create this world with death in it; I created it perfect and good. And even when death came into this world, I made a way back to life. Each person on this earth has an appointed time, and that time is in My hands. Take the blessing that Jenna was to your life and move beyond the pain. You made a promise to Reuben, and now you must keep it. He needed you, and you forsook him. You must forgive him.*"

In her memory of that day at the hospital, Jerushsa saw again Reuben's eyes. They were empty of life, a dark pit. The joy that had once lived there had dwindled to nothing. He was a devastated man. As Jerusha recalled that scene, her heart began to melt and break for her husband.

I'm sorry, Reuben. I'm so sorry...

◇◇◇

Reuben watched as Jerusha left through the front door of the hospital with Bobby right behind her. His tongue cleaved to the roof of his mouth, and his thoughts were chaotic. In a few minutes Bobby came back in.

"You've got trouble, my friend," he said. "Jerusha wants nothing to do with you right now. I suggest you come over to my house for a few days until she calms down."

"Okay."

Bobby came up close and looked into Reuben's eyes. "Reuben, are you alright?"

"She's dead, Bobby."

"I know, Reuben. I wish you knew how terrible I feel for you and Jerusha and for me. This is just awful."

"Jerusha's right. It's my fault."

"Reuben, now is not the time for taking the blame. You did what you thought was right. It just didn't turn out the way you expected. Come over to my place and rest. We'll get this all sorted out."

"I'll need some things," Reuben said.

"I'll take Jerusha to her folks' house for the night. She should be with someone anyway. I'll call Henry and have him pick you up and take you home for your things and then drive you to my place. Reuben, Jerusha just lost her baby. She'll get through this when she's had a few days to accept it."

"She hates me, Bobby. I can see it in her eyes."

"Just calm down, Reuben," Bobby said. "We'll get through this..."

...with the Lord's help.

"She'll never forgive me. No one can help me now... not even God."

"I'll help however I can," Bobby said. "Just don't give up hope, buddy."

After Bobby and Jerusha left, Reuben sat in the waiting room for what seemed like hours, staring at the floor. His hands and feet felt numb. He couldn't get the accusing thoughts out of his head.

I believed You would protect my family if I did everything right, but Jenna died anyway. Now Jerusha hates me and You have abandoned me. I trusted You, I did everything by the book, and now I've lost everything I love.

Suddenly Reuben felt a hand on his shoulder. "Reuben?" Reuben looked up into Henry Lowenstein's face.

"Reuben, I'm...I'm so sorry," he choked out.

Reuben just stared at Henry with a blank look on his face.

"Come on, Reuben," said Henry. "Bobby wants me to take you by your house to pick up some things."

Henry took Reuben's arm and tried to pull him up. Reuben jerked his arm away and stood.

"I'm not a cripple, Henry. I'm just a murderer."

"Reuben, don't say such things!"

"It's the truth. I killed Jenna just as sure as if I put a gun to her head and shot her. You can take me home, but I don't want to go to Bobby's. I've got to sort some things out."

"Well, Bobby said..."

"I don't care what Bobby said!"

Others in the waiting room glanced up at Reuben. A nurse stood up from behind the admitting desk and came toward them. He waved her away and turned to Henry. "Just get me home."

◇◇◇

After Henry took him home, Reuben sat in the darkened and quiet house. Where joy and love and peace had abounded, now there was only despair. He sat on a kitchen chair with his elbows on his knees and his fingers interlocked behind his head. The cradle his daughter had slept in as an infant now sat empty in front of him.

Reuben sat there all night until the morning sunlight began to creep in through the kitchen window. At last he stirred himself and stood up. He went quickly into the bedroom, opened the closet, and dug around until he found a small metal box. He opened it. Inside were several rolls of bills and a sheaf of papers. He put several of the bills in his pocket, looked through the papers, took a pen off the dresser, and signed them on the last page. He found another sheet of paper and began to write.

Jerusha,

I'm leaving. I know you hate me and believe I'm responsible for Jenna's death, and you are probably right. I'm leaving you $5000. It's part of the military pay I saved while in the hospital and never spent.

Don't worry, I won't come back. I hope you will find it in your heart to forgive me someday. I can only wish you truly find a happy life in the years ahead.

Reuben

Reuben went through his drawers and closet and gathered up some clothes and personal items. He packed them into a small satchel and looked around his home one last time. Then he walked out the door and closed it behind him. He walked through the field and crossed the small bridge between their house and the Lowensteins'. He went up on the porch and knocked. After a while Henry's father came to the door.

"Why, Reuben, what are you doing here?" he asked.

"I came to see if Henry could give me a ride back to Wooster," said Reuben quietly. "I have some things I need to take care of."

"I'm sure he can. I'll go get him."

Mr. Lowenstein started to go back in the house but then turned and said, "Come in and wait in the living room. I'm so sorry about Jenna. Is there anything we can do for you and Jerusha?"

"Thank you," Reuben said. "We'll be all right. It will just take some time."

Reuben shifted from one foot to the other while Henry's father went to fetch Henry. In a few minutes Henry came out, pulling on a shirt.

"What can I do for you?" Henry asked. "A ride?"

"If you don't mind. I need a ride back to Wooster to take care of Jenna."

"Sure. I'll take you wherever you need to go. Let me grab a jacket."

They drove to Wooster and stopped at the mortuary. Reuben made arrangements for the mortician to pick up Jenna's body and deliver it to Jerusha's parents for burial. Then they went to the hospital, where Reuben signed release papers. He then had Henry drop him off at a used-car lot.

"Goodbye, Henry," Reuben said as he got out of the car with his suitcase. "I won't see you again. Please keep an eye on Jerusha. She'll need a friend."

"Are you sure this is what you want to do, Reuben? Don't you think you ought to wait?"

"This is for the best."

Reuben closed the car door and walked into the dealership. He asked about a used Ford pickup in the lot and laid a hundred dollars on the counter. The salesman wanted to show him other cars, but Reuben shook his head and pointed to the pickup.

In half an hour Reuben was on the road.

He stopped at a motel on the edge of town and rented a room. After he took his things inside, he went next door to a grocery store and bought a razor and some shaving cream. He went back to his room and stared at himself in the bathroom mirror for a long time, and then he lathered his face and shaved off his beard. He went into the room and pulled a wool shirt and an old jacket out of his suitcase and put them on. He left his hat and black coat on the bed and went out to the truck. He threw his suitcase in the back, climbed in, and started the motor. He sat there for a few minutes with his head down, not moving. Then he sighed deeply, raised his head, and without looking back, pulled onto the highway and headed west.

◇◇◇

Bobby Halverson drove down the county highway thinking about Reuben. He had been gone for a year now. After Jenna's death, he had just disappeared. Henry had come to his house the morning after the tragedy and shared his concern with Bobby.

"I left him at a used car lot in Wooster. He didn't look good, Bobby. He was saying all kinds of weird stuff about killing Jenna and being a murderer. I got a bad feeling about all of this."

I'm sorry I didn't see it coming, Reuben. I knew something happened to you up in that trench on Guadalcanal, but I thought you'd get over it. When you went back to the Amish, I figured you'd be okay. You and Jerusha were so happy, and when the baby came it was like your life got on the right track. But I should have talked to you about it—made you talk about how you were feeling. I guess I failed you as a friend. I sure wish you'd come home. I need your help...and so does Jerusha.

◇◇◇

The last piece of wood from the shed was burned. The light was dying outside, and Jerusha knew the two of them probably wouldn't survive another night without a fire. The cold continued to close in on Jerusha and the little girl like circling wolves. The wind howled as the day crept on into night. Jerusha huddled under the quilt with the child and stroked her brow.

I'm sorry, little one. I tried to save you, but I can't do it by myself. I'm sorry, Lord. I see now that You didn't kill Jenna, and Reuben didn't either. It was this world, fallen from grace and filled with evil and disease. If only I could see Reuben one last time. I would tell him that I forgive him...and that I need him.

Chapter Thirty-Six

A Place to Hide

Lowell Jackson's ranch sat high on a ridge outside Fairplay, Colorado. From his front porch he could see cars on Highway 9 in the valley below him. One day in January of 1950, he watched from his porch chair as an old Ford pickup turned onto his road far below and began the circuitous passage up the mountain.

A light dusting of snow had covered the road earlier that morning, but the afternoon sun had melted it, and now the gravel road was in good shape. Lowell had lived on this ranch since retiring from the army in 1939. He raised horses and some cattle, but mostly he watched as the world went on its way far below. He didn't get many visitors, so the old Ford crawling up the hardpan road was of some interest to him.

"Manuel, looks like we got company," he called out. "Better set another place for dinner."

An old Mexican man limped out on the porch with a fry pan in his hand. He was as grizzled as Lowell and wore a Detroit Tigers baseball cap.

"Why we got to make a place, Señor Lowell?" he grumbled. "I only cook enough beans for you and me."

"Don't argue, you old cactus," Lowell said. "Just put on some of those steaks you been saving and get some potatoes from the cellar. It'll take that truck a while to get up here, so git!"

Manuel went back in the house, muttering as he went.

"And don't you be callin' fire down on my head," Lowell hollered after him. "I speak Spanish, you know."

About twenty minutes later, the Ford pulled up in the front driveway in a cloud of dust. A tall, dark-haired man got out.

"Howdy, stranger," Lowell called from the porch. "What brings you to the Eagle's Nest?"

"I'm looking for Lowell Jackson."

"You're lookin' at him."

"Mr. Jackson, I'm Reuben Springer. I got your name from the man at the general store in town. They said you might be looking for someone who's good with horses."

"Where you from, Reuben?" Lowell asked.

"Ohio," Reuben said, "and I sure could use some work. I've just about run out of money. I'm headed for California. I had a job waiting for me outside Denver, but the man sold his ranch while I was in the Marines, so I'm headed west."

"You're a vet?" asked Lowell.

"Yes, sir," Reuben replied. "I served in the First Division of the Marine Corps in the Pacific theater. I saw action on Guadalcanal."

Lowell considered this and said, "I lost a son on Guadalcanal at the Tenaru River. If you served with my boy, you're welcome at my table. Come on in and sit a spell. Manuel's cookin' up some steaks. We'll talk about a job while we eat."

A smile cracked Reuben's stern features. "That sounds more than good to me, sir."

"Lowell," said the old man as he led Reuben into the house. The walls were made of peeled pine logs, notched and set into place. To the left around a corner was the kitchen, and Reuben could hear someone rattling around in there. Snatches of a song in Spanish and the welcome smell of frying steak drifted into the dining room. There were large windows and the room had a big plank table with rough-hewn chairs around it. To the right was a large open room filled with sagging couches and rustic old chairs set in front of a huge stone fireplace that took up the entire end of the house. A stack of fresh-split pine logs and a box of kindling sat to one side of the fireplace. A stairway went up and around out of the foyer where they stood.

Manuel came out of the kitchen with a two-pronged fork in his hand.

"Hey, mister," he said, looking Reuben over, "how you like me cook your steak?"

"Medium rare would be fine," Reuben said.

"You think this is a French restaurant maybe, señor?" Manuel grumbled as he went back in the kitchen.

Lowell laughed. "Don't mind Manuel. He's just pretending he's polite. He doesn't have a polite bone in his body. You're gonna get your steak medium no matter what you say."

Reuben laughed, but even as he did, Lowell sensed something about him. *Sent me another wounded one, huh, Lord? He's running from something, and I guess You got him up here for me to find out what it is.*

A few minutes later Manuel came in with some plates on a tray. The steaks were still sizzling, and there were country potatoes and some refried beans. Reuben sat down to dinner with more anticipation than he had felt in a long time.

"So where'd you learn horses, Reuben?" Lowell asked.

"On my dad's farm in Ohio. I've broken them, trained them, and everything in between."

"Who'd you say was going to hire you in Denver?"

"Ansel Robertson. He had a ranch between Denver and Fort Collins," Reuben replied.

"Just so happens I know Ansel," Lowell said through a mouthful of steak. "He was one of my best customers before he sold his ranch. I'll give him a call and check out your story. In the meantime, you're welcome to stay here for the night. After I talk to Ansel, we'll see where we go from there."

After dinner, Lowell took Reuben down to the bunkhouse. "Don't have any hands anymore except for Manuel," he said. "I used to have around ten fellas working for me including my boy, but things are a little slow, and I'm getting old enough to where I mostly want to sit on my porch anyway. Put your stuff in here and then come on back up to the house. We'll sit by the fire and have a chat."

After Reuben stowed his clothes and spread out some blankets on a bunk, he went back up to the house. Lowell showed him to a chair by the fireplace and poured him a coffee. "I just got done talkin' with Ansel, and he put in a good word for you. Says you come highly recommended by some friends back in Ohio. So if you want the job, I'm offering it to you."

"That's mighty good of you, sir...I mean, Lowell," Reuben said. "When do we start?"

"Breakfast is at six. After that, we'll see what you can do," Lowell replied. *And I guess we'll find out why the Lord sent you to me.*

◇◇◇

Reuben fit in well at the Eagle's Nest. Within a few days he had demonstrated his ability with horses and his strong work ethic. Soon he was cleaning up old piles of junk and making repairs around the place that Lowell had put off for years. From time to time Lowell tried to strike up a serious conversation with Reuben, but Reuben would only talk about superficial subjects. Whenever Lowell asked him about what had brought him out west, Reuben would clam up or suddenly remember something he needed to take care of. On Sundays, when Lowell and Manuel drove down to the little storefront church in Fairplay, Reuben always begged off or found a reason to stay at the ranch.

And so the spring and summer of 1950 passed as Reuben buried himself in work at the ranch. Lowell took a strong liking to Reuben.

He reminded him of his son—a hard worker and serious but with something eating him. Still, Reuben wouldn't open up.

One night after dinner, Lowell tried again. "So, Reuben," he ventured, "the day you got here, you told me you fought on Guadalcanal."

Reuben looked down at his plate and mumbled an indistinct reply.

"Look, Reuben, I don't want to dig into your personal life. It's just that I thought maybe you could help me."

"Help you?" Reuben asked. "How?"

"Well, like I said, my son died on Guadalcanal at the Tenaru River. I never could get much information from the Corps...just that he had died in battle fighting off an enemy invasion. I wrote the War Department, but they said it was classified information. Since then I've tried a few times, but they don't seem to care much anymore, and I just get passed along to another bureaucrat. I guess I'm grasping at straws by asking you about it."

Reuben paused. He liked Lowell, and the old man's simple request was genuine.

"I wasn't at the Tenaru," he said slowly. "I was...I was..."

It seemed to Lowell that each word caused him great distress. He started to tell Reuben that he didn't have to finish, but Reuben waved him off.

"It's okay," he said. "It's painful for me, but you've been good to me, and I want to help you in any way I can." He thought for a moment. "My friend Bobby Halverson and I were in the scout and sniper platoon, so we didn't see much direct action until the Battle of the Ridge. We heard about the Tenaru though. It was pretty tough going for our boys. Did they tell you any more about where your son was stationed?"

"They just told me he was one of a squad of men defending a sandbar across the river the Japanese were trying to use as a bridge. That's all I know."

Reuben's eyes widened. "What was your boy's name?" he asked quietly.

"Dick," Lowell replied. "Richard. Corporal Richard Jackson. Why, did you know him?"

"No, but every Marine on that God-forsaken island heard about him."

"What do you mean?" Lowell leaned forward.

"Your boy was a hero. Wouldn't they at least tell you that?" Reuben asked. "When he heard that the Japanese were headed their way, he took his squad out on the neck, and they strung barbed wire across to seal it off. While they were finishing the job, a thousand enemy troops moved up from the beach and started trying to cross the sandbar. From what I was told, your son grabbed a machine gun and stayed out in front of the wire, fighting off the enemy troops until his men finished stringing it across the neck. They warned him that he was going to get trapped on the wrong side, but he just ordered them to finish while he held off the Japanese. When he ran out of ammo, he ran for the wire but got caught in it, and an enemy soldier shot him while he hung there."

Reuben shook his head. "If that wire hadn't been strung, the Japanese would have come right across the neck and pushed us all the way back to the other end of the island. As it was, they got caught in the wire trying to cross and were sitting ducks for our troops.

"After the battle, the men went out and brought your son's body back. It's not often that you see battle-tough men cry, but they say there wasn't a dry eye in that platoon when they carried him back to camp. I don't know why he never got a medal, but he should have. What he did was a lot more sacrificial than what I did."

Lowell looked at Reuben for a long time, and then the old man put his head down on the table and wept.

After a while, Lowell reached over and gripped Reuben's arm.

"I can see that it was real hard for you to talk about the war, and I won't ask why, but I got to tell you this. You will never know how much it means to me to hear that my boy died doing his duty. Dick and I had our times, and sometimes I was tough on him, but he was a good and decent boy. Even though he fought me, in the end he stood up for the values I taught him. That does an old man's heart good, and I thank you for it."

Both men sat silently for a few moments, and then Lowell chuckled.

"What?" Reuben asked.

"Barbed wire," Lowell said. "If there was one thing Dick hated worse than rattlesnakes, it was barbed wire. He must have strung a thousand miles of that stuff while he was growing up. He used to come back at the end of the day with bloody scratches all over his arms. He just hated it. One of the last things he said to me before he left was, 'Well, Dad, I guess I won't be seeing much of that blasted barbed wire where I'm going.' Then the last thing he does in this life is string barbed wire."

Lowell's laughter turned again to tears and then back to laughter. Reuben sat silently for a minute and then began to laugh with Lowell, and soon their laughter and tears flowed together and carried them beyond the struggles of this world to that place where pain and joy disappear into the light of blessedness.

Chapter Thirty-Seven

A New Day

After that night, Reuben was a little less guarded with Lowell. He still refused to go to church, but he was willing to sit and listen when Lowell occasionally pulled out the Bible after dinner and read some of his favorite verses. At those times, Reuben sat politely, but Lowell could see that he held most of what was being read in disdain. One evening, Lowell read Psalm 27:9: "Hide not thy face far from me; put not thy servant away in anger: thou hast been my help; leave me not, neither forsake me, O God of my salvation."

When Lowell finished, Reuben muttered something under his breath.

"Did you say something?" Lowell asked.

"I said, that's a prayer that God isn't going to answer anytime soon, at least not if I pray it."

"What is it about the Bible that bothers you so much?" asked Lowell.

Reuben looked at Lowell but remained silent. Lowell pressed on.

"Reuben, you must have had some religious upbringing," he said. "You have values and standards, you respect your elders, and you're a hard worker. It seems to me those are qualities you find most in children who have been raised by God-fearing parents."

Reuben smiled wryly. "If you knew the half of it, you'd be mighty surprised. I have had my share of religion, that's for certain, and I've come out the other end with a firm conviction that believing in God is for weak-minded people, people who need a crutch, people who want to escape—"

"I hope you don't lump me in with all those folks," retorted Lowell. "I regard myself as a pretty independent ol' cuss. What happened to you to make you so negative toward God?"

Reuben began to grow agitated. "I still have some things to do before it gets dark," he said. "I better get about them."

"Okay, boy, don't get all het up. I'll leave it alone," he said gently. "It's just that I see there's something troubling you, something deep down, and I wish I could help. I know if you'd turn to the Lord..."

"I turned to the Lord," Reuben said with an edge. "All it got me was pain and suffering and the loss of everything I loved. I've *been* there, Lowell, and I'm not going back. Now I'm going out to see about that mare that's about to foal, and when I get back I hope we can talk about something else."

"Suit yourself, Reuben."

Lowell watched as Reuben left the room. He looked over at Manuel. "Something is really stuck in that boy's craw, and he won't get well until he comes clean and spits it out."

On another occasion, when they were mending fences, Lowell asked Reuben about his military service. Reuben put down his hammer and looked at Lowell.

"My military service isn't something I'm proud of."

"Well, the only reason someone would feel that way is if they were a coward or a deserter," said Lowell, "and I doubt you were either of those."

"No, Lowell, I wasn't a deserter," said Reuben. "In fact I won..."

"...a medal?"

"Yes, a medal."

"Which one?"

Reuben hesitated. "Well, if you must know, I won the Congressional Medal of Honor."

Lowell stopped and stared at Reuben. "The Congressional Medal," he said with awe in his voice. "Son, I knew you were somethin' special when I first laid eyes on you. How can you not be proud of that?"

Reuben sat down on a pile of posts and passed his hands over his eyes. "I won that medal by shooting, stabbing, and beating Japanese boys who were just like me except for the color of their skin. I still carry a picture I took from a sniper I killed. He had a wife and a child just like me, and now he's a pile of bones out in that stinking jungle. His little boy will never know the father I killed. When I was fighting on the ridge, I saw men become animals, and I was the worst of them all. And for that they gave me a medal? What kind of a world is this, Lowell, that rewards men for going against everything God says is good and right? At least your boy gave his life to save his men. I wasn't thinking about saving anyone. I just wanted to kill. And when it was done they put me up on a pedestal, but inside I knew who I was and what I'd done. So did God, and He punished me for it."

Lowell stood in amazement. He'd never heard Reuben show emotion. Now the passion of this outburst had tears forming in Reuben's eyes. Lowell couldn't think of anything to say. Reuben stood up and walked away, wiping the tears from his face while Lowell stared after him.

There's part of it, Lord, but that ain't all. Show me the rest, Lord. Show me what's eatin' that boy so we can get him healed.

◇◇◇

In the weeks before Thanksgiving of 1950, Reuben spent most of his free time by himself in the bunkhouse. Lowell sensed he could do nothing for Reuben, so he decided to back off for a while and let Reuben continue to work through it on his own.

But matters came to a head before that would happen. On the night before Thanksgiving, the sound of the barn door creaking open woke Lowell. He got up and went to the window and saw a dim light coming through the cracks between the boards. He grabbed his shotgun, slipped on his boots, and walked quietly out to the barn. He went around to the back and peeked through the window. What he saw shocked him. Reuben had thrown a rope over the main beam in the barn and tied it off. He was standing on a stool with the end of the rope looped around his neck.

As Lowell watched he saw Reuben tense his face and close his eyes. Just as Reuben pushed himself off the stool, Lowell kicked open the back door, raised his shotgun, and blasted the rope where it hung over the beam. Reuben fell in a heap and began to weep uncontrollably.

"Let me die, Lowell," he cried. "*Please*, just let me die!"

"Get up. Nobody's getting hung on my spread unless they're a murderer or a horse thief."

"But I am a murderer. I killed my little girl. Please just shoot me and put me out of my misery."

"Not before you tell me what happened. Let's hear your story, and when it's done, if you deserve it, I'll shoot you where you stand."

So Reuben began to tell Lowell the whole story—growing up Amish, leaving his faith and joining the Marines, fighting in the trenches, being wounded, and returning to his home and his Amish faith. And then he wept his way through the story of Jerusha and of Jenna's illness and death and of his flight from Apple Creek and the pain and grief of the wife he had left behind.

"I thought if I obeyed the rules of our Order and did everything the *ordnung* said, I'd be safe. I did everything right, and God still let Jenna die. Either He's not real or He's cruel and capricious, and I just can't face either one of those options anymore. I want to die. I deserve to die, Lowell."

"From where I sit, there are men who deserve death a lot more than you do, yet they still walk this earth. And there are men like my son, who had his whole life ahead of him and died at eighteen in some stinking jungle halfway around the world. Reuben, you're not the one who decides. That's up to God and no one else. And you're wrong—God *is* real and He's *not* cruel or capricious. He didn't kill your little girl; this sin-cursed world did. From what you tell me, it seems your little girl already understood God and His ways, and so her going home means she's with Him.

"As for you killing her, that's just not true. God keeps our lives in His hands, and when it's our time to go, there ain't no one can change that. If you had put a gun to her head and shot her, that would be different, and we'd be on our way to see the sheriff right now. As it stands, you were just trying to do what you thought was best, and it didn't turn out.

"God is trying to show you something in all of this, Reuben. You don't earn points with God by keeping rules. In fact, Jesus pointed out that there are only two rules: Love God with all your heart, and love your neighbor as yourself. It appears that you did neither. You didn't love God. You tried to make Him do what you wanted Him to do instead of just serving Him. And you didn't love your closest neighbor, your wife, like you loved yourself, so you bowed to your pain and forgot about hers. If there's anything you're guilty of, its abandoning your wife when she needed you most."

Reuben looked at Lowell. "I've never really known God, have I?"

"No, son, it seems not," Lowell said. "But that's easily remedied."

"How?" asked Reuben.

"Well, boy, you just climb down off your high horse, ask Him to forgive you of your sins, and then ask Him to come and live with you and be the one who makes all the decisions for your life. He said, 'Take my yoke upon you, and learn of me; for I am meek and lowly in heart: and you shall find rest for your souls. For my yoke is easy, and my burden is light.' You can't do it by yourself, Reuben, you need Him, and you need Him bad. Trust Him with your life. But this time, get to know Him as God, not as a set of rules. Oh, I know the Amish are good folks, but without a relationship with Christ, it doesn't matter how many rules you make up, you can never keep them. You need Christ living in you. Like Jesus said to Nicodemus, 'You must be born again.'"

And so Reuben prayed with Lowell, and as he did, he began to find the peace he had been seeking all his life. He began to understand the depth of his wife's pain and his failure to care for her in her deepest need.

"Jerusha has been alone with no one to help her," Reuben said quietly. "What should I do?"

"Well, son, I think it's time that you get back into that old Ford and point it east."

And so on Thanksgiving Day, November 23, 1950, a year after his daughter's death, Reuben climbed into his truck, waved goodbye to Lowell and Manuel, and headed for Ohio. The truck hummed beneath his feet, and his thoughts turned to Apple Creek.

If I drive straight through, I can make it home by Sunday...

◇◇◇

Dim light came faintly through the window into the room. The first faint hint of Sunday morning woke Jerusha to another day. She had held the little girl close, the two of them wrapped in Jenna's tattered quilt, all through the long night. She checked the little girl's pulse. It was still beating faintly.

Her hope of rescue for them both was fading. Surely if help was coming, it would have come by now. This God she was so angry at only two days ago was once again going to fail to rescue her at her darkest hour. Still, somehow she had worked through the idea that God had failed her. Now it was her own failures that seemed the hardest to bear.

Pride, ambition, anger, faithlessness, fear, selfishness...the things that had slowly but surely drawn Jerusha away from her first love became clear to her, and she cried out to the Lord to forgive her and restore her. And then she prayed for her husband.

"Lord, please bring Reuben home. I need him. I was wrong to treat him the way I did, especially when he needed my love and my forgiveness so much. I do forgive him. If You will bring him back, I will be a good wife to him. I need You, and I need Reuben."

A scripture came to her from the book of Job: "Though he slay me, I will hope in him."

"*Ja*, Lord, no matter what happens now I will always love You and praise You for all You have given me."

And as Jerusha prayed, her beloved *Loblied* came to her lips.

Lässt loben Ihn mit allen unseren Herzen! Weil Er allein würdig ist!

The Fifth Day

Sunday, November 26, 1950

Chapter Thirty-Eight

To Seek and Save the Lost

◇◇◇

Bobby Halverson drove slowly down the county highway toward Apple Creek. It was Sunday morning, and the sun was just coming up. The snow had drifted all along the road, in some places up to thirty feet high. The wind was still blowing at a steady thirty-five miles an hour, but the temperature had risen a few degrees to slightly above zero. A few Ohio National Guard Jeeps followed Bobby's plow, bringing food and medical supplies to folks the storm had isolated.

After three days of searching in vain for Jerusha, Bobby had come to the grim conclusion that Jerusha was no longer alive. She couldn't be. No one could survive this storm out in the open. She must have gotten hypothermia, gone into shock, and wandered away from the car.

As the grim thoughts pushed into his mind, the little caravan crept into Apple Creek. Bobby swung out of line and headed toward the Springer home. Maybe she was there by some miracle.

Bobby pulled up in front of the Springer house. He left his tractor running and made his way through the drifts of snow. He clambered up on the porch and stopped there. In the snow leading up to the front door were boot tracks. Whoever had come up on the porch had gone inside and had not come out. Probably just Hank checking the house out again.

Bobby walked along the porch to the window. The tracks led up from the side of the house…and then he saw an old Ford pickup pulled up in the yard.

That truck doesn't belong to anyone I know.

Bobby brushed the snow off the window and looked in. In the dim light he could see a dark figure seated in one of the chairs facing the fireplace. There was a fitful blaze burning on the hearth, and the flickering light cast the figure's shadow on the wall. Bobby went back to the front door, cautiously opened it, and peered in.

"Hello in there," he said. "What are you doing in this house?"

There was no answer, so Bobby went inside and walked slowly toward the fireplace. He could see that the person in the chair was a man by the breadth of his shoulders. The man had on a long mackinaw and a Western hat, so Bobby couldn't see his face.

"I asked you what you are doing in this house," said Bobby. "If you are trying to get out of the cold, I can take you over to the armory, but you sure don't belong here."

The man stirred in his chair and looked up.

"Hello, Bobby," said a quiet voice.

Bobby found himself staring into a very familiar pair of violet eyes. "Reuben! For goodness sake, man, you're alive! I thought I'd never see you again."

Reuben reached out his hand, and Bobby grasped it firmly. The two men stayed that way for a moment, and then Bobby pulled Reuben up and embraced him. Reuben hesitated but then returned the hug. Bobby pulled back and looked at his friend. His face was tanned, and he had put on some weight. He wasn't wearing a beard, but he was unshaven and looked tired.

"Well, wherever you have been, it looks like you've been doing all right," Bobby said. "You've put on a little weight, and you look fit."

"Yeah, well, that happens," he said, then added, "Bobby, where's Jerusha?"

Bobby looked away. "Jerusha's missing."

"Missing! What happened?"

"Henry was driving her up to Dalton for the quilt fair, but he hit a stray cow in the storm, and they skidded off the road. Henry left her in the car and went to get help. He got hurt, and by the time I was able to get to his car, it was empty. Jerusha was gone. I thought maybe she either tried to walk out or someone found her, so I've been looking for her for three days. But...well, no one has seen her. I'm afraid..."

"Don't say it, Bobby." Reuben put his head down and stood quietly for a moment. Then he looked up at Bobby. "She's not dead. If she were dead I would know it in my spirit. No, Jerusha is alive somewhere, and we've got to find her."

"I've been out on the road since Thursday. I've tried the hospital, her friends, even the jail and the armory, but no one has seen her. She's just vanished. I just don't know what else to do..." Bobby sank into a chair and put his face in his hands and began to weep.

"Come on," Reuben said, putting his hand gently on Bobby's shoulder. "It's time for a little faith."

The light from the fire lit Reuben's face, and Bobby could see a change there. It was somehow unexpectedly peaceful. The anxiety and fear that had held Reuben prisoner for so long were gone. Something was different about him...and then Bobby realized what it was. The smile was back—there, behind his eyes. The old Reuben was back.

"What...what happened to you, Reuben?" Bobby asked. "You've changed somehow."

"We'll talk about that later," Reuben said. He reached down and grasped Bobby's hand and gripped it again.

"First, I want to thank you for being such a true friend. I know you've done everything you can to help Jerusha, and I'll never forget that. But you've got to pull yourself together and help me for just a little while longer. Can you do that?"

Bobby wiped his face with his sleeve and nodded.

"Now give me some details," Reuben said. "Where did you find Henry's car?"

"Over on Kidron Road, about two miles from Mark Knepp's place. When I got back there after Henry told me where to look, the car was empty. I've gone up and down the road a dozen times. I've stopped at every farmhouse between here and Dalton. No one has seen her. She's just vanished."

"Two miles from the Knepps' place?"

Bobby nodded.

"South of there?"

Bobby nodded again. "Not far from the county highway to Apple Creek."

"The Jepsons' cabin," Reuben said quietly.

"What?"

"The Jepsons' cabin. It's off in the woods over there by the old pond. It's been empty for years. It's where I took Jerusha the night before I left for basic training. It's only about a half a mile from where you say the car was. Jerusha's smart. She knew she had to get out of the storm, and she may have gone there when it got too cold in the car. It would have been the closest shelter. Did you look there?"

"I haven't been out there in years—since I was a kid. I thought it had fallen down by now."

"No," Reuben said. "Jepson may have been a bad farmer, but he was a good carpenter. That old house was built to last. Will your plow get us in there?"

"I think so. The snow is piled up really high in places, but I'm pretty sure we can push her through. You can show me where the old road goes in. It'll be tough going. The storm has let up a little since yesterday, but it's still pretty fierce. You'll need some warmer clothes."

"I hope Jerusha didn't throw away my things," said Reuben with a wry smile. "I wouldn't blame her. I left a lot behind when I took off."

Reuben went into the back of the house and searched through the closets. Soon he reappeared wearing warmer clothing.

"Let's go find her, Bobby," Reuben said quietly.

The two men went out to the tractor and climbed up in the cab. Bobby turned the plow around and headed east.

◇◇◇

The fire had been out for a long time, and Jerusha was too weak from hunger and thirst to get up. She felt as if she were inside a freezer, and she knew she and the girl were becoming hypothermic. Her skin was turning blue, and her hands and feet were numb. Outside, the wind howled around the eaves of the house, and snow had piled up almost to the windows. During the night she had heard a sharp crack and a huge crash. The heavy snow and high winds were taking their toll on the trees.

Are we going to die here, Lord? If we are, I think I'm ready. I still don't understand Your ways, but I accept Your will.

Jerusha felt herself beginning to lose consciousness. And in that moment, she remembered a scripture that had been one of her grandmother's favorites. "*You have not chosen me, but I have chosen you, and ordained you, that you should go and bring forth fruit, and that your fruit should remain: that whatsoever you shall ask of the Father in my name, he may give it you.*"

She remembered her grandmother's words to her when she was learning to quilt. "*The first thing that needs to be done before any quilt is made is to decide which kind of design we will use. We must know in our heart what the quilt will look like when it is finished...If the design is not pleasing to the eye from the start, that's wasted time, and to waste time is to try God's patience.*"

You've had a design for my life since before I was born, haven't You? And

I was getting in the way of that design with my pride and my lack of faith. I have not loved You with all my heart and trusted You in all my ways. How I have wasted Your time and how I must have tried Your patience.

Again, her grandmother's words came to her. "*If the design is to be even and pleasing to the eye, each individual piece of fabric must be stitched just right in order for it to fit together properly.*"

You ordered everything in my life, every individual piece, didn't You? Jenna was one of those pieces, and Reuben too. I never realized how perfectly it all worked together. In my pride I haven't let You be the one who puts everything together. I have not let You be God. And if I am to die here, it's part of Your perfect plan, isn't it?

Once more her grandmother's gentle voice came to her.

"*Never hurry, always pay attention, and do the work as unto the Lord. You have been given a way to give back to the Lord, as He has given to you. This is a special gift not everyone is given. But to whom much is given, much is required... That's why we put a small mistake in the quilt before we finish. It's so that we do not make God angry with us for being too proud.*"

You gave me this gift as a way to glorify You, and I used it to glorify myself. I was using it to escape from You. Lord, if I am meant to live, I will use my gift to bless others. If I am meant to die, I will die in peace, knowing that I have at last come to understand in some small way Your plan for my life.

Jerusha's eyes closed. The light in the room began to fade, and the darkness closed in around her. She pulled the little girl as close to her as she could and smiled.

I will see You soon, my precious girl, and I'm bringing you a sister.

Chapter Thirty-Nine

I Once Was Lost...

◇◇◇

Bobby drove out County Highway 188 toward Kidron Road. The wind had picked up again, and the snow was blowing hard across their path. Visibility was down to about a hundred feet, so they moved slowly, looking for markers. The roar of the wind was relentless, and the two men had to speak up to hear each other.

"There's County Road 142," Bobby said as they passed a crossroad where several trucks with flashing lights were parked by a barricade. "The wind blew down some power lines up the road. The power company wants to get in there, but it's just too dangerous to try to put them back up."

"It's the same west of town," Reuben said. "I had to backtrack at least three times to get home."

"I wondered," Bobby said. "You must have driven like a crazy man."

"Let's just say I was determined to get here as fast as I could."

They rumbled on, heading east. Soon they came to another cross street. They couldn't see a sign, but they were both sure it was Carr Road.

"Let me get out and check," Reuben said. "I don't want us to get lost in this whiteout."

Reuben jumped out of the cab and made his way to the corner of the road. A broken-off wooden sign pole was lying in the ditch with a sign that said Carr Road on it. Reuben hurried back to the tractor. "That's Carr Road. One more mile to Township Highway 179, and then one more mile after that to the turnoff to the Jepsons' place."

Bobby nodded and put the tractor in gear. The trees along the road opened up somewhat in the next stretch, which made the going much more difficult. The wind had come sweeping through this open area and piled the snow up all along the road. Several times Bobby had to clear big drifts out of their way. Finally they came to a massive drift that had piled up across the entire road.

"How are we going to get around this one?" Reuben asked.

"We're going to have to back up and go right at it," Bobby said. "Hang on! I'm going to hit it at an angle and see if I can blow the pile off to the side."

Bobby backed up about fifty feet. Then he put the tractor in gear and revved it up. He angled into the drift and hit it at full speed. The plow blade threw most of the snow to the side of the road, and the tractor bumped and swayed up over the rest of the pile and back down the other side. Reuben hung on to the side of the cab and let out a laugh. "It's like a carnival ride. Been a long time since I was on one of those."

"Good to see you laugh again, my friend," Bobby said as they continued down the road.

"It also reminds me of the morning you and me and Sarge were on the troop transport about to land on Guadalcanal," Reuben said. "You looked at me and said 'Stay close,' and then you went over the side. I was scared stiff, and the last thing I wanted to do was follow you into that little boat, but I couldn't just stand there and watch you be the hero. So over I went. Bobby Halverson, no fear; Reuben Springer, shaking in his boots."

"These snowdrifts are nothing compared to that," Bobby said. "The truth is I was scared to death too. If I hadn't gone over the side, I probably would have crawled back to my bunk and hidden under the covers. I was no hero. I just didn't see any other way than to go straight at it."

The two men drove on down the road in silence. Then Bobby spoke. "So you can talk about it now. That's good."

Reuben paused for a minute and then answered. "It still bothers me to think about what happened on that island. But I'm not afraid to talk about it anymore. I had some help out in Colorado from a good man I worked for. He was a World War I vet, and he had a son who got killed at the Tenaru River. Turns out his son was Dick Jackson, the corporal who kept the Japanese from getting across that sandbar at Tenaru. The War Department didn't give Lowell, the old man, too many details about the battle and about how Dick died, so I was able to help the old man out. A few weeks later he returned the favor."

"I remember Dick Jackson. It's pretty amazing that you should end up at his dad's place. What happened?"

"I'd hit bottom and decided I couldn't take any more. I was actually about to kill myself, but he stepped in."

Bobby looked at Reuben. "Wow—I had no idea things had gotten that tough for you."

"It wasn't that long ago. It was getting close to the anniversary of Jenna's death, and I felt like I couldn't go on. Lowell saved me, and then he helped me come to grips with my issues about God. I found out I had built my relationship with God on a faulty foundation. I was trying to keep the rules so I could be holy and be safe from a horrible world. I didn't know that God isn't too concerned that we belong to a certain church.

"Every one of us has the potential for truly horrible behavior no matter what our religious background. It's only when we let Him live His life through us that we have any real chance to live in a way that pleases Him. Keeping rules didn't earn me points with God. I had to find refuge in God, not my religion or my hideout. When I did, I saw that everything that happens in my life can work together for good. That helped me to come to grips with my past."

"Well, I'm happy for you," Bobby said. "But if you have a closer relationship with God...I mean, why have all these bad things happened to you?"

"Like I said, all things can work together for good. We don't know the end of this story yet. Yes, we lost Jenna, and that was the most horrible thing I've ever experienced, even worse than the Battle of the Ridge. But I'm not the only person who's ever lost a child. God never promised that bad things wouldn't happen in our lives, but He did promise that He would see us through them and that if we trust Him, He would bring good out of the most terrible things.

"The point of the gospel is that God lost a child too, but that wasn't the end of the story. Christ's death turned out to have a very good ending in bringing man back to God. I don't know how my story will end. I don't know if Jerusha will take me back or if she'll even talk to me. But I do know that I let her down terribly, and I have to somehow show her that I still love her and that no matter what, I will always be there for her."

"Well, I sure wish I could say that I had your faith that we'll find Jerusha," Bobby said, "but I've been out here for three days, and I'm pretty much at the end of my rope."

"Funny you should use that expression," Reuben said. "Out in Colorado, I literally came to the end of my rope, but God sent Lowell to intervene in the nick of time, and now here I am, and that helps me see that God is at work in all of this. So until I see her body with my own eyes, I'm believing that Jerusha is alive and that we're going to find her."

Reuben's declaration left Bobby without anything to say for a moment. Then he replied. "Okay, Reuben, I'm with you. We'll look until we find her, and I can tell you that I hope as much as you do that she's alive."

Just then they reached another cross street. The sign was still up.

"This is the old Township Highway," Reuben said. "The turnoff to the Jepson place is off Kohler Road. The Jepsons owned that whole piece between Kohler and Kidron. The pond is just off this highway, and the road up to the old cabin turns off Kohler, goes by the pond, and then heads north and comes around behind the house. Kohler is about a mile ahead, but it's not a well-used road and it's not marked. We'll have to keep our eyes peeled."

The tractor crawled on up the road, and both men were silent as they watched for the Kohler Road turnoff. After about twenty minutes, Reuben pointed to their left and shouted, "Right there, Bobby! That's Kohler."

Bobby pulled the plow up to the intersection of the two roads. There had been no traffic up Kohler, and the snow was deep and unmarked. Trees lined both sides of the road, and the passage looked difficult.

"Can she make it, Bobby?"

"We'll make it or die trying." Bobby put the tractor into its lowest gear and started forward up the road, plowing as he went. The old diesel chugged steadily, but Reuben could feel the tires slipping from side to side. They went up the road about fifty yards, and then Reuben pointed to a break in the trees.

"That's the way in, Bobby," he said. "The old driveway cuts around a small hill and back to the pond and then turns north to the cabin."

"Hold on, Reuben," Bobby said. "There's tough going ahead."

Bobby turned the tractor toward the break in the trees and started forward. He could see that the bank sloped up to the left and the road wound around to the right along the bottom of the hill. Soon they came to what looked like a meadow on the right side of the plow.

"Stay left against the hill, Bobby," Reuben said. "That's not a meadow, that's the pond."

As more of the pond came into view, they could see a dark object on the far shore. "What's that?" asked Reuben.

"Looks like a car that flipped," Bobby said. "Look up the slope behind it. Some small trees are knocked down. Looks like it didn't happen too long ago. Someone who was going pretty fast came off the highway and got all the way over the rise and down to the pond before they stopped. We should probably check it on the way back, see if anybody's in there."

Bobby continued around the hill, and then Reuben pointed ahead. "It's pretty overgrown with gorse, but you can break your way through to the meadow."

Bobby put the plow straight into the thicket that blocked the road and crushed his way through. He reached forward and patted the dashboard of the tractor. "Atta girl."

Reuben was watching through the snow when he signaled to Bobby. "There's a big tree down up there. I don't think you should go around it because that's a big swampy meadow out there that the creek runs through. It might be deep mud under the snow. We can leave the tractor here and go on foot. It's only about a hundred yards to the cabin."

"Okay, but I hope she doesn't stall while we're in there," Bobby said. "I haven't been able to charge the battery today, and the charge might be too low to warm the glow plugs if we have to restart the engine.

Bobby set the engine on high idle, and the two men clambered out of the cab. The freezing wind hit them like a sledgehammer, and the snow stung their faces like a million tiny shocks of electricity. Bobby and Reuben worked their way around the tree and started in the direction Reuben indicated. The visibility was down to fifty feet, and the temperature was around zero. The two men struggled through the deep drifts with Reuben leading the way. After a few minutes Reuben pointed ahead. There in the distance was a dark shape against the snow.

"There's the cabin," Reuben shouted.

They pushed ahead through the snow and reached the front porch of the cabin, which was filled with snow up to the windows. The glass had been broken out years before, and someone had nailed up plywood to cover the holes, but there were some small windows above the door that still had glass in them. Reuben pointed to the side of the cabin, and Bobby followed him around. There was a small shed attached to the house by a roofed walkway. Reuben went up to the back door and pushed on it. It swung open, and the men went inside. As their eyes adjusted to the dim light, they looked around the room but couldn't see anyone. Except for what looked like a pile of old rags by the stove, the cabin was empty.

Chapter Forty

...But Now I'm Found

A small amount of light shone into the room through the two small windows above the door of the cabin, but most of the room was in shadows. Bobby and Reuben strained their eyes looking into the room, but seeing no one, Reuben's shoulders slumped.

"I was sure she was here."

"We'll keep looking. There are still some places she might be." Bobby feigned enthusiasm, but inside his hope was draining away.

The two stood silently for a moment.

"Well, we might as well go, we're wasting daylight," Bobby said.

Reuben turned to go with Bobby just behind him. Just as they got to the door. Reuben heard a tiny sound.

"Mama."

"Did you hear that?" he asked.

"Hear what?" Bobby asked. "All I can hear is the wind."

"No, I heard a voice, a little girl's voice, like Jenna's."

"Reuben...You know that Jenna..."

Then Reuben heard it again, just a little louder.

"Mama."

"Whoa! I heard it too!" Bobby cried. "What..."

Reuben turned back into the room and peered into the darkness. And then he stepped over to the stove and looked more closely at the pile of rags.

"Over here, Bobby," he cried as he knelt down beside the stove. The pile of rags next to the stove had a shape, long and narrow. Bobby stood beside him while Reuben reached down and pulled the top layer of the cloth aside. What they had thought was a pile of rags was a large piece of material wrapped around something. As his eyes adjusted to the light, Reuben could see the material was actually a torn and mud-died quilt with someone inside it. Reuben slowly pulled the cloth away from the face of the person in the quilt. There was Jerusha lying in the quilt with her arms wrapped tightly around a tiny girl.

"Jerusha!" Reuben cried. He knelt down beside the still figures and gathered his wife and the little girl into his arms.

Bobby felt for a pulse in Jerusha's wrist. "She's alive!"

"What about the little girl?"

Bobby felt for a pulse. He couldn't find one in her wrist, but when he checked her jugular he found a faint beat there. "She's alive too! They're both alive!"

"But barely," Reuben said. "We've got to get them to a hospital."

"A hospital?"

"I know...I wouldn't have said that before. But we need to take Jerusha and this child where they will get the best care and the most attention. And for now, that's a hospital."

"Okay, I'm with you. I should bring the tractor up here to the cabin so we don't have to carry them through the snow and wind. Is it swampy everywhere around the house?"

"The big tree fell right across the old driveway," Reuben answered. "If you stay to the left and push the tree aside with the plow, you can probably avoid the swampy ground. Do you need me to come with you?"

"No, you stay here with them. Do you have anything you can use to start a fire?"

"No, I didn't figure on staying when we found her."

"Okay, I'm going to bring the tractor up. It'll take me a few minutes."

Bobby hurried out the door. The wind had picked up again, and visibility was down to a few feet.

Bobby made his way through the drifts the way they had come, following their tracks through the howling wind. As he got closer to where they left the tractor, he strained his eyes through the white.

It's right up here, but I don't hear anything.

Suddenly the tractor appeared out of the snow right in front of him. It stood silent and dark. The old diesel had stalled.

◇◇◇

Reuben held Jerusha tightly in his arms and kissed her softly on the forehead. Jerusha groaned and mumbled some indistinct words.

"Reuben? Where are you? I'm so cold..."

"I'm here, my darling, I'm here," he whispered. Tears ran down his face as he pulled his wife and the little girl close to him and tried to warm them with his own body.

Just then the door burst open, and Bobby stood there, shaking with cold.

"The tractor died," he cried. "I tried to start it, but there wasn't enough charge on the battery to warm up the glow plugs. I brought a couple of self-starting flares from the toolbox. Maybe we can at least get a fire going."

"Go look out in the shed and see if there's any wood there," Reuben said. "I'll pull a couple of these wall boards off."

Bobby hurried out to the shed while Reuben laid Jerusha and the little girl down. He went to a place on the wall where some of the boards had already been pulled off and pulled on a board. It didn't budge. Reuben looked around the room and saw the rickety table next to the stove. Reuben grabbed it and broke it apart. He used one of the legs as a lever behind the wallboard and pulled on it with all his strength. The board creaked as the old nails gave way and then pulled loose. Reuben leaned it against the wall and stepped on it with his boot. It broke into two pieces. He did it again and in a few seconds had a pile of pieces that would fit into the stove. Just then Bobby came back from the shed with an arm full of scraps and small pieces of pine.

"This was all that was left," he said. "Jerusha must have gotten a fire going and used whatever was here to stay warm."

"Put it in the stove and use one of your flares to get it going," said Reuben. "I'll break up this table and some more boards."

Bobby put the wood into the stove and pulled out one of the flares while Reuben pulled more boards off the wall and broke them up. Bobby opened the flare and struck the igniter on the cap. It burst into flame and lit the room with an eerie red glow that reminded Bobby of the night on the ridge. He glanced at Reuben but didn't see any anxiety on his face, only a grim determination.

"Yes, Bobby, it's like the battle on the ridge, and we will win this one too! Now get that fire going!"

Bobby stuck the flare into the stove under the pile of wood. Soon they heard the crackle of the pine pieces catching on fire. Reuben shoved some more pieces of broken board into the stove. Soon the fire was roaring, and the sides of the stove began to glow red. Reuben gently laid Jerusha and the little girl close to the stove.

"This is good for now," Bobby said, "but we've got to get them out of here. Maybe I could walk back to the road and flag down some help."

"The road's too far," Reuben said, "And you might wait for hours for someone to come by. No, we've got to find another way to get out of here."

"If I had another battery I could pair it up with the one on the tractor and maybe get enough juice to warm up the glow plugs."

"Where would we get that?" asked Reuben.

"What about that car we saw back at the pond?" Bobby asked. "I bet there's a battery in there, and I've got jumper cables in the tractor. If I could get the other battery back here and warm it by the fire, I could couple it to the battery in the tractor. There might be enough charge between them to do the trick."

Bobby saw the doubt on Reuben's face.

"Come on, old friend. Time for a little faith."

Reuben rose to his feet. "Okay, but I'll go for it. I know the way. I've spent a lot of time at the pond. I'll get the battery and be back in half an hour. You stay here and keep the fire going. Did you bring any tools?"

"There's a toolbox behind the seat in the tractor. It has pliers and screwdrivers in it."

The two men looked at each other and then grasped each other's hand.

"Be careful, buddy," said Bobby. "God go with you."

"No atheists in foxholes," Reuben said as he smiled at his friend. And then he turned and was out the door and gone into the storm.

Reuben pulled his coat tight around him and stepped off the porch into the snow. He followed their tracks south back toward the tractor. Several times he lost his footing and plunged ahead into the snow but quickly got to his feet and pushed on.

When he got to the tractor, he climbed into the cab and looked for the toolbox. He opened it and pulled out a sturdy set of pliers and a couple of screwdrivers. Jumping down off the tractor, he headed back toward the pond, leaning forward into the wind and trudging ahead until he reached the place where Bobby had crashed through the thicket of gorse. He picked his way carefully through the sharp branches.

About ten minutes later, he came to the place where the road ran around the hill. The pond was just ahead. He moved to the right and carefully skirted the flat surface of the pond. He had to push through some thick growth at the edge of the pond, and once he had to backtrack and go up into the woods to get around a fallen tree.

Finally he came to the wrecked car on the far side of the pond. He glanced inside, but it was empty. Most of the front of the car had slid onto the ice. Reuben carefully stepped onto the ice and slowly inched around to the front of the car. The front end was smashed but not totally wrecked. The ice was badly fractured in a zigzag pattern coming out from under the hood.

He went back around behind the car to the driver's side and tried to open the door. It was jammed, so he kicked out the window. He stooped down, reached in, and pulled the hood latch. He heard it click but the hood didn't drop. He pulled it again but still nothing happened. He pulled the larger of the screwdrivers out of his pocket and went around to the front of the car. The hood had dropped down a little but he could see that the wreck had bent the release, and the hood was jammed. Carefully he inserted the screwdriver and began to pry the hood open. He worked his way along the edge until he hit an obstruction.

He peered into the engine compartment through the crack in the hood and saw that the battery had come out of its holder and was lying on the inside of the hood. He worked his way back, straightening the front of the hood with the screwdriver as he went until he came to where the latch held the hood closed. He stuck the screwdriver in and jammed it into the latch. He wiggled it back and forth until he felt the latch start to release. Suddenly the hood latch gave way and the hood fell open as far as it could before hitting the ice. The heavy battery, still attached to one of the cables, fell out of the car and hit the ice, right on a fracture.

There was an ominous cracking sound, and then a hole opened right beneath Reuben's feet. He turned to run, but before he could move, the ice gave way and he slipped into the icy water. As he went down he twisted his upper body and grabbed at the bumper of the car with all his strength. The car rocked down and then back up, pulling him partway out of the water.

Reuben tried to get his leg onto the ice, but the edge broke, and his leg fell back in. The car dipped down again, and he went into the water up to his waist. He could feel the cold begin to penetrate his body as he hung halfway in and halfway out of the pond.

Is this it then, Lord? After all this, am I going to die in this pond?

Reuben closed his eyes. He hung from the bumper of the car and felt his strength fading as the cold began to numb his legs.

He closed his eyes and waited for the end. Just before he let go, something made him open his eyes. He was no longer hanging on the car—he was standing on a hill, and there was something right in front of him. It was a wooden cross. He looked up and saw a man hanging motionless, his hands and feet nailed to the wood. The man's eyes were closed, but he opened them, looked straight at Reuben, and spoke to him.

"*I hung between heaven and earth so you could live. I will never leave you or forsake you.*"

legs [illegible]. He [illegible] and he went into the water [illegible] to his waist. He could feel the sand [illegible] his feet [illegible] around his waist [illegible] of the [illegible].

[illegible]

[illegible] eyes [illegible] the [illegible] his [illegible] began to [illegible].

He closed his eyes and waited for the end. [illegible] he [illegible] opened his eyes. He was no longer [illegible] in the [illegible] standing on a hill [illegible] there was something right in front of him. It was a wooden cross. He looked up and saw [illegible] hands and feet nailed to the wood. The man's eyes were [illegible] but he opened them, looked [illegible] at [illegible] him.

[illegible] you are ready [illegible] come home. [illegible] for you.

Chapter Forty-One

Going Home

Reuben clung desperately to the bumper of the car. The freezing water was up to his waist, draining his strength away.

Jenna, I'll be with you soon, sweetheart.

Just then Reuben heard a sound behind him, something sliding slowly across the ice. He tried to turn his head to see what it was, and then he felt strong hands grip his coat and his arm.

"Let go, pal, I've got you."

Bobby! Reuben felt his friend pulling on him, and he let go. As Bobby pulled, Reuben's legs came up out of the water and onto the ice. Bobby slowly and carefully dragged Reuben backward across the ice and up onto the bank. Reuben lay there gasping for air.

"Where did you come from?" he asked, shaking with cold.

"Well, you always seem to get yourself into trouble, so I figured I had better make sure you got back in one piece. Your wife needs you."

"Is she all right?"

"The fire has warmed her up and she's doing better, but we still need to get her and the little one out of here. We're a little too busy to be taking a swim right now."

Reuben looked at Bobby and then began to laugh. Bobby stared at him and then started laughing too. The two friends laughed hysterically, and then finally they stopped and caught their breath.

"Now, let's get that battery and get out of here before the whole thing gives way," Bobby said.

"I think it fell into the pond," Reuben said.

Bobby looked under the hood.

"Nope, we got lucky. It's still attached to one of the cables. I'll get around on the other side and unhook it. Did you bring tools?"

Reuben reached in his pocket and pulled out the pliers and the small screwdriver.

"I dropped the other one in the pond," he said.

"That was a two-dollar screwdriver, pal. You owe me."

Bobby walked around the back of the car and then carefully stepped out onto the ice. It groaned dangerously under his feet, but he kept going. He slowly worked his way up the side of the car until he got to the front. He knelt and used the pliers to undo the cable holding the battery to the car, lowered the battery all the way down, and then pushed it behind him. He reached into the engine compartment and freed the other cable. The hole where Reuben had fallen through was only a couple of feet from where he was working, and the ice continued to crack and pop.

"You better get off that ice pretty quick, but don't forget to get all the nuts and washers," Reuben shouted.

"Way ahead of you, pal," Bobby replied, holding up the hardware. He held on to the car with one hand and slowly eased his way back to the bank, dragging the battery along by the attached cable. Just as he got to the bank, the ice gave another sharp crack and broke. The front of the car dropped into the crack, and the car began to slide into the pond. Bobby leaped up onto the bank, dragging the battery behind him. Huge bubbles of air escaped out of the broken window as the rest of the car slid slowly down the bank and into the water.

"Timing is everything," said Bobby as he watched the car disappear.

"Now let's get you back to the fire and get those wet clothes dried out," he said as he helped Reuben get up.

Bobby handed Reuben the cables and grabbed the battery. "Let's go," he said, and the two men headed back toward the cabin.

The fire had taken the chill out of the room when they got back, but Bobby added more wood anyway while Reuben checked Jerusha. Her breathing was shallow, but a little color had come back to her skin. She was still unconscious. The little girl lay next to her, quiet and still but alive. He stripped off his wet clothes and set them to dry while Bobby placed the battery next to the fire to warm it up.

"Hopefully it didn't freeze so hard it lost all the charge."

"How long will it take?" asked Reuben.

"About twenty minutes or so. If we can just get enough charge to boost my battery, it will get the glow plugs warm enough to start the tractor. What I'm worried about the most is the shape my glow plugs are in. Dutch said a couple of them are pretty worn out. I was hoping to get some new ones tomorrow, but the storm came in on Thursday and I had to go with what I had."

In about twenty minutes Reuben's clothes had dried enough for him to slip them back on. The battery was warm to the touch.

"When we get out there, we'll have to hook up the batteries and then wait," said Bobby. "We've got to let the plugs warm for at least ten minutes. Then we'll see if it starts up."

Reuben built up the fire and then kissed Jerusha once more. "I'll be back soon, my darling," he whispered.

The two friends went back out into the storm, carrying the battery and the cables. Slowly they made their way back to the tractor. When they got there, Bobby opened up the hood, placed the battery on top of the engine, and then pulled out the screwdriver and scraped off the battery terminals to make sure there was a good connection.

"Climb up in there and throw down the jumper cables," he yelled to Reuben.

Reuben tossed down the cables and climbed down to help Bobby. They stretched the cables from the extra battery to the one in the tractor and then checked the connections to the engine.

"If there's enough charge, the dash light will go on in about ten minutes," Bobby shouted over the wind. "Until then, we'll just have to wait. Get inside."

Reuben and Bobby climbed up into the cab. They sat on the bench seat and watched the dashboard. The indicator on the dash remained dark.

"While we're waiting, can I ask you a question?" asked Bobby.

"Sure," said Reuben.

"This God of yours," said Bobby slowly, "does He ever...well, I mean...do you ever hear Him talk to you?"

"I think I heard Him talk to me while I was hanging onto the car. He told me something I've never really understood until today."

"That's interesting," Bobby said. "Do you want to know the real reason I was there to help you?"

"Real reason?" asked Reuben.

"I was sitting in the cabin with Jerusha, waiting for you to get back, and all of a sudden, I heard a voice...or maybe it was a feeling, I don't know...but it was very clearly telling me to get up and go help you. It sounds crazy, but it was so real, I just got up and went. And when I got there, I found you goofing around with the car."

"Goofing around?" Reuben said with a laugh. And then in a more serious tone he said, "I believe you, Bobby. I do."

As Reuben finished speaking, a small yellow light on the dashboard blinked on. Bobby stared at it in amazement.

"What?" asked Reuben.

"The glow plugs! They warmed up!"

"Isn't that what you expected?"

"Actually, I thought that we had about a snowball's chance in...well you know."

"What now?" Reuben asked.

"I'm going to try to turn it over." Bobby pressed the starter. The diesel jumped and chugged a couple of times and then stopped. He tried it once more. Again it turned over but didn't start.

"Sounds like that battery is running down," Reuben said.

"We've got about one more try," Bobby said. Then a thought occurred to him.

"Hey, look behind the seat and see if there's a spray can back there."

Reuben groped behind the seat and found a can. "Ether?"

"Dutch, I love you!" Bobby shouted as he took the can from Reuben.

"I'm going down and spray this into the manifold port. When I yell, you crank it over."

Bobby climbed down and brushed the snow off the engine. He pointed the spray nozzle into a small hole in the manifold and shot a stream of ether into the engine.

"Go!" he shouted.

Reuben pressed the starter. The engine gave a bang, kicked like a mule, and started. The jerk knocked Bobby down, and he jumped back up as the diesel came to life.

"Ka-chug, ka-chug, ka-chug!" he shouted as he danced around in the snow to the chug of the engine. "You old hunk-a-junk," he shouted. "I love you!"

Bobby climbed up in the cab and grabbed Reuben in a hug. "Let's go home," he said.

◇◇◇

Jerusha slowly opened her eyes. She was in a white room. It was warm and quiet. She was in a bed with warm blankets pulled over her.

Is this heaven?

She slowly turned her head and focused her eyes. A face swam into her field of vision. A familiar face...with a hidden smile behind violet eyes.

"Reuben?" Jerusha held out her arms.

Reuben got out of his chair, knelt by the bed, and took Jerusha in his arms. They clung together tightly.

"Jerusha, can you ever forgive me?" he asked.

"I already have, my love," Jerusha said quietly. "But can you forgive me?"

"There's nothing to forgive," Reuben said. "I just want to be with you and start again. I need you to help me forgive myself, and I need to be there for you. We've suffered a tragedy, but if we stay together, I know we can find healing."

"With the Lord's help?" asked Jerusha.

"Yes, with the Lord's help."

Just then there was a knock on the door. Reuben sat up, still holding Jerusha's hand. "Come in."

Dr. Schaeffer came into the room with Bobby and a nurse.

"Bobby!" Jerusha said. "I know you had something to do with finding me. Thank you."

"If it wasn't for Bobby, you wouldn't be alive today," Reuben said.

Bobby took Jerusha's hand. "I'm grateful to God I was able to help," he said.

Jerusha and Reuben looked at each other and smiled.

Dr. Schaeffer came to the bedside, peered over his glasses, and said, "Well, one of our patients is doing better, I see."

"One of our patients?" asked Jerusha.

"Well, there's this one too. She came in with you."

Dr. Schaeffer pointed to a smaller bed pulled up right next to Jerusha's. A little girl lay in the bed. Her eyes were open and she lay looking at Jerusha solemly.

"You found me," she said to Jerusha. "I was lost, and you found me."

Jerusha stared at the little girl. For a moment she thought it was Jenna. But it couldn't be Jenna. Jenna was gone. And then she remembered everything—the storm, the wrecked car, the cabin. She remembered God's healing touch and holding this little girl through the long nights. Without thinking she held out her arms to the little girl who started to come to her.

Dr. Schaeffer moved forward. "I don't think—"

Bobby tapped the doctor on the shoulder and said, "I think I just heard a nurse calling you, doctor. They need you in the ICU."

The doctor looked at Bobby and then at Reuben and then to Jerusha and the little girl.

"Yes, I believe you're right. I'll be on my way." He turned and left.

Reuben walked around to the little girl and picked her up. He placed her in the bed beside Jerusha.

Jerusha took the little one into her arms.

"What's your name, darling?" she asked softly.

"My name is Jenny."

Reuben and Jerusha looked at each other in amazement and then tears began to flow down Jerusha's cheeks. She pulled Jenny close against her breast.

"Thank you, Lord, oh thank you."

Reuben knelt at the side of the bed and took them both into his strong arms. And though the wind was still blowing and the storm was still raging outside, inside their hearts it was spring in Apple Creek.

Epilogue

◇◇◇

Apple Creek, Ohio, Thanksgiving 1962

The woman pushed the door open and slowly entered the room. Her blonde hair was beginning to show some gray now, and a strand peeked out from under her *kappe.* The years had left their mark on her beautiful face, but not unkindly. She turned up the gas lamp and went to the old cedar chest against the wall. The lid creaked as she opened it and knelt beside it.

Some shawls and other handmade items were on top, and she lifted them out and laid them aside. Finally in the bottom of the chest, she came to the object of her search. It was a parcel rolled in paper and tied with thick brown string. She pulled it out, stood, and went to the rocking chair in the corner, where she sat down and placed the parcel in her lap.

After all these years, I still miss you, my darling Jenna. I have received many blessings since you left us, but in my heart is that place where you will always live. I thank the Lord every day for the four years you spent with us and the joy of having you for my daughter.

The woman untied the string, laid it aside, opened the package, and pulled out the torn quilt. It was still mud-stained, and a corner was missing, but the exquisite design and the expert stitching that had once marked this quilt as the best she had ever made was still evident to her practiced eye.

The Rose of Sharon, I called this quilt. I made it with silk. The rose in the center was blood red...like the blood of Christ. I named it for you, my darling girl.

Just then the door opened, and a teenage girl peeked in.

"Mama?"

"Come in, *dochter*," Jerusha said, and the girl entered.

She was lovely, with reddish blonde hair and a strong face. She came to her mother's side and looked down at the quilt.

"That's my quilt," she said. "The one you wrapped me in to save my life."

"Yes, Jenny, this is your quilt. It's a strange and wonderful story, how it came to be yours."

Jenny knelt down at her mother's feet and laid her head on Jerusha's lap.

"Tell me again, Mama," she said.

Jerusha laid her hand gently on her daughter's head and began to stroke her hair as she spoke.

"I made this quilt for your sister, Jenna. I was running away from God and from my faith. This quilt was my way out. But God led me to you, and I had to make a choice—to hold on to my pride and keep the quilt unspoiled or to use it to save you. I made the right choice."

"And how did you get me?" Jenny asked even though she had heard the story many times.

"No one knew where you came from or who your parents were. When the police went to Jepsons' Pond to pull out the car I found you in, it was already spring. In the bottom of the pond they found the body of a man. He never was identified. He may have been your father, but no one knows. When they checked on the car, they found that it had been stolen in New York City. You were all alone, so we applied to take you into foster care while the authorities looked for some relatives, but that was a hopeless search. So we adopted you, and that's how you became our daughter. And a wonderful daughter you've been."

"Mama, did you ever regret having me instead of Jenna?" Jenny asked, looking up into her mother's face.

"Jenna was a wonderful child. She already had a special relationship with the Lord when she died. It was an easy thing to raise her. You were a stronger child than Jenna, more determined and self-willed. God knew that you needed your *daed* and me to raise you, to bring order to your life, and to give you the opportunity to have a relationship with Him. Who knows what would have happened to you or me or your *daed* if God had not put us together? We all needed each other. And since that day, I have never thought of you as anything but my own flesh and blood."

Jenny laid her head down in her mama's lap again. "Sometimes I dream about being in the car where you found me," Jenny said. "The dreams are sometimes strange, and mostly I don't understand them. You are there, and then you're an angel. And there's a bad man, and then *Daed* is there, and he always makes me feel safe. All I know is that I was lost and you found me. Thank you, Mama, for saving me."

A voice from the doorway piped up. "No, Jenny, it was you who saved us."

A tall man stood there, his hair and beard starting to show gray hairs among the black. He was stern of face but with a smile hidden in his eyes. He took off his black, broad-brimmed hat and came into the room.

"And how are my girls today?" he asked as he reached down and pulled them both into an embrace. He kissed Jenny on the cheek and the forehead and then gave Jerusha a kiss on the lips.

"Husband!" said Jerusha as she lowered her eyes and blushed red.

Reuben smiled and held them both even tighter.

Discussion Questions

I. Dealing with Loss

In chapter 1 Jerusha has experienced a deep personal tragedy in the death of her daughter, Jenna, and the disappearance of her husband, Reuben. She deals with it by letting a root of bitterness into her life that results in hatred toward God.

1. Have you ever had a similar loss in your life? A similar situation?
2. How did you deal with it?
3. What was the outcome? Positive or negative?

Scripture References: Philippians 3:8; Hebrews 12:12-15

II. Family Roots

In chapters 6 and 7 Jerusha learns about the roots of her faith and her family from her *grossmudder,* Hannah.

1. How important is it to understand your family's heritage?
2. How do you gain strength from your family?
3. If you are someone whose family is scattered and out of touch, how does it affect your life?
4. How important are families to God?

Scripture References: Psalm 68:6; Ephesians 6:4

III. Under the Law or Under Grace?

When Reuben returns from the war, he has been so traumatized that he seeks refuge in the church. He learns a great lesson in chapter 37.

1. What did Reuben place his faith in?
2. Was following the law the path to personal peace for Reuben?
3. What did Lowell tell Reuben about earning points with God that broke the bondage Reuben was under?
4. Do you think you are a Christian just because you follow the rules?
5. If you do, is it working for you?

Scripture References: James 2:10; Romans 8:1-2,

IV. Choices

In chapter 25 Jerusha must make a life-and-death decision. One choice will bring glory to God, the other will bring glory to her.

1. Have you ever had to make a decision that meant sacrificing something very precious in order to follow God?
2. How did you respond to the test?
3. What was the outcome?

Scripture References: 1 Peter 1:7; 1 Peter 4:12-14; John 3:16

About Patrick E. Craig

◇◇◇

Patrick E. Craig is a lifelong writer and musician who left a successful songwriting and performance career in the music industry to follow Christ in 1984. He spent the next 26 years as a worship leader, seminar speaker, and pastor in churches and at retreats, seminars, and conferences all across the western United States. After ministering for a number of years in music and worship to a circuit of small churches, he is now concentrating on writing and publishing both fiction and nonfiction books. Patrick and his wife, Judy, make their home in Northern California and are the parents of two adult children and have five grandchildren.

Watch for books two and three in the Apple Creek Dreams series . . .

The Road Home

Jenny Springer is the local historian for the Amish community in Apple Creek, Ohio. As a child, Jenny was rescued from a terrible snowstorm, and when no trace of her parents could be found, the Springer family adopted her. Since then she has had a burning desire in her heart to find out who she really is. When a drifter, John Hershberger, comes to town looking for his own roots, Jenny gets serious in her search for her long lost parents. As she opens doors to her past, she finds the truly surprising answer to her deepest questions. And as John discovers the true story of his own heritage, his growing love for Jenny causes him to reexamine his lifelong atheism, and in doing so he discovers his need for a real home, a family, and a relationship with God.

The Amish Heiress

Rachel Hershberger lives a typical Amish life in Apple Creek, Ohio. Typical, that is, until a stranger comes to town and turns her world upside down. He tells her that the strange, key-shaped red birthmark above her heart identifies her as the heir to the enormous St. Clair fortune. She has also earned the enmity of her long dead grandfather's sister-in-law, Augusta St. Clair, who will do anything to keep the fortune in her own hands and the hands of her grandson. Suddenly her life is in turmoil. Robert St. Clair, her distant cousin comes to court Rachel, accompanied by agents of the St. Clair family. Their instructions are to eliminate Rachel if Robert cannot win her. Caught in the middle of this intense competition is Joshua King, the Amish boy who has hoped to court Rachel. Joshua discovers the danger to Rachel but cannot convince her because Rachel is enthralled by the possibilities that lie before her. As the days go by and her heart is torn between two worlds, she comes to a point where she must choose between enormous wealth and a godless, loveless marriage, or the plain ways of her people and the love of a faithful Amish boy. Her choice could determine whether she lives or dies.

More fine Amish-themed books from Harvest House Publishers

◇◇◇

The Wings of Morning by Murray Pura

Jude Whetstone and Lyyndaya Kurtz, whose families are converts to the Amish faith, are falling in love. Jude has also fallen in love with flying that new-fangled invention, the aeroplane. The Amish communities have rejected the telephone and have forbidden motorcar ownership but not yet electricity or aeroplanes. Though exempt from military service on religious grounds, Jude is manipulated by unscrupulous army officers into enlisting in order to protect several Amish men. No one in the community understands Jude's sudden enlistment, and he is shunned. Lyyndaya's despair deepens at the reports that Jude has been shot down in France. In her grief, she turns to nursing Spanish flu victims in Philadelphia. After many months of caring for stricken soldiers, Lyyndaya is stunned when an emaciated Jude turns up in her ward.

Lyyndaya's joy at receiving Jude back from the dead is quickly diminished when the Amish leadership insist the shunning remain in force. How then can they marry without the blessing of their families? Will happiness elude them forever?

A Promise for Miriam by Vannetta Chapman

Amish schoolteacher Miriam King loves her students. At 26, most women her age are married with children of their own, but she hasn't yet met anyone who can convince her to give up the Plain school that sits along the banks of Pebble Creek. Then newcomer Gabriel Miller steps into her life, bringing his daughter, an air of mystery, and challenges Miriam has never faced before.

Will Gabe be able to let go of the past that haunts him? He thinks he just wants to be left alone, but the loving and warm community he and his daughter have moved to has other plans for him. After a near tragedy is averted, he hesitantly returns offers of help and friendship, and he discovers he can make a difference to the people of Pebble Creek—and maybe find love again.

The Hannah's Heart series by Jerry Eicher

◇◇◇

Book 1—***A Dream for Hannah***

Hannah Miller's Amish faith is solid. Her devotion to her family and Indiana community is unquestionable. Yet her young spirit longs for adventure and romance. As troubling circumstances give her good reason to spend the summer at her aunt's Montana horse ranch, Hannah soon discovers she has much to learn about life and love. Her heart is awhirl with emotion as she dreams about her future. Sam, the boy Hannah has known all her life, is comfortable and predictable. Peter is the wild one, the boy who is on *rumspringa*. And Jake is unpredictable, intriguing, and living in the Montana wilderness. Hoping for a dream come true, Hannah must decide how to fulfill her heart's desire while staying true to her faith.

Book 2—***A Hope for Hannah***

Hannah Byler is now married. She and Jake live in a small Amish community near Montana's Cabinet Mountains, and the rough log cabin is far from everything Hannah holds dear. Anxious about her new role as wife and soon-to-be mother, Hannah understands she must learn to control her anxious heart if her marriage is to survive. Just as the young couple settles into their new routine, Jake loses his timber job and answers the call to ministry. With winter pressing in and money scarce, Jake and Hannah discover hardships can either drive them apart or draw them closer. Determined to find hope, they struggle to survive in this harsh land and bear their responsibilities with grace.

Book 3—***A Baby for Hannah***

Jake and Hannah are adjusting to life in their Amish community in rural Montana. While Jake works long days as a furniture maker and newly appointed minister, Hannah stays busy keeping their home in order. Both anticipate their baby's birth with joy. When word of the Mennonite tent revival spreads and worry about losing church members mounts, Hannah's sister arrives and catches the eye of the young bachelor whose brother left the church during the last revival. At the same time, Jake and Hannah's neighbor—an *Englischer*—announces his interest in one of the Amish widows.